STORME WARNING

Books by W.L. Ripley

Hail Storme
Storme Front
Eye of the Storme

Cole Springer Series
Springer's Gambit
Pressing the Bet
Springer's Fortune

STORME WARNING

A WYATT STORME THRILLER

W.L. RIPLEY

Text copyright © 2015 W.L. Ripley
All rights reserved.
Printed in the United States of America.

ISBN: 1941298664
ISBN 13: 9781941298664

Published by Brash Books, LLC
12120 State Line #253
Leawood, Kansas 66209

www.brash-books.com

For Penny, who makes life more fun.

PROLOGUE

Rory was surprised that the first thing he wanted was a beer. He would've thought it would be a woman. Long time without one. But no, it was a beer. An icy longneck Miller High Life, one of those in the clear bottle so you could see the gold color, sweat trickling down its side. And maybe a shot of Jim Beam beside it. Yeah, that would be nice. Funny what a guy missed. Then a big bleeding steak with that Texas toast and a fat baked potato with steam rising out of it. Served on a tablecloth and somebody asking if he was all right. Calling him sir. Can I get you anything else, sir?

Then a woman. One who smelled of soap and strawberry shampoo. Soft and squeaky clean. In a big bed with a mattress more than a half inch thick. And sheets that didn't feel like something you could file your fingernails down with. Clean and smooth as marble.

Then, find that damn football player and blow his shit away.

It was the football player's fault his life was in the toilet. He'd been somebody once. Nice clothes. The best booze. Good restaurants. Caddy convertible, a cherry-red Diamante with leather seats that Bobby Frank was always telling him was too fucking something. What was the word he used? Ostentatious. Yeah, that was it. He'd looked it up, and it meant pretentious display. Fucking Wop who ate with his mouth open and picked his teeth with his fingernails, all that jewelry around his neck and his shirt open to the navel like it was the seventies all over again, telling Rory he was ostentatious.

"It's a nigger car, Rory," Bobby Frank would say. "You gotta get a lower profile. Get a dark-colored hardtop. Something nice, y'know? Quit acting like you was a colored guy or somethin', huh?" Then, his dipshit flunkies would laugh, all of them sitting around playing pinochle and drinking espresso and wine, sloshing it into water glasses. It was an Ed Sullivan trained animal act. Dipshit Dagos.

But Bobby Frank paid well. Rory couldn't kick about that. Even gave Rory a cut of the take on some of the collections. Sometimes when he didn't even know it. Walk into some place with the persuader, a nine-inch piece of cable insulation with a leather thong at one end sticking out of his back pocket, let 'em see it pushing the tail of his coat up on one side. Ask to talk with the owner, tell him what a nice place he had. No threats. Maybe drop something breakable on the floor. Even pay for it. But let 'em see you did it on purpose. Tell 'em how much you'd like to have a business like this. Wait for his lower lip to start quivering or the muscle at the corner of his jaw to start bunching up, and you knew the deal was done.

Then one day this black guy, owned a specialty coffee place, for chrissakes, gets nervy, says he ain't paying. Not now, not ever. Now, that's not good business. Guy had only one leg in the first place. Some kind of Vietnam vet or some shit. Everybody's a hero anymore. Probably got the money to start the place on some kind of government handout to nigger gimps who'd been in the service. Can't let 'em get away with that, so he gets nine inches of industrial insulation across the chest. Stand on his stomach and pull off the phony leg and throw it through the glass case where the guy kept his coffee and tell him there'd be another visit. Real soon.

Only next time there's this big guy there. Rangy guy built like Gary Cooper or Clint Eastwood. Taller than Cooper, bigger through the shoulders and chest than Eastwood. Shoulders like a fucking lumberjack. Dressed like one too. Carrying a cutdown baseball bat, if you can believe it, like he was fucking Don Mattingly or something. Hard fucking eyes. Blue-gray like car metal. And he had a mouth on him. Said he'd make Rory a deal. Told him his buddy "doesn't want to pay, and you don't want a proctologist to do your dental work from now on." Later, Rory found out a proctologist was an asshole doctor.

Anyway, he tried to sucker the guy, act like he was sorry for the trouble, all a misunderstanding, you know, while he was working the leather thong around his wrist. He'd practiced that move a thousand times and could slip it out of his pocket faster than you could say, "Ouch." Meaning to put it upside the guy's head.

But he'd never seen anything like this big guy. Fucking hands were like lightning. Hit Rory twice with the bat while he was trying to clear the persuader—once on the point of the shoulder and the second one on the elbow, then backhanded him twice with a free hand, kicking his legs out from under him. Then while he was lying on the floor, the football player laid the bat across Rory's throat and started talking shit at him.

"Never come back," Superstar said, acting pissed off about the whole thing. Like he was coming back anytime soon with a dislocated elbow and a broken collarbone. Hurt like a bitch. "You do, and I'll change your whole life." Then the big guy lets the colored guy kick Rory in the ass with the phony leg as he's going out the door.

So now, Bobby Frank's all over him. "You stupid or something?" said Bobby Frank. "You let some off-the-street whitebread asshole take you down? Kick your ass?" Like he could take the guy easy. This is what Rory had to put up with. But Bobby Frank hadn't seen the way the guy could move, the way his hands worked like there were two of him working him over, then picking him up—picking up a two-hundred-pound guy like he was a sack of sugar he was putting in a cabinet and throwing him out the door. Never seen anybody so big move that fast.

Then Bobby Frank and his guys and Rory too started getting pulled over on the interstate by the state rods. Hassling them with speeding tickets and searching the car, busting Bobby Frank for open-container laws, failure to indicate when changing lanes, touching the white line on the side of the highways. Chickenshit stuff.

Bobby Frank blamed Rory for all this too. "What'd you bring down on us, ya stupid fuck? This football player's got the cops busting my balls every time I back outta my driveway. He's friends with one of 'em. Didja know that? Huh? Naw, you don't know shit. They got me standing on the highway with my dick hanging out while some thirty-grand-a-year guy in a park ranger hat's going through my ride. I gotta tell you something. Rory, are you listening, you dumb Polack? I ain't enjoying this shit."

So Bobby Frank cut him loose, and it was hard to get work what with a cast up to his neck for two months. So he took to robbing convenience stores and shaking down pimps and prostitutes. Then he got busted when his nine fouled robbing a jewelry store. They gave him a dime jolt because he used a gun, but he only did a deuce before his lawyer got him a parole for good behavior. The yards were too full, so they had to cut some guys loose. Two years inside and two broke bones. Still hurt when it turned cold, and he couldn't reach behind him without effort. Fucking prison doctors. No more slick moves with the persuader.

So now he was out, and he was gonna look up the football player—superstar, Rory called him—and whack his ass out. But he wanted Superstar to see it coming. Like De Niro did to Nolte in that movie, what was the name of it? Cape something. *Cape Fear*, that's it. Bobby D. was a scary bastard in that one. Better than Mitchum was. Yeah, just walk up to the man, look at him, let him know he was in town. "Remember me, Superstar?" Smile at the guy. Eat at the same restaurants. Shake 'im up a little, make 'im squirm. Then some night when the guy wasn't looking for it, take him down.

But first a beer and something to eat.

And then find Superstar.

What was the asshole's name? Something to do with the weather or something. What was it?

Wyatt Storme. Yeah, that was it.

"Why can't we all ride together and be cowboy buckaroos?"
—Mason Williams (Cowboy Buckaroos)

ONE

Blue-gray clouds swollen with rain hung in the charged atmosphere. The air was heavy with the deep smell of forest and decaying leaves and the clean aroma of freshly cut oak logs. Things change in autumn; it's a time of readiness as nature prepares for winter, a time of beauty and color as the leaves turn. It's a time of dying.

Waiting for Chick Easton. Said he had a surprise.

Chick Easton, an exclamation point with legs, often showed up at odd times, usually with interesting results. But it would be good to see him again. As it always was. It had been six months.

I watched the Jeep bounce and career up the rough lane leading to my cabin. I set my coffee mug on the ledge of the deck. Only a handful of people knew how to get to my Missouri retreat. Fewer would bother to go to the trouble. I only knew one person who would torture a vehicle in such a manner.

As the Jeep neared, I saw the passenger, wide-eyed and strapped in, one hand on the dash, the other hand holding on to his cap. Chick skidded the Jeep to a halt in a spray of dust and chat, a three-acre smile on a face that gave no hint to his age, other than the scar above his left eye where an eyebrow should have been. Chick jumped out with a package in one hand, a foaming bottle of Michelob beer in the other.

"Home is the sailor, home from the sea," he said, "the hunter home from the hill."

I smiled. Couldn't help myself. "What's up, Chick?"

1

"Got something for you," he said. He tossed the package up to me. It pinwheeled through the air, and I caught it with my free hand. "Still got the hands, Wyatt."

I removed the wrapper to reveal the old-gold and red Macanudo cigar trademark. "Thanks."

Chick's shell-shocked passenger unstrapped and stumbled from the vehicle like a shipwreck survivor. He straightened the line of his oilskin drover's coat and reseated the fresh out-of-the-box LA Dodgers baseball cap. He had a clipped brown beard salted with blond and a few gray hairs.

"I'm Geoffrey Salinger," said the passenger, saying it like it meant something. Maybe it did. I didn't get out much, and I didn't keep up either. Maybe he was royalty of some kind, and me with the good china packed away. Always unprepared. Never going to get anywhere socially. Salinger stood there in his crisp Levi's and Ray-Ban sunglasses awaiting my reaction.

I yawned. Sipped my coffee. "Wyatt Storme," I said, then nodded at him. "Nice to meet you."

"Geoffrey's a motion picture director," Chick said, rubbing the side of his nose with a finger.

"Oh," I said. In the distance I could see the thick fingers of rain on the southwest horizon. Could use a break in the weather, I guess.

"A famous Hollywood director," Chick said.

Salinger, the famous Hollywood director, looked at Chick. Chick grinned, enjoying himself, apparently at Salinger's expense.

"Am I missing something here?" Salinger asked Chick.

"A...well, Wyatt's a little, you know, reclusive," said Chick.

"And you think it's funny that he doesn't know who I am?"

Chick tilted the brown beer bottle and drank. He swallowed, looked at Salinger, and nodded.

"Yep," he said.

Salinger ignored Chick and looked at me. "Is he always like this?" Salinger asked.

I nodded. "Unfortunately."

Salinger smiled. "I'm a big fan of yours. Remember when you played. I have a business proposition I wish to discuss with you. May we come in, Mr. Storme?"

"Sure." Even hermits get lonely.

Salinger removed his coat but not the hat when we went inside. I offered coffee to the director, who declined when he discovered it wasn't decaffeinated. California guys. I love 'em. Chick asked if we had any caffeine-free whiskey. I didn't answer, as he was fishing for a straight man, and he knew where everything was anyway.

"Chick tells me you own the site where Bailey's Crossing used to be."

"Yeah."

"They say the James Brothers were in on a robbery that occurred there."

"I've heard that."

"I also heard that Cole Younger hid the loot from the holdup somewhere around here."

"Heard that too. Not sure I believe it."

"I plan to proceed as if it were true. Westerns, particularly those depicting the West as an unlovely reality of dust and sweat and violence, are making a comeback." He leaned forward, gesturing with his hands as if forming something out of the air. "I envision a picture about the James gang with the raid at Bailey's Crossing as a centerpiece, recreating the town on the original site. Cameron Fogarty has agreed to play the lead, and I have Meagan Ames lined up for the female lead."

"I prefer Randolph Scott and western dramas of tightlipped men doing what they have to do," I said. "I'm not sure it was all that unlovely."

It stopped him momentarily. He looked at Chick, who shrugged. "He's this way sometimes," he said. "There's nothing to be done about it."

"Don't you know who Fogarty and Ames are?" Salinger asked me.

"Vaguely."

"They are two of the industry's hottest young stars. Ms. Ames was nominated for best supporting actress last year. Don't you go to the movies? Or watch television?"

"Some."

"Reclusive," said Chick, rummaging behind the bar.

"This is a major production," said Salinger.

"I believe you," I said. I sipped my coffee.

"Sardonic," said Chick, pouring Maker's Mark whiskey into a square rocks glass. Salinger gave Chick a disgruntled look, which Chick reacted to with a satisfied smile.

"What's your proposal?" I asked.

"I wish to shoot the picture on the original site with your permission. I will need a free hand, however. So, if you'll simply sign an agreement I've had—"

I held up a hand.

"Take it easy," I said, thinking about it. I envisioned people milling around and disturbing the wildlife. I had a couple of good deer trails down there, which I would have to forget about if they started hauling in a bunch of equipment. I could hunt elsewhere, sure. But there'd be reporters and autograph seekers, and gawkers and celebrity worshipers tramping around, pointing at things and leaving footprints and litter. Civilization.

"We'll pay, of course," Salinger said. "Enough to make it worth your while."

"It's not that simple."

"I could give you a job as an extra."

"No thanks."

"Perhaps a larger role. Maybe as a secondary character or gang member. Think about that. Your face on movie screens all across the country."

Just what I needed: my face on a thousand movie screens.

"No," I said. "I'd rather not tear up the land. I hunt that area. I like it there. It's quiet."

"Diffident and intractable," said Chick, taking a healthy swallow of whiskey. He held up the glass. "Yet, hospitable."

Salinger placed his hands on his knees and pushed himself into an erect sitting position. "We will be happy to restore everything as it was before we started, so you may resume murdering the animals after we leave."

I looked at Salinger. I let out a breath, then looked at Chick, my lips pressed together. Chick grinned and raised an eyebrow. He really only has one. The other eyebrow was like a sideways apostrophe, the result of his service in Vietnam. He put a hand up, said, "No, don't thank me." Then he produced a cigarette, which he lit with one of his ever-present wood matches.

"Must you smoke that?" Salinger said.

Chick exhaled smoke. "I must." Chick smiled, blew a blue smoke ring toward the ceiling.

"I have a strict no-smoking policy for all my employees."

"You working for him?" I asked Chick.

"Bodyguard work."

"He's not protecting me," said Salinger, whose tone was beginning to annoy me. "I've hired him to protect Fogarty."

"I'm also doing some stunt work," Chick said. "Chick D. Easton. The *D* stands for 'Danger.'"

"Now you're a stunt man," I said.

"Thought I'd add it to my repertoire. May get a small part in the movie too."

"That hasn't been decided," said Salinger.

"I'm photogenic. The camera loves me. Don't miss this opportunity."

"Why does Fogarty need protection?" I asked.

"There have been threats," said Salinger.

"What kind of threats?"

"Phone calls. Letters. That sort of thing."

"What do they say?"

"That his life is in danger. That he deserves death, and they will kill him."

"Do they say why?"

"No, they don't. I already have most of the interior shots filmed. I need the location shots and cannot afford to have anything happen to him or the picture at this point. I would have to recast and reshoot."

"Not to mention what it would do to Fogarty's schedule," I said. I pulled out a pocketknife and slit the wrapper on the cigars Chick had brought. Salinger watched, probably fearing I'd light one. I unwrapped a cigar as Chick thumb nailed a wooden match, which popped and sizzled merrily. I took the match from him and rolled the cigar above the flame. Remembering my manners, I offered one to Salinger.

Salinger stroked the bottom of his beard with the back of his hand and declined the offer. He shook his head and smiled. "Okay, you win. But you've not given me an answer. Will you allow us to shoot on your property?"

"I'm giving it some thought."

"I need this location," Salinger said. "I will pay you very well. There are many people who would jump at this opportunity." He thrust a hand into his coat pocket. I could see the outline of his balled-up fist against the fabric. He wasn't used to being put off.

"Don't jump much," I said. I looked at Salinger.

"What do you want then?"

I held up my cigar and looked at it. "If I let you use the land, you'll have to agree to certain conditions."

"Which would be what?" Salinger asked petulantly.

"First, when you're done, the land is returned to its original state. Second, you take the rent money, divide it into equal amounts, and give it to a public school and two churches, the names of which I'll supply. Do so anonymously. And Chick will be allowed to smoke—"

"And partake of adult beverages," said Chick, interrupting.

"Whenever he wants," I said, finishing.

"What do I tell the other employees?"

"Chick works best when left alone. He'll get the job done. You try to put constraints on him, he'll drive you crazy. And he'll do it on purpose. He's already started, in fact. He's going to do what he wants anyway, so I'm saving you the headache."

"Maybe I won't require his services. I can get someone else."

"That's fine. He doesn't work, you don't get the land." I doubted Chick needed the work. It was more likely other reasons, which were usually his own. "Which brings me to my final condition. I don't like crowds all that much. Anybody that I find objectionable, I'm going to run him off. I don't mean your crew or the actors, I'm talking about tourists, hangers-on, and even the media, if they become annoying."

He gave a sidelong look at the floor. Then, looking at me, he said, "I'm not used to being told how to run my affairs."

I looked at my cigar and waited.

I watched him struggle with it. The power of his position had insulated him from having to negotiate with lesser mortals. He didn't like it much either.

"There is another problem, however," he said.

TWO

The other problem was Cameron Fogarty.

"Fogarty has an entourage of sycophants who have leeched themselves to him," said Salinger. "They get drunk and stoned and keep Fogarty out late, partying, which makes Cameron late for first call. He shows up hung over, stumbles over his lines, and irritates the rest of the cast. Worse, there are times when the makeup people are unable to hide the bloodshot eyes and the other…well, other effects.

"They are parasites," said Salinger, continuing. "They cause problems with the locals when we shoot location. They damage things, wreck vehicles, and get arrested. They create problems with the cast, intimidating them and harassing the females. They started a fight with the stunt men on one set. For their trouble they received the beating of their lives."

"Why does Fogarty go along with them?" I asked.

"He doesn't go along, he's the instigator of these incidents. His toadies do nothing without his say-so. They are devoted to him." Salinger opened his hands and shook his head. "It is a constant difficulty, keeping Fogarty out of jail and out of the headlines. Assault charges. He did thirty days in LA when he struck a photographer. That served to dampen his escapades for a short period, but he doesn't fear jail out here in the sticks. He's the type who wears out his welcome with great speed."

"Why put up with him?" I asked.

He smiled and pushed the baseball cap back on his head. "He's very good at what he does. He's charismatic, and it comes across on the screen. He's different once the camera rolls. Professional. He's the perfect Jesse James—the little bad boy with the soft blue eyes and the challenge in the set of his shoulders. Not many have it. McQueen had it. James Dean. So does Fogarty. Right now he's white-hot, and kids will shell out their gas money to see him. As will their parents; his appeal blurs demographic lines. And that makes for big box-office receipts. I have to have him for this part. No one else comes close. I know he's an insufferable shit, but I must have him, and I must have the location. Well, at least I'm stuck with him. Can't start over. But now these threats are problematic because he refuses to give up the poison lifestyle. He will prove difficult to protect."

"I don't see what that has to do with me," I said.

Salinger leaned back, surprised. He looked at Chick, then back at me. "I thought you would assist Mr. Easton. I'd really like that. Seriously, I was a big fan when you played for the Cowboys."

I looked at Chick, who made a show of looking at the ceiling. I waited. Finally, Chick looked at me, shrugged, and smiled.

"I've got things to do," I said. "I don't have time to babysit some Hollywood jerk-off confused about his manhood."

"You'll be well paid," said Salinger.

"We've been across that territory."

"What if one man isn't enough?"

"Chick is like having a team of bodyguards," I said. "Though he pretends to be disaffected, when he's moved to action, you will be amazed."

"Aw shucks, Wyatt. Stop, you're embarrassing me," said Chick, fanning the air in a palm-up, give-us-more gesture.

Hard not to enjoy yourself when Chick was around. Hard.

"What if something unforeseen occurs?" Salinger asked.

"Then I call Storme," said Chick.

"He said he wasn't interested."

"No," Chick said. "He said he wasn't for hire. You gotta listen better. I need him, he'll be there."

Salinger looked at me. "Is that true?"

I nodded.

Salinger took his hat off his head and ran a hand through his hair. Shook his head and smiled.

"And I thought actors were crazy," he said.

The blue-gray clouds had turned a dark purple and began dumping rain. I saw Chick and Salinger out and watched them leave, then returned to the cabin and put on an old Michael Nesmith CD. I made a fresh pot of coffee, and I listened to Nesmith's quirky lyrics and soothing voice as the rain washed over the cabin, making a nice rhythmic patter against the windows. While the coffee was brewing, I settled into an overstuffed chair and started reading a James Lee Burke novel, puffing on my cigar occasionally. Not bad. There are worse ways to spend a rainy autumn afternoon.

After a couple of chapters of first-rate prose, I closed the book and retrieved a cup of coffee. I took my coffee, walked over to sit in the bay window, and through rivulets of rainwater cascading down the glass, I looked out across the valley, which stretched and fell away from my cabin like an impressionist painting.

Soon Chick would call, not because he needed help, but because he thought it was his job to break me loose from the social hibernation that was my chosen lifestyle. Sometimes he was right to do so. There were times when my life stagnated, but often enough it was everything I'd imagined—peaceful and quiet and fulfilling in a meandering way, like a country stream bubbling across rocks—separate and apart from the main artery.

It hadn't always been this way.

Once it had been a twentieth-century sideshow of different hotels in different cities, waking up to chase down footballs, plucking them out of the sky while heat-seeking gazelles with twenty-inch biceps tried to separate me from the ball and consciousness as drunken accountants and oil workers screamed from rented seats.

It was almost like real life, except for the crazy parts.

At each stop on the search to find out where I was going, the ennui would subside and be replaced by a deep-seated fatigue—a settled disposition of distaste for society in the last quarter of this century. Civilization had rapidly become too constrictive for living. The more we screamed we were free and enlightened, the more we became enslaved and indoctrinated. Every town the same, every slogan a screed, everyone a victim for one hour.

So, being a bold coward, I fled. Retreated to the freedom of solitary life in the forest and hills of imagination. The longer I stayed away, the more the stench of our frantic culture slipped away from me.

I liked it out here. Sometimes I ventured back. Sometimes I was dragged back.

Chick would call. He always did. He didn't want to hang out alone. And there were times when I didn't wish to either.

THREE

Finding this Storme guy was going to be harder than Rory figured. First, he had to go to rural Missouri, which was filled with halfwits in pickup trucks and tractor hats. Nobody he talked to knew where the guy was or what he was doing. The only thing said was the guy used to play for the Cowboys. The guy left no other trail. It was like he'd disappeared into the atmosphere or something. Rory checked out a public library in a little town called Peculiar, if you could believe it.

Since he hadn't been in a library on purpose since junior high, he had to get help from a tall woman wearing lilac perfume with a lavalier chain on her glasses. She looked like she was two thousand miles overdue for a lube job. She punched some keys on a computer while Rory looked around, not understanding how somebody could spend her life in such a place smelling like his third-grade teacher. The computer scrolled some lines, then the librarian led him to a bookcase of magazines, pulled down a sleeve of *Sports Illustrated* magazines, and gave him some dates to check.

He sat at a wood table, looking through the magazines, until he found a picture of Storme in his Cowboy uniform. The guy was stretched out to full length as he dove for a football, looking at the ball with those nasty, gun-metal eyes wide open, like someone had goosed him with an electric cord. The caption underneath the photo said, "Storme, en route to game MVP honors, was thunder and lightning, catching nine passes for 127 yards and two touchdowns, including this one, which tied the game in regulation."

Another article in a different issue talked about Storme retiring from the NFL. There were no quotes from Storme. The Cowboys brass announced that Storme had called and notified them that he was coming to summer camp and that he was retiring. The Cowboys president said it had nothing to do with salary.

The *SI* writer talked about the retirement as "the loss of an American sports original—a man who didn't say much, Storme was the personification of the 'Lonesome End'—split wide from the pack, thundercloud eyes staring downfield before whirling into the secondary like an autumn tornado, leaving a wake of destruction and broken hearts. His touchdown catches were a ballet: acrobatic, slashing, his hands those of a magician or a concert violinist. 'The fastest hands in the West.' Hands as sure as a bank deposit. And at the end, no shake-and-bake dance, no ball spiking, no celebration, his demeanor as calm as a man stepping off an escalator, as if to say, 'I've been here before.'"

"The son of a bitch 'looked' like a cowboy," said Dallas quarterback Murphy Chandler. "I don't mean he wore cowboy clothes. I mean it was like he just come off a movie set where he shot all the bad guys and rode off into the sunset. Hell, when I got in trouble back there, I just hung it out in the sky in his general vicinity and let him figure it out."

Rory looked at the picture of Storme that went with the article. Guy had his helmet off and holding it in one hand by the face mask, smudges of lampblack under both eyes, hair messed up and slick with sweat. They didn't have any pictures of the guy off the field. No mention of the guy's plans or where he lived. What kind of celebrity's that, huh? How can you be famous if nobody knew nothing about you?

So, what the hell was he doing busting people up with a cut-down baseball bat? No figuring a weird guy like that. But he was gonna find this guy. There was no doubt about that. He just needed a handle, a starting place. He'd done some shylocking for Bobby Frank and some independents and he knew how to find people.

Just a matter of time.

FOUR

Wednesday, as I returned from a morning hunt, the phone rang. I answered without identifying myself.

"This is Mike Franklin of KSTL Radio in St. Louis. Am I speaking to Wyatt Storme? The Wyatt Storme who used to play for the Dallas Cowboys?"

"No," I said, "you have the wrong number."

He ignored me. "Mr. Storme, I realize you like your privacy, but I just have a couple of questions about the Geoffrey Salinger production. I understand it is being shot on some property you hold title to. Is that true?"

"You have the wrong number," I said again and hung up. When it began ringing again, I ignored it. It quit after the tenth ring, and I hooked up a recorder to screen the calls. The cell-phone service was hit-and-miss at my cabin, so I had to use the landline more often than not. Within the hour there were three more: one from a different radio station and two from newspapers. The recorder was set to kick in after the seventh ring, so the caller had to be persistent to activate it.

The phone rang again, and a familiar voice said, "Pick up, Wyatt. I know you're there, and you have nothing else to do." It was Chick.

"What do you want?" I said.

"You need some work on your phone etiquette. Try saying 'hello' or even 'good morning' when you pick up the phone."

"I'll try to remember. You giving out my phone number? I'm getting a bunch of calls."

"You know better."

I did.

"Guess who is an asshole of epic proportions?" Chick asked.

"Cameron Fogarty."

"Protecting him is a joy. Only people hate him are everybody he meets. Hell, I hate him, and I'm supposed to protect him. His mother should be ridden down and hanged for bearing him."

"So, what's the problem?"

"You know, no problem. But what do you think about coming over here and hanging out for a while? Nobody's shot the guy yet, and it's almost noon. What else you got to do? Only take about thirty minutes to get here. You gotta see this guy and the human hemorrhoids he hangs with."

"I'm pretty satisfied here," I said. "Sandy's coming by tomorrow."

"You don't have to stay over. It's not a camping trip. Bring me a bottle of Jack Daniel's when you come."

"Are you listening to me?"

"Yeah, sure. Could you stop and get me a pack of Camels too? I think one of Salinger's gofers pinched mine when I wasn't looking. You can't trust reformers."

I hung up the phone and smiled. Maybe I'd run over there in a couple of days. After Sandy left. I hadn't seen Sandy Collingsworth in two weeks. Our long-distance romance was in its seventh year. Maybe that was good luck. It wasn't always easy with her alternating between Colorado and New York City and me doing the same between Colorado and Missouri.

My migration turned upon the weather, the hunting seasons, and personal whim. Sandy's was determined by how many spots—live or canned—she would have to shoot for her ten-minute daily spot "Morning Coffee Break" for *Fox and Friends*. She would fly into New York on Sunday night, shoot three to five shows, then return to Colorado Thursday afternoon for the weekend. They allowed her to film some of her segments in Denver at their local affiliate. Sometimes she'd fly back and stay at my place until Sunday. Sometimes I'd drive out to Denver to meet her at the airport. Once in a great while, I'd fly out to Denver.

I had never gone to New York with her.

When I played for the Cowboys, we would play in New York once a year as they were in the East Division of the NFC with us. Actually, we played in New Jersey. The other guys would hit the night spots of the Big Apple, though it was frowned upon by management. I went with them a couple of times. Usually I'd buy a few cigars at an antiquated tobacco store, run by a nice Jewish couple I became friends with, the Zuckermans. Mrs. Zuckerman always asked about my family and would chastise me for not wearing a hat in the cold weather. It was always nice to see them, like a family away from home. I still receive a Christmas card from them.

They had a real cigar-store Indian out front. I'd buy a few cigars and return to the motel bar or my room, smoke a cigar, think about what I had to do the next afternoon, and turn in early. I'd seen concrete and steel before and remain unimpressed.

Not that I was a saint in those days. Sometimes I would find a metropolitan girl to accompany me back to my room for a night of heavy breathing and early-morning regrets. That was then. Back when I was another guy I didn't know. People change.

I showered, shaved, and was toweling off when I heard the phone ring again. After the seventh ring, I heard Sandy's voice.

"Pick up if you're there, Wyatt," she said, her voice filling the room and my head. "If not, then call me back at two-one-two, eight-eight—"

I picked the phone up off the cradle and said, "Hello, Sandy."

"Hello, handsome," she said, and I could hear the smile in her voice. "What are you doing?"

"I just got out of the shower."

"And me two thousand miles away."

"Don't start this, I have enough trouble sleeping."

"I have great news," she said. "The FOX Network is interviewing me for a bigger spot on an afternoon news show."

"Hey, that's great, Sandy. When you get here, we'll celebrate."

"Well," she said, "that's the bad part. They're going to interview me Friday morning, so I'll have to stay over. Then I have to meet with the producer and some other executives Saturday morning. But I'll fly in Saturday evening, and we'll do it then. I'll leave my flight time on your machine if you're not around."

"That doesn't give us much time if you have to go back Sunday."

"I'll see if they'll let me off Monday."

"Sounds fine," I said. "Chick's been after me to come over and see him on this movie set where he's working." I told her about Chick's job and Geoffrey Salinger's visit.

"Geoffrey Salinger came to your cabin?" she asked.

"Yeah, I'm having the chair he sat in bronzed."

"Hard to imagine you two in the same room."

"Neither could he."

"Where you your usual self?"

"What is my usual self?" I asked.

"Let's see," she said. "Misanthropic, atavistic, annoyingly smug. Did I leave out anything?"

"I offered him coffee and a cigar," I said. "And I'm going to look up misanthropic, and it'd better mean warm and hospitable, or I'm going to sell naked pictures of you to *Penthouse*."

"Wyatt, this interview is big. It's what I've been working for all my life. I'm nervous about it. What if they don't like me?"

"That's not possible," I said. "They're going to love you."

"I hope so."

"Why wouldn't they? I do."

"Thanks. Say a prayer for me."

"You got it."

"Gotta run. Love you."

I put the phone down slowly. Oh well, there's always Chick.

I stopped at Frank's Trading Post to make the purchases Chick requested and headed for Bailey's Crossing. It was a day that would make Thoreau smile. The air was clear and as crisp as a freshly cut pumpkin; the rolling hills were ablaze with trees washed in warm oranges and butter-soft golds. The Allman Brothers sang "Southbound" on the stereo as I turned off the dual highway and onto the two-lane county blacktop.

It would be great for Sandy to get this job. It was what she wanted. Going national. What did I want? I wanted what was best for her. But back in the rusty cell where I kept the selfish part of my personality, a voice, faint and distant, was trying to get my attention. What would it mean if she got the job? What would it do to our relationship? I liked routine and had become used to the long weekends we enjoyed. Had learned to deal with the days and distances apart. We had been through a lot together. She was a fully realized woman who was maybe strong enough to no longer require the company of a certain ex-football player. Don't go there, Storme. That is the place where the egocentric and pitiful go to feel sorry for themselves. Nothing's happened yet.

Yet.

I thought about other things. In the late 1800s, Bailey's Crossing had been a conduit for westward-bound dreamers who had followed Horace Greeley's advice. Even then Americans were victims of fashion. Wagons loaded with dry goods headed for Dodge City, stagecoaches looking to link up with the Santa Fe Trail, and young men headed for Colorado and California with heady daydreams of adventure and gold fever throbbing in their heads had all passed through a century ago.

Now it was a row of rundown buildings, its single avenue grown over with weeds and saw grass.

Bailey's Crossing sat on seventy-five acres and had been left to me by my Grandfather McGee. I bought the two hundred acres adjacent to it, most of which was timber. I rented the eighty tillable acres out to a local farmer who rotated corn and milo and beans, affording the wildlife a nice alternative to acorns and wild berries. The agreement was that he would leave two rows unharvested for the wildlife.

I arrived on the movie set with a carton of Camel cigarettes in one hand and a fifth of Jack Daniel's in the other, feeling like the Midwest distributor for bad habits. There were vans and trucks strewn about and electric cable rolling and intertwining like huge snakes on the grass. Too much of it on the grass, in fact. But a deal's a deal.

The ground teemed with people—actors and extras in century-old clothing, technicians with headphones across their backward baseball caps, various gofers carrying various items, and men in yellow windbreakers with "Security" stenciled across the back. The rundown buildings had been given false fronts, and extra buildings had been constructed. Had to admit it looked pretty good. I half expected to see Clint Eastwood walking down the street in a poncho, a cheroot in the corner of his mouth. It had a nice nostalgic ambiance. The magic of movie land.

Chick was dressed in cowboy garb—hat, vest, and holstered Colt. As he approached, he pushed back his hat with a gloved thumb and said, "Howdy, partner. See you brought the red-eye and the smokes."

I looked at his costume. "You look fairly authentic."

"I am a damn cowboy. Yup, yup, yup."

"You got a part?"

"Walk-on. Some stunt work, stand-in for Fogarty. I am, of course, magnificent and steal the whole picture."

"I'm sure they're grateful," I said. "Where's Fogarty?"

He pointed in the direction of a well-built young guy with a slender face and the kind of features that would always make him appear younger than he was.

"That's him over there. Guy dressed like me." Fogarty was talking to Geoffrey Salinger, who was dressed like he was on safari. They appeared to be arguing. Soon they were shouting at each other.

"How am I supposed to get inside this character?" said Fogarty. "The way you want me to play him, it's like he was a cigar-store Indian."

"That," said Salinger, "would have more to do with your acting ability than the part. Jesse James was a Midwestern farm boy from a religious family, not an MTV cartoon character. Subtle is best. See if you can resist the urge to overplay the part."

"I'm overplaying the part?" said Fogarty, his head tilted back.

"You seem to want to play him as if making an appearance at a James Dean festival. And it would be nice if you could manage to show up on the set without first sticking your head in the medicine cabinet."

"What does that mean, Geoffrey?"

"Oh," said Salinger. "Pardon me. I forgot that nuanced conversation escapes you. It means I would rather you weren't drunk, stoned, or hung over for every call."

"Yeah, well, fuck you, Geoffrey," said Fogarty, stomping off.

"What's all that?" I asked Chick.

"Daily occurrence. Salinger tells him to do something, Fogarty throws a tantrum, then they take a long lunch together, and Fogarty does what Salinger tells him. You're going to have to get used to Hollywood ways, pilgrim. Salinger is good at what he does and handles it."

"How are you getting along with Fogarty?"

"I follow him around and try not to wince when he talks."

"How do you stand in for him? You don't look alike."

"I imagine how an open sore would think if it could. That, and keep my hat pulled down and my face away from the camera."

"Where are his buddies?"

"It's only two o'clock. They're not up yet. You're going to love them, though."

But I didn't. Love them, that is. Probably didn't try hard enough.

Fogarty's gang shrugged loose from their hibernation looking as if the light burned their eyes. There were three of them.
All decked out in the latest in LA gotta-have-it-if-you-wanna-be-
somebody attire, the kind of stuff you'd imagine the characters
in a Dickens novel would wear if they wanted to be contempo-
rary. Armageddon chic.

The trio staggered around, poking shirttails into pants,
yawning, rubbing, and scratching, their mouths sticky from
sleep and indulgence.

"Cursed be the wants that sin against the strength of youth,"
I said, borrowing from Tennyson.

"They should be put to sleep," said Chick. "Want to meet them?"

"Not just yet."

"Don't know what you're missing."

"Some pleasures are better postponed."

They shuffled off, a trio of space creatures as out of place in
the autumn woods as an oil refinery on Walden Pond.

The rest of the day was mostly standing around while
Salinger and the stunt gaffer choreographed a fight scene outside the false-front saloon. Cameron Fogarty and the stunt men
walked through the scene several times in slow motion, then half
speed, before shooting a faster tempo.

Fogarty moved well. He was athletic and fluid and quick. At
the end of one take, Fogarty continued to move, jumping into
a fighter's stance and throwing a decent sidekick, followed by
a series of short punches before retreating into an Asian pose,
hands curled, legs apart. Then he relaxed, smiled, and slapped
the stunt man on the shoulder.

I looked at Chick.

"Oh yeah," Chick said. "Kid thinks he's Chuck Norris. Thinks
him and me need to do some sparring between takes, so I'll
know he's a tough guy in real life. 'How about you and me going
a couple rounds sometime, Eastwood?' Calls me Eastwood, and
I really like that a lot."

"So indulge him."

Chick smiled as if thinking of a good meal. "I don't have time for kid stuff. Besides, I'm supposed to protect him, not shorten his life-span."

Fogarty walked up to us, swaggered actually. You don't see a good swagger much anymore. Pretty entertaining.

"See that, Eastwood?" said Fogarty as he got closer. "I can take care of myself."

"Yeah," said Chick. "If the killer walks up to you and tries to beat you to death, rather than shoot you, I'd say you had a decent chance."

Ignoring Chick's remark, Fogarty looked at me and said, "Who are you?"

I looked at him. "A little indelicate in your approach, don't you think?" I asked.

"I forgot, he's rude too," said Chick. "He's the whole package. No doubt about it."

"You still haven't answered my question," said Fogarty.

"I'm waiting for Emily Post to swing by and rap you smartly on the knuckles."

He didn't like that. "How would you like it if I put you off the set?"

"Be hard to do," said Chick. "Even if he didn't own it."

Fogarty cocked his head to one side. "You Wyatt Storme?"

I nodded.

He shrugged. "I didn't know."

"I understand you're receiving death threats."

"What's that to you? Why am I talking to this guy, Eastwood?"

"He's a huge fan of yours," said Chick.

"Who wouldn't be?" I said.

"That," said Chick, "and he's got a head for this kind of thing."

"Yeah?" said Fogarty. "What is he, some kind of private investigator?"

"Nope," I said. "Just something to do."

"Wyatt can help, Cam," said Chick.

He spat theatrically, off to one side, then looked back at me. "Okay," he said. "Yeah, I've been threatened. I gotta couple of calls. A letter."

"What did they say?"

"Said they wanted to kill me. What do you mean, what did they say? What kind of question is that?"

"Did the voice sound familiar? Did you notice an accent, any unique dialect or diction traits? Was it male or female?"

"I don't know," he said, oddly evasive. "Male. Could have been female, maybe. Can't tell. They were disguising their voice."

"Did you keep the letter?"

"It's back in LA."

"Do the police have it?"

"No. I threw it away."

He threw it away? I filed that away for now.

"You didn't tell the police about any of this?"

"No," he said. "What would they do?"

"Investigate. Ask questions. They're good at that. They might even find out who's doing it. It's what they do. And they do it better than I ever could."

"So why am I talking to you, then?"

"Beats me," I said.

"You're just a washed-up football player."

"That's me. Want to see me limp around and say duh?"

He smiled to himself, turned around and walked off.

"He's a beauty, isn't he?" said Chick. "And he's all mine."

"You think he likes me?" I asked.

"Took to you right off."

"What I thought too. Maybe he'll give me an autographed picture."

"You play your cards right, anything's possible."

FIVE

Geoffrey Salinger kept a personal trailer on the set, but he had also rented out the president's suite at the Holiday Inn in Paradise when he felt like getting away from the location. And fresh air. And wildlife. But I was getting used to Salinger and liked him. Like Chick said, the man knew what he was doing, and that was why he was successful. Salinger kept things on schedule and had a nice touch with the crew and the actors. He understood he was dealing with people who were used to being treated like royalty but wasn't afraid to chew them out and then pat them on the back.

On the day I arrived, Salinger had contracted the banquet room at the Holiday Inn for a dinner and impromptu party—a break from the grind. The menu was exotic: shrimp bisque and trout almandine, along with some unidentifiable vegetarian dishes. Chilled wine and three types of coffee, all freshly ground, and several kinds of imported beer. Waiters and waitresses in white shirts and red bow ties made sure glasses didn't stay empty long. Two off-duty sheriff's deputies were posted at the door to keep out the undesirables.

But I was there anyway.

Salinger had hired two music groups—a string quartet to play Mendelssohn and Brahms and Mozart before and during dinner and then a DJ spinning music when the partying started.

There was a pecking order to the seating arrangements. The secondary actors sat at a couple of tables near one side of the room. The technicians and camera crew sat at four tables at the east wall. Geoffrey Salinger and Cameron Fogarty sat with the two female leads, Meagan Ames and Valeri Darnell, at a private table. I recognized Darnell. She was one of those rare beauties whose face grew more interesting with maturity—the emerging lines accenting the character in her face.

Meagan Ames, on the other hand, was the type of disposable beauty that Hollywood cranked out like bubble gum. Thick mane of cotton-blond hair, slender pink-white tongue, cherry lips, exercise boutique figure, and eyes like blue jawbreakers: eyes desperate with hunger and overstimulation. She would not wear well and would leave no aftertaste when Hollywood was through with her.

The most animated group sat at the stunt men's table, which is where Chick and I ended up. Chick introduced me around, and I shook hands. They joked and told stories and juggled fruit and silverware. They passed around Chick's bottle of Jack Daniel's, drinking it like autumn cider, enjoying the esprit de corps of shared danger, much like pro athletes and cops—a camaraderie that cannot be adequately explained, creating a bond between them, while quite often placing them outside the circle of mainstream life. These were men who jumped off buildings, fell from galloping horses, crashed cars, set themselves on fire, and performed similar acts of calculated insanity all for the sake of a few seconds of celluloid magic. And occasionally their performance cost them their lives.

Halfway through the meal, I noticed a tall black man come into the banquet room. He was slender-hipped, and his handsome face looked as if it had been chiseled from a block of frozen cappuccino. I recognized him as an old friend. Michael LeBeau. He'd been a running back for USC, then later for the Rams before doing color commentary for NFL games. We had met at the Pro Bowl game in New Orleans when we played on the NFC squad. I wasn't surprised Michael had gravitated toward Hollywood, as he possessed a charismatic dignity and strength that raised the level of performance around him.

LeBeau accepted a glass of wine from a waiter and surveyed the room. His impassive eyes passed over the Salinger table, though Salinger gestured at him, and continued to pan the room. His eyes met mine, and a smile like diamonds lit up his intelligent face. He walked in the direction of our table, slowly shaking his head.

"Wyatt Storme," he said. "What the hell are you doing here?"

"Hello, Michael. Good to see you." I held out my hand, and he shook it. Chick and I made room between us for him to sit. I introduced Chick.

"Been a long day," Michael said. He yawned. "This getting up before dawn is a rough way to make millions of dollars. Worse than summer training camp. Though Southern California in August was a bitch, man."

"Try West Texas," I said. "You could see the heat shimmers before the sun came up. No air conditioning, no phone, nothing to do at night but sweat. Your skin broke out in heat rashes. Guys irritable all the time. We heard the coaches wanted to bring in concertina wire, but it was back-ordered."

"Those were the good old days for sure," said Michael.

"You've done well for yourself," I said.

He shrugged. "Money's good. Company you keep's not always the best. What are you doing now?"

"Little of this, little of that."

Michael laughed. "Same old Storme. Still the mystery man. You never change. It's good to see you, man." He turned to Chick and said, "You should have seen this boy catch the ball. Didn't matter where they threw it or how hard they hit him. Like he was magnetized or something." He turned back to me. "Wyatt Storme, the *legend*." He said the last word in a mock-serious voice. "Our secondary threw a party when they heard you retired."

"What's your part in the movie?" I asked.

"I'm Deputy Sheriff Quintain Robinson. Pretty good part too. They let me speak like a man instead of Stepin Fetchit. Lot of people don't realize there were a lot of brothers in the Old West."

"Sure they do," I said. "The James brothers, the Earp brothers, Dalton Brothers."

"You still haven't explained what you're doing here," Michael said. "You're not doing stunt work now, are you?"

"No," I said. "I'm visiting Chick."

Michael leaned back, turned his head sideways, and looked at me from the corner of his eyes. "You're the hick Geoffrey's been talking about. The one who owns the property." His smile was big, amused. "Wyatt Storme, land baron. Geoffrey likes you but says you're kind of a smartass."

"I thought I was merely misanthropic."

"You still dating Sandy?"

"Yeah."

He whistled, then adopted a street dialect. "She be fine. I saw her the other day on a commercial. That's a pretty woman. Got her some long legs. Why does she hang with you, when a handsome Afro-American stallion such as myself would be better for her?"

"It is a mystery," said Chick.

"I'm surprised you didn't sit at the head table," I said. "Where you'd have a better audience. And maybe you could do Eddie Murphy for them instead of wasting it on us."

"You mean Cameron and Meagan?" he said. "Give them a chance to feel all virtuous by letting the darkie jock sit among them?" He smiled again. "I thought about it. But I don't feel like talking about Europe and fashion design and the country club and how bad things'll be for us po' colored folk if those demon Republicans get control of Congress again. We're with you, Michael," LeBeau said in falsetto, imitating Meagan Ames. "It's a wise African American who trusts none of you palefaces."

"I don't care if you join the country club," I said.

"Easy for you to say. You don't even belong to one."

"They found out I had some African blood in my background."

"Explains why you were the only white boy who could go long."

"I thought it was my classic moves and dazzling speed."

"Naw. The brothers said it'd been so long since they'd seen a Caucasian more than ten yards past the line of scrimmage, the novelty paralyzed them. They thought you'd come off the sideline, illegally."

Chick lit an after-dinner cigar and smiled, the smoke trailing off behind his head.

"Geoffrey doesn't like smoking," said Michael.

"Yeah, I know," said Chick, settling back in his seat contentedly.

"You got another one?" asked Michael.

"Sure," Chick said. He handed Michael a cigar.

"Thanks. Now we are all together in our rebellion," Michael said. "You're the bodyguard, aren't you? The one Geoffrey hired to guard Cam the ham."

"That'd be me."

"You know anybody who'd want to kill him?" I asked.

"Sure," said Michael. "Everybody here. Including me."

"Why do you say that?"

Chick held out a flaming match so Michael could light his cigar. After Michael got the cigar started, he said, "Because Cam's a shit stirrer. He likes to mess with people. He's the kind of guy who'll hit on your woman, play with your head. He's a punk."

"How did he get this far?"

"He knows when the camera's on. He has a feel for when the reporters are around. Like he's two people or something. He does these environmental commercials, then throws beer cans and shit all over the lot. Talks about tolerance, but calls me 'America's favorite nigger' behind my back. He says it to my face, there will be a delay in shooting. Of course, that's nothing new to the industry. Most of them talk that tolerance bullshit, but I'm from Louisiana, and the worst cracker there at least treats me like a man, instead of a child they can pat on the head, get in my way with their 'help,' then forget me."

There was some heat behind the words as Michael ended his comments. Not much, as Michael was a very controlled individual, but if you knew him as I did, you were able to discern the nuances of his emotions. Michael's background was Deep South Creole. He had worked on the loading docks in Baton Rouge as a teenager to help support his family after his father was injured when a boom chain snapped and whiplashed the older LeBeau's legs, permanently crippling him. Michael was an intense competitor who burned with the kind of low flame the great ones have. Not even a grimace when he was hit. Michael LeBeau was certified tough.

"Fogarty has received some threatening phone calls," I said. "Some letters."

"Yeah," said Michael. "Heard that. Even been on the news. He did a couple of interviews back on the coast before we headed out here. You know, 'ain't he all brave' and 'the show must go on.' That kind of crap."

"Interviews?"

"You don't think Geoffrey and Cameron lose an opportunity to cash in on something like that, do you?"

"Don't you read *Variety* or *People*?" Chick asked. "What are you, some kind of unenlightened heathen?"

I sipped some coffee, then said, "Police have any theories about the threats?"

"In Hollywood, California?" Michael said. "They think the usual stuff. Some crazed fan. That's what they think."

"What do you think?"

"I think I hope I'm there to see it. So I can laugh and shit." He said it without emotion.

I looked at Chick, who shrugged and tipped back the bottle of Jack Daniel's.

SIX

Thursday

Salinger gave the cast the next morning off while he reviewed what "was in the can." He had been called back to the coast, which was a regular occurrence. After lunch the media, which had descended on the set, prevailed upon Salinger to grant them an audience while the crew set up for a scene where the James gang was to ride into town to reconnoiter the town prior to robbing the bank. Michael LeBeau wasn't required for the scene and had returned to his trailer.

"Tell us about the threats on Cameron Fogarty," asked a female reporter. "Are you taking any precautions?"

"Of course," said Salinger. "I have contracted a bodyguard who has experience with movie stars, including Linda Sterling, among others."

"What have the police done?" asked a hatless male reporter, with a tape recorder in one hand.

"There is little they can do at this point," said Salinger. "LAPD and the California State Police are checking files and records for possible suspects, but they have no physical evidence other than one letter, which they have been unable to trace. The local sheriff's office has been helpful as well."

"Regarding the movie itself," said another. "What about the love scenes planned between Michael LeBeau and Meagan Ames? There are people who say that it is out of place in a James Gang movie."

"I believe we are way beyond the kind of limited intellect that considers an interracial relationship to be news. It has been decades since Raquel Welch and Jim Brown in *100 Rifles*."

There was a burst of questions, but the female reporter who had asked the initial question pushed forward and said, "There are rumors that you had trouble getting backing for this production."

Salinger's eyes narrowed. "That's all it is. A rumor."

"They say you need a box office success, or you're in trouble. Especially after your last two vehicles bombed financially."

"They were not bombs. They were misinterpreted. H.L. Mencken was correct when he observed that 'no one ever lost money underestimating the intelligence of the masses.' With *The Night Riders,* we are making a traditional, yet intelligent movie that hopefully transcends the genre."

"They say there is mob money backing this production."

"That's untrue," said Salinger. "And you can quote me."

"Who is backing the movie?" asked the reporter, boring in.

"They wish to remain anonymous at this time. It is a group of businessmen who donate large amounts of money to charitable organizations."

"What charitable organizations?" asked a voice in the middle of the pack. "The AFL-CIO and the Preserve Las Vegas Foundation?"

The other reporters laughed. Geoffrey didn't.

Before Salinger could reply, there was a commotion at the back of the set. Two four-wheel drive vehicles had pulled onto the property and regurgitated six men, all with razor-slick bald heads and wearing leather, camo, and Ranger jump boots. The six men formed a dark knot at the rear of the set. One of them carried a sign that read:

NO NIGGERS IN THE JAMES GANG

Skinheads.

I hadn't heard of any skinhead activity in the area, but I wasn't that well informed about anything. I wanted to believe that I lived in a land of pastoral beauty filled with country people who went to church every Sunday and raised their children to be kind and respectful of others.

The security people moved in that direction, but they were largely made up of people unused to dealing with violent situations. I started walking toward the commotion. Chick moved closer to Cameron Fogarty, his eyes panning the scene and keeping his body between Fogarty and the neo-Nazis.

"We got a right to protest, guaranteed by the Constitution," said a tall, knuckly intruder whose body was a knot of bone and sinew. He had no upper lip, and his prominent ears made him appear sinister and alien. "Jesse James was a son of the South and a Confederate freedom fighter."

"Look, sir," said one of the security men, "we don't want any trouble here. I'm going to ask that you leave or at least stay back until we get this shot finished."

"No niggers in the James Gang," said a thick-bodied skinhead, and the others picked up the chant. The security contingent looked at one another, confused.

The media had picked up the scent and were gathering. Photos were taken as I stepped through the press of bodies and walked directly to the tall skinhead leader. The chanting stopped as the racists sized me up. The skins' leader glared at me. These guys wanted trouble. It was what they did in place of a meaningful existence.

"Get back in your vehicles," I said, "and leave."

"Whatta we got here?" asked the leader. "Another nigger lover?"

I felt my teeth grinding. I took two steps in his direction so I could look him eye to eye. He was only an inch shorter than me. With my peripheral vision, I saw his henchmen bunch tighter behind him.

"One more time," I said. "And then things start happening you're not going to believe. This is my property, and I want you gone. Right now."

"Why don't you throw us off, nigger lover?"

"Hey, hey, hey," said Chick, moving into view. "What's going on here? Wyatt, you gotta learn to be more gracious with guests."

"The fuck're you, man?" said the leader, looking Chick up-and-down.

Chick cocked his head to one side and rested a hand on the pommel of his Colt .45 six-gun. "Why, I'm Randy McNally, fastest gun in the West and geography expert. And I'm here to tell you and the rest of your radioactive shitheads to saddle up and ride out of Tombstone before you rile me."

"You want a piece of me, mother—"

Chick drew the wheel gun and fanned off three shots in the direction of the intruders. The skinheads reacted by throwing themselves to the ground and looking surprised. The skinhead leader fell backward onto the ground.

Chick twirled the pistol and rammed it back into the holster. "All right," he said, "who loaded my hog leg with blanks?" He looked down at the fallen leader. "Boy, you look really stupid sitting in the dirt like that."

The movie people and reporters began to laugh.

The knuckly leader jumped up and came at Chick. Chick set his feet, relaxing his shoulders and raising his hands. The skinhead threw a roundhouse punch, but Chick chopped the neo-Nazi's wrist with a closed fist, following that with a quick punch to the groin. The leader groaned, and his body folded. Chick used the momentum of the groin punch to rebound an elbow into the intruder's face. It struck him hard on the nose. The racist sat down hard on the ground with an audible "whoof."

The other skinheads began reaching into jackets and pockets. But they were too slow.

Chick produced a semiautomatic .380 Colt as quick as a thought and pointed it at the skinheads. I never knew how he managed that. One moment he didn't have it, the next he did.

"Get your hand out of there," Chick said, pointing the pistol at a skinhead, whose hand froze inside his jacket. "Empty. Bet there's no blanks in this one. Holds seven of those nasty little hollow points. One for each of you and another to shoot off in the air in celebration."

"He ain't gonna shoot anybody," said the leader, sitting back on his hands, legs splayed out, blood trailing from one nostril.

Chick looked back at me and smiled. "Love it when they think I won't shoot." He swiveled his head back and offhandedly, as if spitting a sunflower seed, squeezed off a shot that slapped the ground like dropping a stone in a shallow pan. The leader jumped, startled, shrinking back at the sound.

"What do you think now, Curly?" Chick said, raising the pistol and pointing it at the middle of the man's face. "Think I won't shoot? The rest of you morons better turn to stone. No sneezing, no scratching, no unfortunate thoughts. You twitch, and your buddy gets a third nostril. The better to smell himself with." He smiled at them, then slowly shook his head. "God, I'm good at this. I believe that's your cue, Wyatt."

"Get out of here," I said. "Don't come back."

"Okay," said the leader, getting to his feet. There were dust sprinkles on the blood trickling from his nose. "We'll go. But this ain't the end of it. We'll be back."

"I advise against it."

"The sheriff is on his way," said Salinger. "Just called."

"Better if you kids go fill up on Jim Beam, listen to some Hank Williams Jr., and reflect on your unproductive ways," Chick said.

They loaded up in their vehicles and left, spraying dirt and rock. The media enclave surrounded Chick and me. I pushed my way through them, ignoring their questions. One reporter grabbed my arm but let go when I stopped and looked at his hand. Camera flashes and more questions. Chick pushed through to locate Fogarty.

Giving up on me, the media hounds turned to Geoffrey Salinger, whose expression was a strange mix of irritation and surprise. He held up his hands and tried to quiet the reporters while Chick and I moved away. I watched the two skinhead-infested vehicles get smaller, little plumes of dust trailing their retreat. Off in the distance, I noticed a man standing outside a car. His arms were raised and close to his body, as if holding something to his face. Binoculars?

Salinger caught up to us after the press had left. He came striding up, purposefully. He was a purposeful man. "I'd prefer firearms were not discharged on the set," he said to Chick.

"Might make a western a difficult production," said Chick, smiling.

"You know my meaning. You shot off a live round."

"What did you expect, Geoffrey? You think I was going to write letters to the editor to protect my client? The gun's part of the job."

Salinger held out his hand. "Give me the gun, please," he said.

Chick looked at me. There was merriment in his eyes. "Is this a unique guy or what?"

"Interesting the way his mind works," I said.

"Either give up the gun or find another job."

"We've already discussed this," I said. "It's tiring to have to bring it up every time I see you. Either Chick works, or you pack up the circus and head back to California."

"Then that's what we'll do." Geoffrey had his chin out like a six-year-old refusing to eat his vegetables.

"Okay." I shrugged. "So," I said to Chick. "Nice day. What do you want to do with the rest of it? Got a couple of nice deer stands across the creek."

"How about a twelve pack of Budweiser and some CCR?" said Chick. "You drive, and I'll drink and share strange visions with you."

"How come I always have to play chauffeur for you?"

"Because you don't drink, and I do."

"Knew it was something," I said. Then to Salinger I said, "You have twenty-four hours to pack up and leave."

"What about the money I paid?"

"You didn't pay me anything. You gave it to charity, remember? Won't look good if you ask for it back."

Salinger looked bewildered. "So that's it?" he said. "You're just going to walk away?"

"Sure," said Chick. "Our lives are chock-full of things to do."

"All right then," Salinger said. "Have it your way. I'm sorry." He looked off at the set. "I'm just tired. Just please try to keep your gun out of sight."

"Had a lady friend once," said Chick, "made the same request."

Salinger started to say something, changed his mind. Shaking his head, he walked off.

"We need to do something nice for old Geoffrey," said Chick. "He's a good sport."

"He's okay. Probably never seen anything like that before that wasn't scripted. I don't blame him for being upset."

I was looking at the man standing outside the car. What was he doing? He put something inside the car, then got in himself and drove away. I watched the car drive away, then walked off to join Chick.

SEVEN

Rory looked through the pawnshop binoculars and focused the lenses on the tall, rangy guy. Had to be him.

Found the son of a bitch.

There he was. He hadn't changed much. Looked like he could still be playing football. Right now the guy was looking right back at Rory, causing him to pull the glasses down abruptly, wondering if the guy could see him from that far away. Naw, he couldn't, could he? But the guy was looking right in Rory's direction. Wonder what the guy was thinking? Don't let 'im spook you. He's nothing. A punk. Caught you by surprise the other time. Be different this time. Yeah, a lot different.

Rory put the binoculars in the backseat of the Caddy he'd stolen in the city, not as nice as the one he'd had before they'd thrown him inside, of course. He got in it and drove off.

Guy'd been hard enough to find. Like he was hiding out back here in the woods. How'd anybody stand to live out here? Rocks and trees and bugs and snakes and bears and who knew what else. Not a decent restaurant or club in a hundred miles. Might as well be on the moon or Ura-fucking-anus.

And all the local clodhoppers had some slow kind of talking that wasn't quite Southern, like they had shit in their mouth, and when he'd talk to them, they'd look at him like he was from another planet. Like *he* was the one had the funny way of talking, telling them he was looking for this guy Storme, see, an old buddy, so he could see how he was doing. Like that. Simple, huh? But not for these thickheaded, country yucks. They'd scratch their heads and frown and tell how they knew some completely other guy named Stone or Stokes, like their ears was fulla shit and they couldn't hear what he was saying in plain English. Driving him crazy.

Then he'd run across one old boy who said there'd been some trouble a few years back in Paradise County, and rumor was Storme was involved. So that led him to the Paradise County Library and the newspaper archives. There'd been some killings. County sheriff got whacked and a couple of KC hitters got blown away by the feds. But an article in the *Kansas City Star* had it different. Said there were a couple of anonymous guys involved. Storme was one of the guys whose name was floating around, but nobody could find him to ask.

One thing led to another, and Rory was finally able to track him to this movie location, even though Rory couldn't figure how the guy was involved in the movies now. He didn't see the guy acting. Mostly, the guy stood around watching, except when he fronted the skinheads. That took some 'nads. All the security ass-holes standing around with their hands in their pockets like it was Disney World or something, and the baldheads were crashing the line on the submarine ride. Not Storme, he got right in the guy's face, then his badass buddy in the cowboy duds put one of them on the ground like it was nothing. The badass could be trouble. Seen some of the baldies in the slam. Aryan Brotherhood cons with swastikas and those weird double S's like lightning bolts tattooed on their arms, all of 'em juiced on liquor from fruit or potatoes stolen from the cafeteria and hidden in plastic baggies in their toilets. Always messing with the other groups, especially the nigger gangs inside. They left Rory alone, since he had protection from Bobby Frank on the outside. They respected the organization.

What the hell were those punks doing here anyway?

Wonder if there was a way to use them?

Something to think about over a shot of JD and a High Life.

EIGHT

T *hursday evening*
   After Salinger and the actors involved finished shooting the recon scene, and the actors and technicians had retreated to their trailers and motels, I decided to head back to my cabin.

"Might as well stick around for a while," Chick said. "Never know what'll happen next. You won't know anything about Sandy's interview until tomorrow night. If nothing else, you can sit around and watch me give CPR to a bottle of Chivas while I ruminate on the amorphous state of life in this foul decade. It'll validate you."

But we didn't do that. Instead, we accompanied Cameron Fogarty and the Lost Boys for a night on the town.

"Hell, I gotta stay with him," said Chick. "It's my job."

"Not mine," I said.

But I stayed anyway. It was either that or sit around the cabin and miss Sandy.

Fogarty rented a limousine and driver from a service in Paradise. Most of the driver's experience had been with teenagers inflamed with youth and cheap beer en route to the senior prom. This would be a little different. High school kids had more propriety.

Fogarty and his friends rode in the limo while Chick and I followed in my Jeep. On the way Chick filled me in on what he had learned thus far.

"It's been hard to narrow the field," said Chick. "Like LeBeau told us last night, about the only guys who don't want to kill

Fogarty are his buddies in the limo. He makes a habit of being the classic self-absorbed movie asshole."

I watched the taillights on the stretch limo ahead of me.

"Have you found out what was in the letter?" I asked.

"Usual stuff. A little dramatic, maybe. 'I'm going to make you pay for what you did. This will be your last movie.' That kind of crap. Typed on plain typing paper."

"Somebody knew how to get a letter to him," I said. "That should narrow it down a little."

"What I figure too. Movie stars aren't very accessible. Has to be someone thinks he can get close."

"Or she."

"A woman would have less trouble. Kid spreads himself around like peanut butter."

I watched the limo swerve, then straighten itself.

"See that?" Chick said. "Bet they're messing with the driver. Be my luck he dies in a car wreck. That's something to put on your bodyguard résumé."

"What about the phone calls?"

"He doesn't remember much about them. Says they came early in the morning, before sunrise, when he was sleeping off a drunk. Made to Fogarty's place in Bel-Air. Man's voice, supposedly, but it sounded electronic like a computer. Used something to garble the voice. Same stuff as the letter. 'You're through fucking me. When the curtain falls on *The Night Riders,* you're dead.' There was an article about it in the *LA Times* last week. Salinger and Fogarty refused comment. Article quoted 'an informed source.'"

"A leak."

"Right. Probably provided by Salinger." Chick rolled down his window two inches. "You know, though, this is going to sound funny, but something's not right. After doing this so long, you start to get vibrations about this stuff. And I don't feel any."

"Like they cooked the whole thing up?"

He shrugged and pushed in the truck's cigarette lighter.

"Publicity stunt?" I said.

He lit the cigarette. "Maybe."

"What about the skinheads?"

"Coincidence. May have nothing to do with it."

"Why guard him then?"

"It could be real. It's something to do. Besides, it's gainful employment."

"You catch that about Salinger being in trouble in the industry? What do you think about that?"

"I heard it," said Chick. "Geoffrey's last two movies, he tried to be avant-garde and progressive. Saw one of them. It was like playing strip poker in the dark. Wasn't bad, but the money people aren't into bullshit that doesn't pay, so Geoffrey's got to come up large this time out. He's not going to go broke or anything, but that's why he's putting up with Fogarty."

"Have you talked to any of the people on the set?"

"Naw," said Chick. He took a drag off his cigarette and let the smoke trail off through the opened window. He looked at me. "Thought I'd leave the detective work for you. Know how much you like it."

I slowed for a curve in the highway.

"I've got other things to do."

Chick laughed. More of a chortle, actually. Few things are more irritating than a chortle at one's expense. "You got nothing to do except sit around your cabin and mold."

"Maybe I like that," I said.

"It's not all bad."

"So where are we going, right now?"

"Chicken hawking."

"What?"

"It's what Fogarty and his band of social cripples call it when they're cruising for local talent to woo back to his place for a night of drug-addled debauchery."

I looked straight ahead. "Great."

"Yeah. He's a fucking delight, for sure," said Chick. "A real dead ringer for something like you never want to see again."

We followed the limo to town and into the parking lot of a hamburger place with hot-and-cold-running teenagers. The limo was too big for the diagonal parking slots, so the driver pulled to the side and parked. Chick instructed me to pull in behind the limo, and I did so.

The trio of young men I'd seen for the first time that afternoon got out of the limo and began circulating among the parked cars. Fogarty stayed in the limo.

"They're picking up teenyboppers," I said. "How do you stand this?"

"My job's to keep him from getting killed," said Chick, "not prevent him being charged with statutory rape."

"Quite an attitude."

He shrugged. "You give way too much thought to moral dilemmas. Slows you down some." He swallowed what was left of the beer he'd been drinking and opened another. "But it's what I like best about you."

I folded my arms and leaned on top of the steering wheel. Watched the trio work the girls. Twenty minutes later they had rounded up a half-dozen girls of various sizes and hues. They hustled the girls back to the limo. A window slid down, and after squeals of recognition and delight, the limo door opened and swallowed five of the girls. One girl, a skinny blonde with a nice face, walked back to her car. She looked close to tears.

"Culling the herd," said Chick. He took a huge swallow of beer.

One of Fogarty's entourage, whose name was Kerry Kane, walked back to my Jeep. He was a slender kid, narrow shoulders, and fragile bones with long, wispy, blond hair.

"I need to ride with you, okay?" said the kid.

"Been looking forward to it," I said. "Get in." Kerry walked around the truck to get in on Chick's side. I looked at Chick. "Now I'm a chauffeur."

Chick smiled.

Kane got in the backseat, and we resumed following the limousine.

"How come you're the one had to ride with us?" Chick asked Kane. "Draw straws?"

"Just the way it shakes out, man," said Kane.

"Don't you get to court one of the little sweethearts?"

"What? Oh, wait a minute—Yeah, I got it now. Sure. Cam takes first pick, and we take what's left, unless Cam decides he wants three of them, then Volts and Peter get the other two."

"Pretty magnanimous of old Cam," said Chick. "What was wrong with the blonde? Too skinny?"

"Naw. She had a harelip. Cam don't like defects."

My hands tightened on the steering wheel.

I watched our guest in the rearview as the Jeep rolled down the highway. Kane fumbled in his jacket and produced a cigarette that was fat in the middle and twisted to a point at both ends.

"You got a light, dude?" he asked.

Chick looked at me and smiled.

"Two things we need to get straight," I said, looking in the rearview. "First, my name isn't dude. Second, you put that doob back in your pocket, or you'll be wearing it like a tampon."

"Hey, relax, huh?" He put it back in his pocket. "See?" He showed me his hands. "It's cool. Could I bum a cigarette off you, man?" he asked Chick.

"You're not smoking either," I said.

"He's smoking," said Kane.

"You're right," I said. "He is. That's very observant. You still don't get to."

"All right. All right. Just chill, du—I mean, okay."

Chick, still smiling, said, "You are exceedingly overwrought, partner. It's a beautiful night. Try to enjoy it."

"Shut up," I said. "I'm riding shotgun for a herd of pederasts, and it's your fault. So your job for the rest of the evening is to not come up with any more suggestions about what I can do with the beautiful night."

"What's a pederast?" asked Kane.

NINE

After a roadside pit stop for the idiots to hike their legs and relieve themselves, we pulled into the parking lot of a roadhouse called the Lone Horse. Pickup trucks with gun racks and Confederate flags in rear windows were randomly parked in the gravel and dirt parking lot.

"Not the best place to protect someone," I said.

"No worse than anywhere else," said Chick. "Public. Parking lot's congested. Hard to pop him and get away. Nobody followed us. But I'd appreciate it if you'd wait here a few minutes and see who pulls in."

"That's fine," I said.

"You care if I get out?" Kane asked.

"I'd prefer it," I said. Chick opened his door, and the kid got out and walked across the lot to join his friends. Chick went with him. I watched them. Chick stopped the group at the entrance to the bar, walked in ahead of them, then came back outside and allowed them to enter ahead of him.

I listened to Bob Seger on the radio and waited, watching to see who pulled in. If anyone did, I was to take note of the license plate and how many were in the vehicle. Seger sang "Brave Strangers" and "The Famous Final Scene," and nobody came. I lit a cigar and thought about what Sandy might be doing. Wondered if she was thinking about what I was doing. Wondered how egocentric my thinking was becoming regarding Sandy. Next thing would be wondering if she'd wear my letter sweater, which is peculiar thinking for a man my age. Maybe just give her my class ring.

Five more minutes passed, and still nobody had entered the lot. Place was a gold mine. Seger finished, and Wilson Pickett started singing "I'm in Love." I bailed out of the truck before I started getting maudlin and weepy and exhibiting behavior unbecoming to a man who had seen *Dirty Harry* seven times.

I locked the truck and walked to the Lone Horse Bar and Lounge. Never understood the difference between bar and lounge, but apparently the proprietor of the Lone Horse did. Maybe he'd explain it if I engaged him in conversation. Maybe get him to explain other wonders of the universe.

Inside the Lone Horse, it was loud and half-filled with patrons who looked as if they'd just left the bowling alley. Or a tractor pull. John Deere baseball caps. Hanging beer sign lights dim through a Marlboro haze.

Fogarty and his court sat around two tables they had joined together. The girls sat as close as they could to the movie star without sitting on top of one another. There were sidelong glances of curiosity from the other patrons—partly because Fogarty and his three buddies were positively overdressed, or underdressed, for the Lone Horse, and partly because of the bevy of underage cuties. Chick was standing near a wall, a long-neck Busch in one hand, checking out the patrons and the layout of the bar. When he saw me come in, he joined me at a table nearby Fogarty's.

"Eastwood," said Fogarty, waving a hand at us as we sat. "C'mon and join us. I'm buying."

Chick looked at me and grinned. I shrugged, and we took seats at the table with the children.

"Ladies, this is Chick," said Fogarty. "He's a bodyguard. The big guy is Wyatt Storme. He's kind of a minor celebrity. Used to play football for the Dallas Cowboys."

"Do you know Tony Romo?" asked one of the girls, a strawberry blonde with too much eye makeup.

"No," I said. Wyatt Storme, master conversationalist.

"Wyatt, this is Peter Braithwaite," said Fogarty, indicating a big guy, early twenties, with a weight problem. "And this is Volts." Volts was a dark-haired young guy who looked like he belonged in a Quentin Tarantino movie—lazy eyes, faint mustache, long lank hair shaved close at the temples and pulled back into a knot at the back of his neck. He had a smug expression pasted to his face and the overbearing mannerisms of the street. Braithwaite and Volts sat on either side of the girls.

"Volts has done time," said Fogarty.

"How nice for Volts," I said.

A waitress in a cowboy hat, cowboy boots, and dark hose sidled up to take our order.

"Coke for me," I said. "Chocolate shakes and bubble gum for the ladies." I received dirty looks from a couple of the females. Maybe they preferred vanilla. Can't please everybody, I guess.

"Bring the ladies a couple of bottles of champagne," Fogarty said.

"We don't have any champagne. Sorry, sir."

"Then bring them some wine."

"I'll need to see some ID for the ladies."

"I understand," said Fogarty. "Volts, show the lady some ID."

Volts reached into his jacket and pulled out a wad of bills. He peeled off two hundreds and handed it to the waitress.

"Be another one when we leave, you keep it coming," said Volts.

"I don't know…about this," said the waitress. "The manager, he might not like it."

"No problem," said Fogarty. "Something for the manager guy too." Fogarty reached into his jacket, produced a G-note, and handed it to the hesitant waitress.

The waitress gave a look around like a watering doe, snatched the proffered bills, and left to fill the order.

"Hey, Storme," said Fogarty. "I got a hundred dollars says the manager never sees the thousand. You in?"

I shook my head.

"A hundred too steep?"

I tapped the long ash of my cigar in an aluminum ashtray. "I don't have any interest in playing with people who work for a living."

Fogarty leaned back in his chair, smiling. "Is that some kind of comment?"

"Nearly everything we do is."

"You're probably right," he said. "Hey, Kane, hop over there to the bar and get me some smokes."

Kane got up and carried out the imperial directive. The waitress returned with the drinks and passed them around. There was no talk of checking ID, just the faint blush of diminished integrity in the waitress's cheeks. Kane returned with two packs of cigarettes and handed them to Fogarty.

"What's this shit, Kerry?" said Fogarty. "You know I smoke Luckies."

"They didn't have any," said Kane.

"Maybe if you'd picked up a couple cartons like you were told, I wouldn't be out."

"I did," said Kane. "But we got in a hurry to leave and—"

Fogarty held up a hand. "No fucking excuses."

"Okay," said Kane, nodding and looking out the corners of his eyes at the girls. He looked like a third grader being chastised for not doing his homework. "You're right. My fault. Sorry, Cam."

"But, what the fuck, huh?" said Fogarty, who raised his hands like a Baptist preacher. "Take the little chicklets here, for instance. They look eager and willing, don't you think? You girls ready for some fun?"

The teenyboppers looked at one another and giggled and brushed back hair with slender hands. One of the girls, a black girl with her teeth set in an even line, considered Fogarty with an unamused expression.

Volts and Peter Braithwaite smirked like constipated hyenas.

"Maybe we oughta have us a competition between the little dollies, Cam," said Volts. "Sort of like dueling bitches." Cam smiled. For a brief second, I thought Braithwaite seemed embarrassed, but if he had been, it passed quickly.

The black girl stood up.

"Where you going, babe?" asked Volts.

"I'm leaving," she said. Her ebony eyes were hot, and her jaw was set.

Volts reached up and grabbed her arm. "Relax, little girl. Nobody's gonna bite you."

She tried to pull away, and Volts tightened his grip.

"Let go, asshole," she said.

"Will you look at this," said Volts. "This one's got a little fire in her hole."

"Take your hands off her," said someone. Whoever it was sounded like me.

Volts turned his attention to me. "What's it to you, old man?"

I stood up.

"Oh boy," Chick said.

"Just let go of her arm," I said. "Now."

"Let her go, Volts," said Fogarty.

Volts considered me with fierce eyes. He held the struggling girl's arm toward me, then released her. She rubbed her forearm and looked at me.

"What have you got up your ass, man?" Volts said.

"I don't like the way you treat people."

"Whatcha gonna do about it?" Volts said, standing up.

"Whatever's necessary."

"Sit down, junior," Chick said to Volts. "Everybody's looking at you. Which is bad, because pretty soon they'll come to the sick conclusion that I'm with you by choice."

"What?" said Volts, looking down at Chick. Other people in the bar were looking at us now.

"I'm doing you a favor, kid," said Chick. "Storme's the last musketeer, man. He's got this hang-up about honor and integrity and shit."

"What the fuck's that to me?"

"Ya gotta listen closer. You see, he'd rather risk personal injury than watch you mistreat the girl. Doesn't make any sense to me either, but that's the way he is. Personally, I think it's old-fashioned."

"Maybe I'll have to see what he's got."

"What he's got," said Chick, "is more than you've ever seen. So, sit down, and don't let a burst of stupidity ruin the rest of your life."

Volts continued to look at me, raising his chin a half inch. "What's she to you, anyway?"

"She doesn't want to stay here and be degraded," I said. "Maybe the rest do, but she doesn't."

"You think you can take me?"

"Haven't given it much thought. Doesn't matter either way. I'm through talking to you about it."

"Hey, come on," said Fogarty. "Let it go, Volts. Sit down, dammit."

Volts slowly sat, giving me his best tough-guy mean mug as he did. It's a look the empty little city boys have developed. Chick chuckled to himself.

"Sorry about this," I said to the girl.

"It's okay," she said. "My name's Sharra."

"You need a ride home?" I asked her.

"No, I can call a friend," she said. She gave a disdainful look to her friends at the table. She looked back at me and said, "Thank you anyway."

She left our happy little circle of revelers, produced a cell phone, and made a call.

"How fucking heroic," said Volts. "How's it feel to be a hero, Storme?"

I watched Sharra hang up her cell. She smiled and waved to me before going out the door, and I felt the satisfaction older males feel when we can make young ladies smile.

"It has its moments," I said.

TEN

Friday morning the actors had a 5:30 a.m. set call, and Cameron Fogarty was late. He wasn't just late. It was already 5:50 a.m., and Fogarty wasn't even out of bed yet. It was even early for me. I usually didn't get up before six unless I was hunting.

Chick and I were sitting in folding chairs outside Fogarty's trailer. Michael LeBeau was there with us, drinking coffee and rocking back and forth on his feet, his teeth chattering.

"Baby, you get a black man up before dawn, you better have your white ass there. Jesus, ain't even up yet. Damn."

I was drinking coffee and watching the sun, reddish-orange with heat, break over the oak and walnut trees lining the ridge, pushing back the blue-black night. Chick smoked a cigarette and worked a crossword puzzle, his cowboy hat pushed back on the crown of his head.

"What's a seven-letter word for *succinct*?" Chick asked. "Starts with an *l*."

"Laconic," I said.

"That's a hell of a thing for a guy who used to wear a jock-strap to work to know," said Chick, writing it in the little squares.

"You think if we set fire to his trailer, he might get up?" said Michael.

"No," said Chick. "But it's a warm thought."

Geoffrey Salinger came striding up. Today's outfit was English riding pants and boots with a leather bomber jacket and one of those sloped English gentleman caps that buttoned on the bill of the cap. He looked like a pilot in the Lafayette Escadrille. He even had the silk scarf. Where did he keep all that stuff?

"Where is he?" demanded Salinger.

"You mean where's Fogarty?" said Chick.

"Goddammit, you know what I mean," said Salinger. "Why don't you have him up and on set?"

Chick took a languid draw on his cigarette and rubbed a sleepy eye with the palm of his hand. He squinted at me and shook his head as if trying to shake something out of his ear.

"Boy, Geoffrey, I hope when I turn around, there's somebody behind me you're talking to with that tone of voice," Chick said in a low voice. "'Cause if there isn't, I'm going to be severely distressed."

"I'm sorry, but I hired you to look after him."

"You hired me to protect him. Not to be your gofer. Not to be his alarm clock. And not to listen to any foolish talk before breakfast." Chick smiled at him. "Now, come on, Geoffrey. Be courteous. You can do it. Ask me nice to go over and awaken the crown prince of pedophiles."

"Who do you think you're talking to?"

"A guy who doesn't have anybody else wants to wake up Fogarty."

"Then," said Salinger, "go and get him."

Chick sipped his coffee, sat the cup down, then crossed his legs. Smiled. Waited.

"Hurry. We're losing the light," said Salinger.

"What's an eight-letter word for *annoy*?" Chick asked me. "Third letter is *r*."

"Director?" I said, watching the sunrise.

"I don't have time for this kind of shit," said Salinger, his fists on his hips now.

"It's irritate," said Chick to me, writing it on the crossword sheet. "The word's irritate. Shall I use it in a sentence? The rude director, dressed like Errol Flynn, began to irritate the handsome bodyguard."

Salinger looked mad some more. Chick waited some more. Salinger looked at me. I shook my head at him. Salinger took a couple of deep breaths. He looked at LeBeau, whom he knew better than to send after Fogarty, and then back at Chick.

"Would you...as a favor to me, could you please have Cameron on the set in fifteen minutes, Chick?" Salinger said it as if he were swallowing a ball of wax.

"Love to," said Chick. He tipped the back of his cowboy hat forward and walked into Fogarty's trailer. Salinger looked at us briefly, his lips pressed together, and without another word, turned on his expensive heels and walked to wherever directors go.

"Never heard anyone talk to Geoffrey like that," said LeBeau. "I think old Geoffrey pissed off your buddy."

"Not that easy to do either," I said.

"Geoffrey's an okay dude, though," said LeBeau. "He's up against it about something. Worked with him before, and he wasn't this edgy."

Five minutes later Chick returned, a pair of cowboy boots in one hand and Cameron Fogarty slung over his shoulder as if carrying a wounded soldier. Fogarty was mumbling obscenities when Chick dumped him in the middle of wide-eyed technicians and grinning stunt men. Fogarty's jeans were unbuttoned, and he fell unceremoniously on his rear end.

"Ta-da," said Chick. "And with ten minutes to spare."

"You son of a bitch," said the prostrate actor. He staggered to his feet and struggled to secure his pants. Chick tossed the boots at his feet.

"Mr. Son of a Bitch to you," said Chick.

Fogarty took two steps toward Chick and threw a punch at Chick's head, which Chick blocked with a quick slap of his hand against Fogarty's wrist. Fogarty yelped in surprise, then recovered and threw a side kick at Chick's chest. Chick moved aside like a matador and slapped underneath Fogarty's ankle. The actor ended up in the dirt once more.

This time there was laughter.

"Quit playing around and get dressed," said Chick.

"I've got a headache," said Fogarty.

"And all this time, I thought you were only a carrier," said Chick. "Take a couple aspirin and suck it up. The show must go on."

"I need a cigarette." Chick handed him one. "And a cup of coffee."

"Someone get Mr. Fogarty a cup of coffee," said an assistant director.

"Shit," said LeBeau after things settled down. He looked me up-and-down as if seeing me for the first time. "How is it you know somebody like him, Wyatt? What have you been up to since you retired?"

The sun was up now, glowing with an incandescent brightness in the blue horizon. There was a bank of clouds forming in the southwest.

"You wouldn't believe me if I told you," I said.

The morning shoot progressed well. Fogarty composed himself, then comported himself well. He was able to switch gears immediately and get into the character of Jesse James. It was remarkable. Was acting a talent or the absence of a core personality? As effective as Fogarty was as Jesse James, Geoffrey Salinger was as masterful at his profession. He pleaded, flattered, cajoled, scolded, instructed, bullied, and exhorted the actors and crew to perform at their peak. It was an impressive performance.

The afternoon shoot was delayed when an autumn rain struck. An angry Salinger stood in the middle of the downpour looking up at the Missouri sky as if willing it to stop.

God was unimpressed. It rained harder. A gofer ran up with an umbrella and held it over the stubborn director.

"Dammit," said Salinger, as if he'd just busted at the black-jack table. "Take a break."

Actors and extras scattered like ants in all directions. Cameramen and technicians covered equipment with plastic covers and canvas. I found myself under the shelter of the mess tent next to Michael LeBeau, watching water drip off the canvas, smelling the rain-washed afternoon.

LeBeau produced a couple of cigars from under his cow-boy vest and handed one to me. "Geoffrey's preoccupied," said LeBeau. "I'm willing to risk it, if you are." I smiled, and we lit the cigars, puffing on them as rain pattered merrily against the canvas. A nice moment. You don't get all that many.

"Michael," said a female voice. I turned and saw the face of Valeri Darnell. A face I'd seen in close-up and ten feet tall in a dozen theatres. It was no less impressive in person. Her dark-brown eyes sparkled with the luster of polished gems. Her hair and clothes beaded with moisture, as if the rain knew better than to spoil her elegance.

"Hey, Val," said LeBeau. "I want you to meet a friend of mine. Wyatt, this is Valeri Darnell. Valeri, this is Wyatt Storme. I'm the token black, and Valeri is the token human being."

"Every movie should have at least one," I said. "Nice to meet you, Valeri."

She shook my hand. Her handshake was firm, her hand warm.

"They tell me you used to play football, Mr. Storme," she said.

"About four thousand years ago."

She smiled. "I've never been to Missouri before. It's beautiful. I love it. Everything about it. The trees, the sky, even the rain. I miss the rain. We don't get much of it in Southern California. No wonder you live here." She shivered involuntarily, then hugged herself. I removed my jacket and draped it over her shoulders. She didn't protest.

"Thank you," she said. "Rare to meet a gentlemen on a movie set. Counting Michael, that gives us two for this production." She put an arm around LeBeau's waist and placed her cheek against his shoulder.

"What's up, kids?" said the voice of Cameron Fogarty from behind. Valeri looked as if a smelly mongrel dog had just entered the tent. Fogarty was carrying a pint bottle of Wild Turkey in one hand and a strange-looking cigarette, unlit, in the other. Chick was with him, standing in the background, smoking a cigarette and watching Fogarty's back.

"Hello, Cameron," said Valeri without warmth.

"Well, look at this, Eastwood," Fogarty said to Chick. "America's sweetheart rubbing up against America's favorite Afro-American." Chick arched the half eyebrow and turned away to look at the rain.

"And witnessed by America's most obnoxious bore," said Valeri.

"What's eating on you, Val-e-ri?"

"I don't like it when you call Michael that."

"America's favorite Afro-American? Hell, he is. Everybody knows that. I don't mean anything by it. Mike knows that. Isn't that right, Mike?"

LeBeau looked at Fogarty with a neutral expression as if Fogarty weren't there. Michael LeBeau was nothing if not cool. Our defensive players used to talk about how calm and tough LeBeau was when we played them.

"You can ring his bell, knock the crap out of him, even cheap shot him, and the guy doesn't even change expression. Just gets up and runs it again." And usually he'd break one loose that would break your team's back. It was always better to leave him alone.

"Yeah," said LeBeau. "I also know what you call me when I'm not around."

"Aw, I don't mean anything by it. Just kidding around. You know that. As far as acting ability goes, I have a great deal of respect for you as a ball carrier."

LeBeau smiled bemusedly. He hadn't missed the insult. He turned to me.

"This is one stupid white boy," he said.

I nodded, keeping an eye on Fogarty. I remembered his outburst with Chick earlier. Reason and decorum had little effect on his actions.

Fogarty took a swallow from his whiskey bottle, looked at all three of us individually. "Well, guys," he said, "much as I'd like to hang with you old folks, gotta run now. Spread myself around."

"Careful you don't spread yourself too thin," said LeBeau.

"I'll try to remember that, Mikey," Fogarty said. He walked out into the rain. He took a few steps, stopped, laughed loudly for our benefit, and continued on.

I looked at Chick, who shrugged and followed the movie star into the rain.

Michael shook his head. "I don't know about that boy."

"He is intolerable," said Valeri. "I'm sorry I irritated him. I know he's unpredictable. He usually lashes out at someone, anyone, when he's mad. One way or another."

"You ever work with him before?" I asked.

"Yes," she said. "And it was every bit as enjoyable."

"Why work with him again?"

"He's hot. His last two movies went through the roof. That's why Geoffrey is willing to endure his conduct."

"Anybody else on this set work with him before?"

"Several of us. Salinger, of course. Michael too."

"You worked with him, Michael?"

"Yeah. Makes you wonder what I was thinking when I signed on for this gig, doesn't it?"

"Were there any incidents?"

LeBeau gave me a funny look. "Nothing big," he said. "He just ran off with my girlfriend for a few days. That, and I broke his nose and he sued me."

"He win?"

"Settled out of court. I had to apologize. I really liked that."

"And you're working with him again?"

"Like Bob Dylan says, 'Money doesn't talk, it screams,'" said LeBeau. "Nobody's paying me to run off-tackle anymore."

The gofer that provided Salinger with the umbrella came running through the rain. He stopped a respectful distance from us and said, "Ms. Darnell, Geoffrey would like to see you if you're available."

"All right," she said. "Thank you."

"I'll walk you," said LeBeau.

"Thank you, Michael. Oh," she said to me, "you'll need your jacket back."

"I'll pick it up later," I said. "I'm fine."

She thanked me, and they hurried together through the rain.

I puffed the cigar and thought about people who would involve themselves with people they couldn't stand to be around.

Decided it was beyond me.

ELEVEN

Saturday morning

The rain kept up for the rest of the day and all of the next. Chick and I practiced target shooting and played cards with the stunt men to pass the time while Salinger met with the cast.

During one target session Saturday morning, Chick unzipped a long, exotic-looking pistol from a nylon gun cover. The weapon had wood stocks and an ornate, modified, heart-shaped trigger guard. It was single shot and loaded from the breech like a double-barrel shotgun.

"Thompson-Center Contender," said Chick, handing the gun to me. "Thirty-caliber Herrett, specialty game load. Got two other barrels for it. A .357 Max barrel and a .270. The Herrett and the .357 I had ported by a gunsmith."

"I've seen one like it before."

"I can hit out to three hundred yards with it. Accurately."

"Nobody can hit anything with a pistol at those distances. Not even one of you spec-op crazies."

"I can," said Chick. "See the marks on the front sight?" He pointed at two narrow, horizontal lines painted into the blade front sight.

"So?"

"That's so I can judge the drop. First one is two hundred. The second is three hundred yards."

I looked at him.

"You don't believe me?" he said.

"I don't think you'd allow the truth to stand in the way of a good story," I said.

"Ha!" said Chick. "I am a deadly marksman of some repute. I can knock the antenna off a soldier ant at fifty yards. Shoot between the wings of a hummingbird. Shoot the eyes out of—"

"See that stump down there?" I said, interrupting him and pointing toward the creek. A ridge rose up behind it. "The one next to the dead oak tree."

"Yeah. I see it."

"How far you think it is?"

"Two thirty, maybe two hundred thirty-five yards."

I nodded at him. "Hit that."

"May have to walk the shots up."

"What?"

"I'm a little out of practice estimating distance. I may have to shoot once or twice to get the range."

"Whatever."

"Five shots, then we'll go take a look. I hit four, you owe me a bottle of scotch. The good stuff, no blends."

"Deal."

"It's raining, you know," Chick said, loading the handgun.

"I'd think a big pistolero like yourself would laugh at the elements."

"Rain makes it different. Long-distance shooting is an art. It's not like shooting coffee cans with a shotgun."

"Pretend you're shooting between the wings of a hummingbird."

He walked over to a nearby tree and sat at its base, his back against the trunk. He drew his knees up and rested his elbows on the inside on his knees.

"Prepare to be amazed," Chick said.

He let out a half-breath and gently squeezed off a round. The long handgun bellowed. Chick reloaded and repeated the process four more times. Whether he hit the stump or the trees around it, I couldn't tell through the rain. His concentration was intense. Almost frightening. It was as if he existed on another plane.

"Get your money, son," he said. "I'm in the mood for Glenlivet."

"We'll see."

We walked across the sodden field. Our boots sank in the rain-saturated earth. Reaching the stump, I saw the muddy trail of a bullet channel at the base of the hollow stump. Looking closer, I found the four holes and four splintered exit wounds through the back of the stump. The four hits were within twelve inches of one another.

"I was low on the first shot. But, as you can see, I come as advertised. Chick Easton, long-range gunner. The bad guys aren't safe at any distance even if wearing a condom."

"Pretty good shooting," I said.

"It's better than that."

"All right," I said. "It's the best shooting I've ever seen."

He closed his eyes and smiled as if savoring the moment. He opened one eye to look at me. He smiled.

"Gun does the work," said Chick. "All you gotta do is hold it steady. Uncle Sam gave me a specially worked Remington XP-100 once. Won't tell you what year that was. Looked like a spaceman ray gun. Easier to pack than a sniper rifle. It even had a little sling for it. I could shoot that thing three hundred yards. Further, if I could find a stable rest. Carried a fifteen-shot Browning like yours and a twenty-two Colt auto with a silencer for close work. I liked to be prepared. Y'know, I wasn't over there very long before I determined they were trying to kill me."

"I try not to think about it," I said.

"Sometimes," said Chick, "I can't think of anything else."

Fogarty decided he wanted to eat lunch in town. Salinger lent him his Jeep, and Chick and I followed behind in my Jeep. Five miles from Paradise, a white Cadillac roared up behind us, then settled down to a trailing speed. It was the same car I'd seen the day the skinheads had shown up.

"Saw that car the other day," I said.

"I remember it," said Chick.

"You think he's following us?"

Chick turned around in his seat to look. "I don't know. Could be. Could be following Fogarty too."

Fogarty pulled into the back parking lot of McNaughton's, Paradise's best restaurant. Chick had called ahead and arranged for Fogarty to come in the back way and eat in a private room. When we parked, the white Cadillac pulled in behind us.

"Look at this," said Chick. He took his .380 Colt out of his shoulder holster and put it down beside his leg. We got out. Chick moved closer to the Jeep, sliding between the Jeep and the driver of the Cadillac.

A heavy-set guy, five foot ten, jet-black hair, black eyes got out of the Caddy. He was wearing a dark-gray sharkskin suit, white shirt, no tie. I didn't even know they made sharkskin suits anymore. He looked familiar in a cloudy way, but I couldn't place him.

Chick had his hand in his pocket as Fogarty and his buddies got out of the Jeep. I locked the doors on the Jeep.

"Wyatt Storme," said Sharkskin Suit.

"That's right," I said, facing him. "Can I help you?"

"Remember me?" There was a strange smile on his face as if he harbored some inner glee.

"You've got the advantage of me," I said.

The man's eyebrows knitted, and he tilted his head to one side. He took a couple of steps closer. He had a slight limp. "You sure? Think about it. You don't know who I am?"

"No, sorry," I said. But I was starting to.

He put his fists on his hips and looked at the ground, then around the lot. He muttered something to himself, then looked at me.

"Well, that's fucked up," he said. "You will remember me. Think about it." He turned and jerked open the door to the Cadillac, slammed the door, started the car, and squealed out of the lot.

"Another of your many fans?" asked Chick, slipping the Colt back under his jacket. "Hard to remember all the little people, I guess."

"I remember him now. Just came to me. Used to be a leg breaker in Denver. They called him 'Glory' Rory. Rory Marchibroda. He tried to go independent and collect on a friend of mine. I broke his kneecap and shoulder with a baseball bat."

"Louisville Slugger?"

"Nellie Fox model. Thirty-four inch. Cut down to about half that. Ruined the bat. A real collector's item now."

"You always do things with style."

"Same old story. There's no appreciation for the finer things."

"World's full of peasants."

"Besides being a leg-breaker, Rory's a killer. Funny he should show up now with Fogarty being threatened. Another thing I found out. Did you know LeBeau and Fogarty had a fight on another movie?"

"Who won?"

"LeBeau."

"Good."

"Then Fogarty filed suit and got an out-of-court settlement."

"That chickenshit. He has no honor."

"Fine way to talk about your employer."

"He's my client. Salinger's paying the bill."

"Saw how you treat him too."

"They love being abused."

"I'm sure they do. Either way, LeBeau doesn't like Fogarty. But it wouldn't be Michael's style to make anonymous threats. He's more up-front."

"But he was up-front once and got sued for it. Might make him decide to be sneakier next time."

Which was something to think about.

"How do we get involved in these things?" I asked.

"Personally, I'm just in it for the sport," said Chick.

TWELVE

"**A**sshole football player," Rory muttered to himself as the Caddy splashed and careened down the rain-slick street that led to the room he had rented. It was a piece-of-shit converted attic close to the abandoned train station, but it was cheap, he only slept there, and it was out of the way. Tony Bennett was rolling on the tape deck. Cassettes were no longer the thing. Now kids walked around with iPods, music they recorded on their computers. Had been in stir too long. Rory stopped in front of the house where his apartment was and picked up his gun. He got back in his car and headed back to the place where they were shooting the movie so he could watch the big-shot football player.

So he didn't remember me, Rory thought. That son of a bitch. Just some guy he'd beat up with a baseball bat, like he did it so much, it was hard to remember which one Rory was. Who'd he think he was? It had ruined the moment. Greg Peck remembered Robert Mitchum. Nick Nolte remembered De Niro. This guy needed to remember Rory Marchibroda.

Now, the first meeting was wasted. There was no fear in the guy's eyes. Rory wanted to see fear in Big Shot's eyes. Fear and recognition. Wanted the guy to know his life was going to change.

He'd already been knocked out watching the other guy shooting that weird pistol he had. They hadn't seen him doing that. What the hell had his buddy been shooting at? That's what Rory had asked himself, sitting up on the hill with a raincoat on, looking through the binoculars. Then he watched the two of them walk over to look at a stump, like they had nothing to do but admire dead trees. Couple of morons. Then he'd glassed the stump and saw the splinters sticking out the back and the two men pointing at them. The guy had been *aiming* at the stump, for chrissakes. Never seen nothing like that before. Nobody could shoot like that, could they? Shit.

Who was that other asshole? Maybe have to do Storme when his buddy wasn't around.

Or?

Or take the other guy out first.

But how to whack a guy who could kick your ass up close or bust a cap on you a half mile away?

Very fucking carefully, that's how.

Or get somebody else to do it, which was worth thinking about.

Tony Bennett's voice suddenly started speeding up, sounding like Alvin and the Chipmunks, followed by a high-pitched squealing sound coming from the tape deck. Rory stabbed at the ejection button with his thumb. When he did, he took his eyes off the road, and the Caddy careened into a ditch, taking a chunk of real estate out of the bank. Some old fart came out on his porch to look. Rory gave him the finger.

"Fucking spic car," said Rory aloud, backing the car up. The stereo had eaten Tony Bennett, the tape hanging out of the mouth of the dash like spaghetti. He was glad now he'd popped those guys. Couple of beaners wearing handkerchiefs on their heads like they were pirates or something, bobbing their heads and talking shit out the side of their mouths.

"Watcha doin' lookin' at our ride for, man?" one of them had said while Rory was deciding whether to steal the car or not.

"Yeah, what you doin' this part of town?" said the other. "You lost or somethin,' bitch?"

"Just looking at your ugly piece-of-shit car," Rory'd said, cool-like, scratching his head with one hand while reaching for his gun with the other. "Thinking about borrowing it."

"You thinking about what? Man, are you on something? Get the fuck away from the car before we mess you up."

That's when Rory had cleared the Taurus nine from the holster and shot both of them in the chest. Then one more apiece in the face. The Taurus was made in Brazil. Two spics whacked by a gun made in spic-land. Then with the two guys lying there bleeding, he'd said, "Either you taco-eating greasers care if I borrow your vehicle? Don't say nothing if it's okay." He watched the blood spread on the concrete. "Thank you."

Just like De Niro woulda done it, huh?

Then he'd driven off in it. Car smelling like reefer and some kinda sweet shit he couldn't identify—liked to gag smelling it—and the seats strewn with that salsa music sounded like someone taking a dump and strangling a cat at the same time. He threw all that shit out and headed for where he was now, which was the jumping-off point for the end of the world.

Now the tape player had gone to hell, and the engine was making a funny sound. He stopped at a convenience store in the middle of nowhere and examined the damage to the car. It wasn't much. Mud caked under the rear quarter panel. He checked the oil. It was about two quarts low. He was tired of the car, and he needed one with a tape player that worked anyway. But he couldn't just leave the car anywhere.

That's when he met the two kids, who asked him if he'd buy them a six-pack.

"We got the money," said one of them, a kid wearing a letter jacket with a G on it.

"I'll do better than that," Rory said. "I'll pay for it and give you twenty bucks if you do something for me."

"What?"

"I need to drop this car off for a friend in KC, y'know? You drive it up there for me and leave it."

"Leave it where?"

Shit. He hadn't thought about where. Think, Rory. Yeah, he had it now. Genius. "The airport. Park it in the long-term parking lot. Put the keys in the glove box."

"Drive it to the airport?"

No, you little jerk, he thought, I want you to fly it there. "Yeah, the airport."

"That's a long way from here. 'Bout a hundred miles."

"Yeah? Well, I'll give you forty, and I'll throw in another six-pack and a half pint of Jim Beam. How's that?"

Letter Jacket Boy looked at the other kid, some Opie Taylor-looking dork with zits that made his face look like pimento cheese. "Whatta you think, Neil?"

Neil, the big thinker, shrugged. "I don't care. We can call Jimmy or Josh, have them pick us up."

"Okay, we can do it," Letter Jacket said. "How about another twenty for Jimmy?"

You believe this? Twerpy kid was trying to shake him down. "What I look like? Huh? A fucking ATM machine? Fuck Jimmy. You want the job or not?"

"All right, mister. But how you gonna get home?"

"I gotta ride coming."

Rory bought the beer and the Jim Beam and two quarts of oil and gave them each a twenty. When they left, they waved at him like they were going to write each other or something.

Kids. No wonder the country was going to shit.

He smoothed the side of his hair. He was going to need another car. But first he needed to make a withdrawal. He patted the Taurus and walked into the convenience store for the second time.

THIRTEEN

Monday, after taking Sandy to the airport, I returned to the set location. The rainstorm had broken, the sun was shining magnificently, and the crew rushed to resume production, as the forecast was for more rain later in the week.

Sandy's visit had been conversely wonderful and bittersweet. Nothing was resolved—that is, nothing was resolved in spoken words—but the sense that something had changed hung in the air between us like a sentient being whose name could not be uttered.

"We can work this out," Sandy had said, lying against me, her bare legs streaming away from me on the sofa, her head against my neck. Her voice trailed away from me as if from another room, another time.

"Sure."

She sat up, looked at me. I turned my head to look at her face, a face I loved. A face I wanted to always have with me.

"You don't sound convinced," she said. "Why won't it work?"

"I can't live there, and you can't live here."

"Why not?"

"For the reasons we've talked about before."

"You could give New York a try."

"Have. Didn't work. Won't work."

She sighed deeply in her breast, and the scent of her, heady and alluring, entered my head. "Then we live here, and I take a job at a local station."

"There aren't any close by."

"I'll commute."

"That won't work. I'm not from your world, and you would soon tire of this world."

"Star-crossed lovers?"

"It's more than that. I love you. I know that, but I'm not sure that will be enough."

"Love conquers all," she said, starting to smile, playing with me now.

"Not ready to give up on tired clichés, huh?"

"They're apropos," she said, lifting her chin. Warming to her theme, she said, "The course of true love never did run smooth."

"Love is a smoke made with the fume of sighs," I said.

"That's a heck of a thing to know, for a man who made his living wearing a jockstrap."

"I paid attention in class."

"A jock with a brain."

"Who loves a media babe with a heart."

"I talk about it, you talk around it," she said. "Why?"

I looked away and then back at her. "I don't know. Scares me a little. I'm better with you but worse out of my element."

"This? The woods? The trees? Owls hooting at night?"

"I have an aversion to concrete. Claustrophobia sets in."

"Not the 'man's gotta do what a man's gotta do,' please."

"Okay, so we'll try," I said. "Stay with me here for a month, and we'll see how it works out."

Her mouth, her perfect mouth, started to form the words, then stopped. She chewed on the corner of her lower lip before saying, "Well, I've got appointments this week…and I signed a contract, so…Don't look at me like that."

"Like what?"

"With that little eyebrow thing that says, 'See, I'm right.'"

"I wasn't aware I was giving any kind of look."

"You always know what you're doing. That's one of your problems."

"One of my problems?"

"Your biggest problem is that you're a macho shithead."

Stopped me for a moment. Thought about it. "May have to give you that one."

"And you're often insufferable in your convictions."

"Maybe that too."

She looked at me. Searched my eyes with the face that millions watched and trusted.

"God, why did I pick you to love? And don't say anything charming or sweet or cute. Don't make me laugh…and don't make me cry."

Very quietly I said, "Okay."

"Don't talk," she said. "Just hold me."

———

Once again Chick was waiting outside Fogarty's trailer while his entourage tried to sober him up.

"This looks like action-packed duty," I said.

Chick was slouched in a folding chair, a beer bottle in hand, his cowboy hat pulled down over his eyes. He tipped the hat back when he heard my voice.

"Bodyguarding is fast-paced and invigorating," he said "Not for the fainthearted. Mr. Hollywood's been on a two-day toot. Bennies and tequila and marijuana. Then he forgot about the bennies, and the big sleep jumped all over him." He pulled the brim of his hat back down.

It was then that the charcoal-gray Mercedes-Benz pulled into the crsatz city limits of Bailey's Crossing. Two guys the size of Coke machines got out of the car. The passenger-side monster stepped to the rear of the vehicle and opened the rear door as Geoffrey Salinger approached the car.

"Hey, Chick," I said, nudging him. "Take a look at this."

Moving only one arm, Chick lifted the front of his cowboy hat. "Looks like Geoffrey's got company. Maybe it's the producer or a Hollywood exec of some standing."

A nattily attired man stepped out of the backseat and adjusted the line of his jacket. Dark tan, hair slicked back like Andy Garcia; slender, an inch short of six feet tall, capped teeth shining whitely against the tan. Mediterranean features. The last time I'd seen him, he had a Frankie Avalon haircut and dressed like disco would never die. Now he dressed like a Fortune 500 executive.

"Neither," I said.

"You know him?"

"Yeah, I know him. Just can't figure out what he's doing here."

"Old friend?"

"Hardly," I said. "That's Bobby Frank Ventura. He used to be a lowbrow hood back in Denver."

"Looks like he's improved his lot. How come you know him?"

"Rory Marchibroda used to work for him. I stuck my finger in his eye once."

"And you're still here. How'd you work that?"

"I have a winning personality. People like to see me happy. That, and I had permission from his boss."

"How'd you manage that?"

"Guy was a big football fan. Loved the Jeeps and the Cowboys. I caught a pass that knocked Houston out of the play-offs and let Denver in. He won a bundle of money when I made that reception. So he looked me up. Said if I ever needed anything to ask him, and he'd take care of it. Just thought he was another fan until I found out he controlled the action in Denver. But the whole thing worked to my advantage. I sicced a trooper buddy onto Ventura, and he got some of his fellow law enforcement officials to lean on him and Rory." I told him the rest of the story.

"You know," said Chick when I finished, "you're always blaming me for getting you into these things, but it sounds like you don't need the help."

I watched Ventura and Salinger. They were chatting like old college roommates. A mobster and an Oscar-nominated Hollywood film maker.

"What do you want to do?" Chick asked.

"I want them off my property."

"I can pick them off from here. You've seen me in action."

"A little extreme. You've done enough showing off already."

"Then what?"

"Bet they're carrying illegal weapons."

"And," Chick said, "as bodyguard to the stars, it is my sworn duty to secure the area."

"Exactly."

"You don't mind if I bring my gun, do you? The one with the real bullets in it."

"I'm taking mine," I said, reaching into my bag and pulling out the Browning nine-millimeter pistol. I slammed a loaded clip into it, racked the slide, set the safety, and stuck it in the back of my jeans. "Let's go."

Chick was whistling the theme from *High Noon* as we walked across the street.

Rory lowered the field glasses down and rubbed his eyes. Then he lifted the binos and looked through them again.

What was Bobby Frank doing here?

How was that possible? Shit.

And now Big Shot and his badass buddy were walking across the street toward them.

Bobby Frank Ventura. That cheap bastard. Why here? Why now?

Rory slammed his fist down on the hood of the red rental Cadillac. He'd taken the money he'd boosted from the convenience store to make the payment on it. The dumb ass running the convenience store was an ex-con. Jailhouse tattoos on his forearms. One of the dispshit skinheads that he'd seen the other day on the set. Guy wanted to work a deal where they shared the take, and the guy would give the cops a phony description.

But you can't trust cons. Especially skinhead cons. Guy hadn't banked the day's money like he was supposed to when Rory knocked the place over. Probably skimming the take. The score was over two grand. Not bad. Almost hated to waste the guy. But business was business, and witnesses were a liability.

Besides, he was doing the owner a favor. Guy was ripping him off.

The new Caddy had a CD player in it. He'd bought a couple of CDs to listen to. Another Tony Bennett and a Frank Sinatra. These singers anymore. They can't sing. Fucking Beatles' fault. If he had enough money, he'd let a contract on McCartney. And that Dylan guy and—

But what was he thinking about that for? Deal with the problem at hand, huh? He had the two guys he hated most in the world down below and…Wait a second, Marchibroda.

Maybe this was a good thing. Square away all accounts at once. Yeah, that's the way it could go, guy played it right. He was starting to think clearer. First, there was the genius of having the two kids take the car to the airport, then the luck of the ex-con store clerk not banking the take. Yeah. Things were going his way now. This was just a continuation of the way things were going to be from now on. Maybe the punks down there would take each other out for him.

But there wouldn't be any satisfaction in that.

Or, maybe there would be.

He'd have to think about it.

FOURTEEN

Chick switched from *High Noon* to *The Good, the Bad and the Ugly* by the time we reached the Mercedes and Salinger and the well-dressed hoods. Chick's sense of humor was more developed than mine. The song playing in my head was John Prine's "Please Don't Bury Me."

"What do you two want now?" Salinger asked when we got close enough. The two gorillas had taken note of our approach and moved to a spot where they could move if they were needed. The guy closest to Chick was dark-skinned with jet-black hair pulled back into a two-inch ponytail. The other man had a burr haircut, thick lips, and a lavender polo shirt under his loose-fitting Armani suit. He looked like Howie Long's evil twin. There was enough material in their clothing to make three suits.

"A date with Scarlett Johansson would be nice," said Chick. "But I'll settle for whatever the two grad students have under their jackets."

Bobby Frank Ventura looked up, and I saw his eyes widen in recognition and surprise. Recovering, he said, "What is this about, Geoffrey?" Ventura opened his arms, palms showing. "I come to see you, and this is the kind of welcome you give me. What have I done to deserve such treatment?"

"I apologize, Mr. Ventura," Salinger said. "There have been threats made against Cameron Fogarty, and Easton here is his bodyguard. Sometimes he's a little overzealous."

"Intrepid," said Chick, correcting him.

"Please give him my assurance that he has nothing to worry about from my associates. And call me Robert. Mr. Ventura is so formal."

"You heard him," Salinger said to Chick. "I'll vouch for Robert and his employees."

Chick looked to me. I shook my head.

"Why are you looking at him?" said Salinger. "You are working for me."

Chick turned to Ventura. "Sorry, Geoffrey. But to do the job right, I'll have to check anyone who comes on the set. Union rules."

"You can't mean—" said Salinger.

"Everybody."

"Especially these guys," I said, looking at Ventura.

"Who's in charge here, Geoffrey?" said Ventura, smoothing the side of his hair. "I make a friendly visit, and I get Wyatt Earp and this guy. Who are you?"

"He's Wyatt," said Chick. "I'm Doc. Want to hear me cough?"

"I know which one is Wyatt," said Ventura. "Nice to see you again, Storme."

I nodded.

"Come on, Wyatt," said Salinger. "I said these gentlemen are with me and shall be allowed to conduct their business unmolested. Now, please leave us."

"I don't want them here," I said.

"I paid for use of this property."

"You donated money to charity," I said, correcting him. "The land is still mine. The agreement was that Chick would be given a free hand and that I would determine who was allowed on my property. These men are armed, and I don't like it."

"So," said Chick, "Jughead and Archie can hand me their guns and you can go about your business, or I can frisk them or—"

"You ain't touching me," said Ponytail.

"Or I can take them," Chick finished. "So, choose. Makes no difference to me. Result's the same."

"That's enough, Easton," said Salinger. "Come on. This isn't necessary."

"Naw," said Chick, his eyes on the muscle. "Not in the mood."

"You're a badass, are you?" asked Ponytail.

Chick smiled. "Just a friendly guy enjoys his work. What's it going to be?"

"You don't want this, Ventura," I said. Neither did I. It would be a lot of trouble to manhandle this pair. "Don't have any confusion about the situation. Chick can take the guns. And there's not a thing anybody can do about it."

"I don't think so, Storme," said Ventura. He nodded at the short-haired thug. "Hayworth, show them why they will be unable to take anything we don't want them to have."

"What is going on?" said Salinger, apprehensive now. Ventura raised a hand to silence him.

Hayworth smiled at Chick and I as he walked over to the ponytailed tough. "You ready, Farley?" Hayworth asked his partner.

Farley nodded, set himself, and Hayworth punched him in the gut. Hard. Hard enough to move Farley back with the impact. Hard enough that I would have been lying on the ground gasping for breath. But Farley gave faint facial indication that he even felt it.

Hayworth turned and smiled at Chick, showing his teeth like a big carnivore.

"So," said Ventura, wiping his hands together as if dusting them off, "let's not have any more talk about who will take what from whom. We have wasted enough time here."

"My sister hits harder than that," said Chick. "Why didn't you just kiss him, Hayfever?"

"Maybe you think you can hit harder?" said Farley. His voice was deep, gravelly.

"If you don't mind, of course?" said Chick.

"Go ahead, asshole," said Hayworth.

"Why, thank you, Hackworth," said Chick as he moved closer to Farley. "You ready, Fartley?"

Farley's face reddened, looked at Ventura, then nodded, and set himself.

Chick took a stance with his left foot forward, then placed his right fist close to Farley's stomach as if to measure his blow. Then Chick twisted at the waist, warming up by taking a couple of slow-motion punches.

"Come on, we ain't got all day," said Hayworth.

"You still ready?" Chick asked Farley.

Farley nodded, and Chick uncoiled out of the twisting motion, but instead of punching Farley's stomach, Chick lashed out with the edge of his left hand, catching Farley across the throat.

Farley grunted and fell to his knees, hands to his throat. Gagging sounds emanated from his mouth. Hayworth took a step in Chick's direction, but Chick pivoted and side kicked Hayworth's knee. There was an ugly crunching sound like walnuts cracking, and Hayworth yelped in pain, like a wounded bear, grabbing at his knee as he joined Farley on the ground.

"Six pounds of pressure," said Chick to Hayworth. "All you need to take out a knee. Hardly seems fair, does it?"

While Hayworth writhed in pain and Farley was coughing and wheezing, Chick disarmed the pair. Farley made a weak effort to grab Chick's arm, but Chick slapped the ponytailed man's hand away and said, "Stop playing around, Farto. You know better." Then Chick reached inside the man's jacket and removed a Colt Python. "Carries good stuff," said Chick, holding up the revolver. "You expecting to be jumped by buffalo?"

"You didn't hit him in the stomach," said Ventura.

Chick shrugged. "Didn't stipulate." He stepped toward Hayworth. "Now, give me yours, Hayfever."

Hayworth, teeth clenched, looked to his boss, who nodded. Hayworth handed his gun to Chick, glaring as he did.

"Now there's a genuine, tough-guy mean mug if I ever saw one," said Chick. "Sends shivers down your spine, doesn't it? Less effective when you're rolling around on the ground, though."

Ventura looked at me.

"Told you," I said.

"Get up," Ventura said to his injured bodyguards. The pair struggled to their feet. Ventura turned to Salinger. "I wish to offer my apologies for our behavior here, Geoffrey. I did not mean for this to happen."

"He meant for it to happen to us," I said.

Geoffrey looked like he'd swallowed a fish bone.

"There is no need for animosity between us, Storme," said Ventura.

"Then why did you come here with the muscle?"

"Business."

"Is that why you sent Rory around to intimidate me?"

"Rory?" Ventura said, puzzled. "Are you talking about Rory Marchibroda?"

"Give him a part, Geoffrey," I said. "He's outstanding. You know what I'm talking about, Bobby. Your pet gorilla, Glory Rory, is hanging around, and now you're here. Coincidence?"

"Rory don't work for me no more," said Ventura, the practiced diction slipping momentarily. "I got rid of that cluck a long time ago. What's he doing here?"

"You tell me."

Ventura gave me an odd look, then turned to Salinger and said, "This is not the best time, Geoffrey. Perhaps we can meet later and discuss our business." To me, he said, "We won't bring weapons next time. I can see we'll be quite safe here."

"You'll need permission before you return," I said.

"So, I ask you, huh?"

I nodded.

Ventura smiled wolfishly. "You're often in the way of things, Storme. Why is that?"

"Naturally disagreeable, I guess."

Geoffrey Salinger sat in his trailer and drummed his fingers on the arms of a director's chair. His trailer wasn't appointed like something you'd find in a mobile home sales lot. There was a media center that occupied an entire wall—two thirty-one-inch television screens and a small nineteen-incher, Bose speakers, two recorders, laptop computer on the table, along with a business phone with more buttons than a Japanese sports car. There was a full bar and custom furniture. Roughing it.

"Would you care to explain to me, please, just what you two juvenile delinquents were trying to accomplish?" Salinger asked Chick and me.

"I thought we accomplished it," said Chick. "They had guns, we didn't want them to have guns, and we took the guns. Seems simple enough to me."

"You injured two men. One of them, quite possibly, is permanently injured."

"You're right," said Chick, nodding to himself, "that probably was the best part."

"Why are you involved with a lowlife like Bobby Frank Ventura?" I asked.

"I don't appreciate your accusatory tone."

"Where'd you learn to talk?" I said. "You read too many scripts. I just want to know how you got hooked up with a piece of raw sewage like Ventura."

"You mean Robert," said Chick.

"He is interested in this project," said Salinger, but his eyes averted mine.

"Does his interest involve drugs, prostitution, or breaking elbows?"

"Of course it doesn't."

"Then he's out of his element."

"He is one of the principal investors," said Salinger.

"That's certainly a career move on your part," I said. "Why didn't you just get John Gotti or somebody big?"

"Robert Ventura is a legitimate businessman."

"Took the words right out of his mouth. Why do you think he travels with armed bodyguards, Geoffrey?"

"Half of the people I deal with have bodyguards."

"You're naive, Geoffrey. I've seen some of his work. He had a guy killed in Denver by sticking the guy's head in a vise, then sewing his lips and nostrils shut. He's a psychopath who'd give no more thought to killing me, or you, than what he was going to have for breakfast."

"Regardless," said Salinger. "His money is good, and there are levels of depravity in the industry that would astound your backwoods sensibilities. I live in LA, Storme. I can handle Ventura."

I looked at him. Waited.

Salinger shook his head. He looked tired. "All right. Okay. You deserve an explanation. I hate it, but I'm up against it with this project. It's either make it work or do lesser movies with smaller budgets, if I work at all. I need this picture, Wyatt. I realize I'm dealing with shady people. That's one of the reasons I wanted you along with Easton."

"Okay," I said. "I understand. Were you aware of problems between LeBeau and Fogarty when you hired them?"

"Yes. But they are professionals paid large amounts of money to submerge their differences. Many people have had difficulties with Cameron Fogarty. He is a difficult person of immense talent and charisma. He has his moments where he is charming and even enjoyable company. There are many like him in the business. One of the hazards of working with icons is that you must endure some of their eccentricities." Salinger settled back in his chair. "I am paid to manage and balance personalities and egos."

"Whatever happened to Jimmy Stewart and Gary Cooper?" Chick asked.

"Michael LeBeau is not the only person on the set who has an unfortunate history with Cameron," said Salinger.

"Who else?"

"Valeri Darnell and Rance Caraway," he said. "Perhaps others."

"What's between them?"

"It would be their place to share that information. I'm sorry I can't say more. You both are honest men, and I do admire you both. Right now, though, I've got to review the dailies and call the coast, so I'll have to do that, if you don't mind." He picked up a remote control, turned on one of the big screens, and proceeded to ignore us.

Which I didn't think was all that easy to do.

FIFTEEN

Leaving Salinger's trailer, Chick went to change clothes while I walked over to Valeri Darnell's trailer and knocked on the door. She let me in. The trailer was neat and comfortable. Valeri was wearing jeans and a sweatshirt. She seemed more like a next-door neighbor than a movie star as she bustled around preparing coffee. A really gorgeous next-door neighbor.

"You seem surprised by something," she said. "Is everything all right?"

"I wasn't expecting you or this place to be...ah..."

"So domestic?"

I shrugged. "I guess I expected it to be more self-indulgent. You know, eleven-by-fourteen photos of you wearing a satin gown and dripping with jewelry, smiling into the camera. Maybe a little white dog with a diamond-studded collar and a perm. That kind of thing."

"I'm really just a small-town girl at heart," she said. She kicked off her Top-Siders and sat on the couch, her legs folded under her. She smelled of soap and perfume. "I'm from Muncie, Indiana, originally. I was a cheerleader, and I was in love with the captain of the football team. My goal was to go to college to get a teaching degree and a husband who would give me two-point-five children and an SUV. Does that sound corny?"

"Sounds nice."

She smiled a wry smile. "We always want what we don't have. Things didn't work out that way. I've been through two bad marriages and a dozen bad relationships with men who were forever sneaking sidelong glances at their reflections. I envy the simpler life. Every girl wants to be a movie star, and now I wish I lived in the suburbs and attended PTA meetings."

I knew the feeling. Near the end with the Cowboys, I felt that way every time some media person stuck a microphone in my face or asked a question I'd heard a hundred times before. Every time somebody flashed a camera in my face. I too had wished I were somewhere else. Wished my wife and baby daughter were still alive. Wished I was Joe Citizen and lived in mind-numbing anonymity, absorbed into the great American Milky Way.

"Too late for that now, isn't it?" she said. There was remorse in her voice. The coffee stopped dripping, and she got up. She poured coffee into plastic imitation cups and handed me one, resuming her previous position on the couch. She was somewhat closer to me this time, her knee nearly touching my thigh.

"What brings you by to see me?" she asked.

"I don't know any way to do this except straight ahead. Salinger mentioned some past difficulty you may have had with Cameron Fogarty. There anything to that?"

"What makes that your business?" she said, leaning away from me, her heart-shaped face coloring.

"Somebody is threatening to kill Fogarty," I said. The walls of the faux cup in my hand were as fine as an eggshell. I was afraid it might break in my hand or from the weight of the coffee.

"Good. I hope they're successful."

"Pretty strong reaction."

"He's a weasel."

"You'll get no argument from me." I took a sip from the cup. It didn't crumble. It was going to hold up just fine. "Why do you dislike him so intensely?"

"Take your pick," she said.

"More specific."

"I still don't understand your interest."

"Chick's job is to protect him. My job is to be Chick's friend and watch his back."

"And he watches yours."

I nodded. "That's the way it works."

"You two seem very close. Like brothers. What causes two people to trust each other so much?"

"I know where he's going to be."

"That's fairly oblique, don't you think?"

I shrugged. "The more we know about the situation and the interrelationships around here, the easier it will be for Chick to protect himself."

"And Cameron Fogarty," she said.

"No way around it."

She pursed her lips. Narrowed her eyes and looked at me. She touched a perfectly manicured fingertip to her lips and looked off behind me. The muscles in her finely etched jaw worked. She sighed.

"Cameron was married to my sister, Darla Lodge, for a short time. Darla is her stage name. Her real name is Margaret Darnell. She took Darla from our last name." She gave a noiseless laugh, which lifted her shoulders a quarter inch.

"A very short time, which turned out to be far too long," she said. "She was married, he wasn't. It was the classic 'good girl who loved a man who was no good.' She was crazy about him, but he treated her like a piece of meat. He would stay gone for days without explanation. 'Business,' he said. But he'd be off on drug and alcohol binges with those brain-dead leeches he hangs around with, and he was sleeping with everybody in town. Everybody in the business talks about his escapades, but you couldn't tell Darla anything. The whole marriage was a dream come true for her. Her pictures in magazines. Partying with celebrities."

"I'd think she wouldn't be that impressed. Her sister is a celebrity."

"That was part of the problem. Why she changed her last name. She felt like a failure. I couldn't tell her different. She started getting better parts after she married him. She had very low self-esteem, even though she's much prettier than me."

"Hard to imagine."

She smiled. "She was runner-up for Miss Indiana. She was so innocent. That's probably putting it kindly. She was naive. She caught him sleeping with other women. All kinds. Groupies, starlets, rock singers, even some big-name stars. That isn't even the worst thing. He developed a taste for teenage girls. He's a slug."

"Why did she put up with it?"

"He would make up to her. Promise her it wouldn't happen again. That he loved her and that it was just part of the business. That the women didn't mean anything to him. She always believed his crap. Then, she started drinking..." She looked down at the floor. Lifted her cup, started to drink from it, and then changed her mind. I said nothing. Waited for her. There was more.

"He beat her. That bastard hit her, locked her in her room like a child. She called the police, but this was 'Cameron Fogarty you're talking about, lady.' That's what the jerk police would say."

"They wouldn't arrest him?"

"They would answer the call. They even took him in once or twice, but nothing came of it. She was pregnant. He wanted her to abort it, but she wouldn't. She...she miscarried. I'm sure it was because of the abuse, but she wouldn't prosecute, and she wouldn't kick him out."

"What finally caused her to divorce him?"

"He divorced her," she said. "After she had a nervous breakdown. He told the media she was having an affair and that she was an addict. That was bullshit. She didn't believe in being unfaithful. I know that may be hard to believe, but it's the truth. She's in a clinic now, drying out. She's in the loony bin while the miserable coward goes free and gets his photo on the cover of

Entertainment Weekly. He won't even help with the clinic bills, so I pay them." She looked me square in the eyes.

"There it is," she said. "If you're wondering if I have a reason to wish the bastard dead, there it is." Her eyes grew damp with emotion. "I've thought about a thousand different ways of doing it. Some way to make him suffer for the way he treated Maggie. But…" She let it hang.

"But what?"

"I can't conceive of anything fitting. Anything that seems satisfying enough."

"Why work with him?"

"The chance to work with Geoffrey Salinger. I need to work, and Geoffrey is a wonderful director. I'm not getting any younger. Besides, I'm not the type to lie around the pool and let the scotch and sun bake my brains out."

I sipped the coffee.

"You make good coffee," I said.

"I can cook too," she said, smiling. "I'm a catch."

"I don't doubt that."

"Do you have someone?"

"Yeah," I said, nodding.

"What's her name?"

"Sandy Collingsworth."

"What?" It was her turn to look surprised. She considered me as if I had suddenly sprouted wings and was flying around the room. "You don't mean Sandra Collingsworth, of 'Morning Coffee Break'?"

"Is that what she's doing?" I said. "I told her she needed to find gainful employment. I'm kind of shiftless and lazy."

"I thought you were a retired football player."

"I am. There's a game Sunday, and I'm not playing."

"How do you maintain a relationship with her? I mean, she's in New York and you're out here. No offense, but this is kind of remote. How do you do that?"

"It's not easy," I said.

She turned her head sideways and looked at me. "How serious is it between you and Sandra?"

"Very."

She smiled the wry smile again. "You're an interesting man. I don't meet many interesting men in this business. There's a difference between interesting and narcissistic. I never bought that retired jock thing from the first moment I met you. I knew there was more, much more, percolating under the Eddie Bauer wardrobe and the laconic conversation. There's something else behind your eyes, something deep inside that you keep hidden. You seem, to borrow from Elizabeth Browning, 'a little sunburnt by the glare of life.'"

"Don't ascribe complexities to me," I said. "I'm fairly uncomplicated."

"Just a simple guy."

I nodded.

"A simple guy whose girlfriend is a celebrity journalist," she said, "and whose best friend is a bodyguard. A simple guy who walks right up to a group of racist toughs and tells them to get out, and they do so."

"Chick's the one made them leave," I said. "I was—"

"Don't interrupt when I'm in the middle of a monologue," she said. "You back talk one of the most powerful men in Hollywood. Then the rest of the time, you hardly say anything as if you wish you could melt into the landscape. Yes, there's nothing complex about you, all right. Hardly anything. You're almost a cipher."

Her knee brushed my thigh, and I caught the scent of her perfume. I leaned away. Imperceptibly, I thought.

"Calm down," she said. "I'm not going to attack you."

"Didn't think you were."

"It might not be all that bad if I did, you know. You might even like it."

"That's what I'm afraid of."

"Probably the only thing," she said. "Are you foursquare and true blue to your lady love?"

"I'd better go," I said. "Thanks for the coffee."

"I'm just playing with you," she said. "I'm not trying to offend you."

"You're not. You're a very nice lady. You deserve better than what you've received from this business."

Her face softened. "Thank you," she said. "I don't get much sincerity. But then you're not capable of much else, are you?" She struck a mock coquettish pose on the couch. "Come back sometime. The door's always open." She smiled, pleased with her playfulness.

Thoreau says man is rich in proportion to the number of things he can afford to leave alone. I would tend to agree with him. So I left.

Alone.

———

Walking back from Darnell's trailer, I saw Fogarty's toadies—Volts, Braithwaite, and Kane—talking to Rance Caraway, a character actor. In this production he was playing the town marshal.

The exchange between Caraway and the trio seemed heated. Volts had his hand out, and Caraway turned on his heel and walked away, throwing his hands down in disgust as he did. Kane reached out and grabbed the lanky actor's elbow. Caraway whirled around and pointed his finger in Kane's face. At that point Cameron Fogarty walked up. Caraway turned to Fogarty and said something before walking off.

After Caraway left, Kane said something to Fogarty. Kane's arms were stretched outward as if pleading his case. Abruptly, Fogarty slapped the smaller man upside the head. Kane staggered, nearly falling, but managed to keep his feet. Volts and Braithwaite followed Fogarty as the trio left Kane behind to lick his wounds.

I filed the scene away in my mind.

Not everything was sunny in Bozo-land.

I followed Caraway across the lot, watching him walk in his trademark stride of a hundred movies, a bowlegged sort of gait with his forehead tilted downward a half inch. I caught up with the character actor at the stable where they kept the horses. He was leading a tall roan horse by the bridle.

"Mr. Caraway," I said. "You got a second?"

Caraway stopped and turned his head sideways. He had a classic western face—weather-beaten, with lines at his eyes from squinting into the sun, sandy hair peppered with gray. A two-day growth of stubble on his jowls. He was in his sixties, but still looked every inch the Montana cowboy he had been when he had been discovered unloading a string of horses off a railroad boxcar. He wasn't handsome by movie-star standards, but possessed the type of rugged looks the big-screen cameras loved. As with Valeri Darnell, it was remarkable to run across someone I had only seen as a two-dimensional character on a movie screen.

"What do you need?" he asked. He began to brush down the roan with a large brush with a leather strap that looped around his left hand. The air smelled of horse and leather. Good smells.

"I noticed you had a problem with Fogarty's entourage."

"Yeah," he said. He continued to brush the animal with long strokes. "Saw that, did you? Don't believe I caught your name."

"Wyatt Storme." I was starting to get tired of talking to his back.

"What the hell've you got to do with anything? You working for this production? You a fan?"

"I don't work for anybody," I said. "And I'm not a fan, though I will admit to an admiration for some of your work, so you can turn off the patronizing tone. I don't want your autograph."

He stopped what he was doing and turned to look at me. He used a leather-gloved thumb to push back the brim of his cowboy hat.

"Well, shit," he said, finally, nodding at me. "You 'n me are going to get along fine." He removed his right glove and extended his hand. "Rance Caraway," he said. "Pleasure to meet you, Wyatt."

I shook his hand.

"Sorry about my attitude, partner," he said. "Sometimes I forget to act like I was taught by my folks and start acting like a regulation Hollywood asshole."

"No problem," I said.

"Seen you around here," he said. "If I can put this in the right words, how are you connected to this picture?"

"The land belongs to me. That, and Fogarty's bodyguard is a friend."

He looked around. "Nice place. I like working location when it's out in the open like this. Reminds me of home. What can I help you with, Wyatt?"

"The exchange with the three stooges. What was that all about?"

He smiled a big smile. "That's what we call 'em too. I can remember when people like that got thrown off the set. Those sons of bitches were jumping my tail, saying I was upstaging Fogarty. I told them I didn't discuss my work with culls. Then that little popcorn fart grabbed my arm, and I almost forgot I was an old man."

"You look like you could still handle them. How is your relationship with Fogarty?"

"Professional," he said. He reached up and stroked the roan's nose. "Other than that, I don't want anything to do with him."

"Mind giving your reasons?"

"You've been around him, haven't you?" he asked, tossing his head like a stallion in the direction of Fogarty's trailer. "He's horseshit."

"Did you know that before you accepted the part?"

"Sure. We worked together on another movie when he first started climbing the ladder. He was late on the set one morning, and I told him I didn't appreciate standing around freezing to death. He smarted off, and I grabbed him by the collar." He smiled, thinking about it. "Shoulda seen the look on his face when I pulled him up on his toes. He tried to get me fired off the picture, but the director was an old friend."

"Why work with him again?"

He hooked a thumb in his belt. He shook his head. "I don't know," he said. "Don't need the money." He cocked his head. "Because it's a western, that's why. They don't make all that many anymore. Hell, still like to get up on a horse with a six-gun strapped on my leg. I've become a crazy old geezer."

"Was that movie your only experience with him?"

"Nope."

I waited. He looked off behind me and patted the horse again.

He shrugged. "What the hell," he said, holding the horse's bridle. "Everybody knows about it anyway. He was—I can't ever say that F-word, though everybody around here uses it. He and my wife—my second wife, that is, my first wife died of cancer. She was a fine woman…Anyway, Fogarty had himself an affair with my young wife. They took to running together. She was thirty years younger than me. Shoulda known better. My children were ashamed of me. She ran off with him. To New York City. Least she got to go there. I sure wasn't going to take her. Worst thing was, she took a pair of matched Colt forty-fives that Eastwood gave me. Now, ain't that a hell of a thing to do to a fella? Son of a bitch sent me pictures of them together in bed. His way of getting back at me, I guess."

"That's a tough loss."

"Yeah," he said, shaking his head, a smile playing at the corners of his mouth. "Sure do miss those pistols."

SIXTEEN

found Chick and told him what I had learned talking to Valeri Darnell and Rance Caraway.

Chick listened attentively, twirling his prop six-gun around his finger, then into his holster over and over until it slid into the holster as if oiled. When I was done, he said, "Protecting Fogarty from people who wish him harm is an epic undertaking. LeBeau, Darnell, Caraway, and the ghost of Jesse James all have reason. A guy could retire selling Cameron Fogarty voodoo dolls around here."

"Looks like it."

"Not to mention we just tweaked the nose of Bobby Frank Wannabe," said Chick.

"Don't forget Rory," I said.

"Our plate is full," said Chick, twirling the gun into the holster once more. "Nothing left to do but kick back and admire God for keeping us in mind."

"Haven't talked to Meagan Ames yet," I said.

"A dangerous mission. I volunteer. You're far too valuable to this team."

"Uh-huh. Let's try her another day. I think I'll head back to the cabin this evening. I'm getting too old to hang out with you. Think I'll sit in front of the fireplace and drink Ovaltine laced with Geritol."

"How can you give this up?"

"You know," I said, "it occurs to me life would be less complicated if you hadn't come by my place with Salinger."

Chick nodded. "You mean less interesting."

I returned to the set the next morning. During the lunch break a maroon Ford with the words "Truman County Sheriff" in silver pulled onto the set lot. A short, dark-haired man with a slight paunch from too many of his wife's fried chicken dinners got out of the car with his hat, a tan Stetson, in his hand. He settled the hat on his head and walked toward us.

"I heard you were out here, Wyatt," said Sheriff Carney Statler.

"Good to see you, Carney," I said. I shook his hand and introduced him to Chick. "What brings you out here?"

He pushed the brim of his hat back, then placed a hand at the small of his back and stretched. "Getting harder to sit in that car all day. Had a robbery out at that convenience store on B Highway. You know the one. Sits out there by itself in the middle of nowhere. Catches the lake traffic on the weekends. Knew sooner or later it was bound to happen. Too isolated. Clerk got himself killed. Two shots in the face, all the money gone. Killer took the guy's car. We had a bulletin out on it, but I'm sure we'll find it ditched somewhere."

"Why kill the clerk?" I asked.

Statler pulled a Dutch Masters cigar from his pocket. He unwrapped the cellophane, which made a crackling noise like bacon sizzling.

"Doesn't make sense to me," said Statler. "Maybe it was somebody the clerk recognized. Clerk was a two-time loser. Nothing big. Assault and B and E. Just got placed in this job by his parole officer." He stuck the cigar in his mouth and lit it with a silver lighter.

"Thing is," he said, after he got the cigar started, "that boy got hisself killed was just here the other day. Name was Leamon Cosgrove."

Chick and I looked at each other. Chick shrugged.

"I hear you two run him off," said Statler. "Him and some of his buddies."

"He was one of those skinheads that was here?"

"Yep. He wasn't supposed to be consorting with them. Bunch of lowborns from down around the lake. Would have got him violated had he lived. There's been a bunch of weird shit going on around here. Two boys from up around Gilman got picked up on drunk driving charges clear up on I-435 by the highway patrol. Good boys. Not troublemakers. Said they were taking the car to the airport for a man who gave them twenty bucks apiece and a twelve pack of beer."

"Boys will be boys," said Chick.

"Thanks for contributing the cliché," I said, making me think of Sandy.

"Always glad to help."

"That's not even the weird thing," said Statler. He puffed his cigar. I waited. "When the state traced the car, they found out it belonged to a drug dealer got himself killed two days before. Shot down on the street with one of his lowlife buddies."

I looked at Chick. Chick whistled lowly.

"But those things are out of my jurisdiction," said the sheriff. He picked a tobacco flake off the end of his cigar. "Got a call from the FBI. They wanted to 'apprise' me—no fooling, this is the words they used—that 'an operator they suspect of organized crime ties' was in my county. Fella named Ventura. Got himself a weird first name."

"Bobby Frank Ventura," I said. I was sure Statler knew his first name. He was fishing. "He was out here yesterday."

"What was he doing here?"

"The director, Geoffrey Salinger, knows him."

"And you don't?"

"I know he's dirty," I said. "And I know he has money invested in this movie."

"Well, that beats anything I ever heard," said Statler, rubbing his chin with thumb and forefinger. "Haven't got enough trouble without some Hollywood director importing known criminals into my jurisdiction. What about you?" he asked Chick. "You know him?"

Chick shook his head.

Statler's cigar had gone out. He fumbled in his pocket for his lighter. Without looking up, he said, "What is it you do, Mr. Easton?"

Chick stopped playing with the six-gun, smiled, then chuckled. "I hang out with Storme some. Do some bodyguard work, a little skip tracing. And sometimes," he said, "on social occasions only, of course, I drive my Chevy to the levee and drink whiskey and rye."

"Anything else?"

Chick nodded. "Yeah. I do my best to drive the mental patients at Fat Butts Incorporated crazy by not telling them where I am or what I'm doing."

Sheriff looked at Chick for a moment, then to me, then back to Chick. He relit his cigar and laughed. "Guess I need to polish up my subtle act."

"It wasn't too bad," said Chick.

"Maybe I'll try it out on that Salinger fella," said Statler.

"You'll have an advantage with him," I said. "He's a pretty good guy but already thinks everyone in Missouri wears overalls, drives a pickup, and marries their first cousin."

"That right?" said Statler. He hitched up his belt. "Point me at that old boy. Think I'm going to enjoy this one."

"Care if we watch?" asked Chick.

"Matter of fact, I don't."

Salinger frowned when he saw us and grudgingly let us into his trailer while he finished up a phone call. He hung up the phone then I introduced Statler.

"What is it you want, Sheriff?" asked Salinger.

"Just want to visit with you a little."

"Well, I must apologize. I'm just a little busy here."

"Now, hold on, Mr. Salinger," said the sheriff. "I'm not going to take much of your time."

"Five minutes work," said Salinger.

"Well, best not waste it then. I want to know about a man named..." Statler made a show of squinting at a piece of paper he took from his pocket. I don't think it had any writing on it. "Yes, here it is. A man named Bobby Frank Ventura. You know that fella?"

Salinger looked at me. "Did Storme put you up to this?" Salinger asked.

"Is this going to count against my five minutes if I answer?" said the sheriff. Statler got a fresh cigar out of his pocket.

"I'd rather you didn't smoke, thank you," said Salinger.

Statler put the cigar back in his pocket. "Sorry. Forgot my manners. And no, Storme did not put me up to this. You managed that all by yourself, Mr. Salinger."

"I know Robert Ventura."

"What's he doing in these parts? He a friend of yours? An acquaintance?" He paused for a second. "A relative?"

"What is the nature of these questions?"

"There you go again, Mr. Salinger," said the sheriff. "Asking questions on my allotted five minutes. But that's okay. I just want to ascertain what in the hell a big-city hood like Ventura is doing here."

"I don't believe Mr. Ventura is a criminal."

"Well, now, the FBI has a different take on the matter. They think—mind you, I'm talking about the Federal Bureau of Investigation here, and not myself—they seem to think this man is some kind of gangster."

"Well, treat people as they deserve and not according to some preconceived notion."

"An admirable practice. Are you in business with him?"

"In a manner of speaking," said Salinger.

"What manner of speaking would that be?" the sheriff asked, leaning forward in his chair.

"He's an investor in this movie project," said Salinger.

"Oh," said the sheriff, leaning back in his chair and nodding. "He's an investor. Does that mean he has any say in how the money is spent?"

"He's one of a half-dozen investors. He does not control a majority of the picture."

"But he's allowed to come on the set and walk around, right?"

"He has the right, or at least I should extend the courtesy to allow him to observe how his money is being utilized."

"Well, then help me with something," said the sheriff. "I'm not familiar with how these movie things work. Does this courtesy include bringing thugs carrying concealed weapons into my county?"

"Of course not. The question is insulting."

"Then I apologize for that and in advance of my next question. Are you in any financial difficulty, Mr. Salinger?"

"I am not."

"Are you under any pressure to see that this picture is a big success?"

"A director is always under pressure to produce a successful picture. Some of it comes from the studio. Some from your peers. But I feel that most of the pressure a good director experiences comes from within. There is a pressure to compete with one's self, to create the desired vision, to interpret the—"

The sheriff held up a hand. "Sorry to interrupt, but we're on the clock here. I just want to know if there is any pressure peculiar to this particular project."

Salinger's face colored. Interesting. "Are you purposely attempting to exasperate me, Sheriff?"

"No, no," the sheriff said, shaking his head. "No, I wouldn't do that, no sir. Let me go at another way. Do you like intrusions, Mr. Salinger? I ask that, because you see, I don't. And I consider you bringing a gangster like Ventura into my jurisdiction an intrusion. In fact, I consider it an affront to the people who elected me. And I just want to know that you're not bringing trouble into the county."

"I don't see what any of this has to do with me. I cannot control the movements of Mr. Ventura, nor do I intend to."

"Do you know a man named Leamon Cosgrove?"

Salinger seemed surprised at the question. "No. I don't."

"You don't know a Leamon Cosgrove?" the sheriff asked again.

"No, dammit."

"Well, that's funny," said the sheriff. "Because a man matching your description was seen talking to him just a few days ago."

"What is your point? You do have a point, don't you, and plan to reach it while I'm still in my forties?"

"Mr. Cosgrove got himself killed the other day. We kind of frown on killing around here, though maybe it's a daily occurrence where you're from. I have information, corroborated by these two men here with us that Mr. Cosgrove was on the movie set with a bunch of mental deficients who think the color of a man's skin has something to do with his worth. I don't like those people around here either. So, what I have is you showing up to shoot a movie, which attracts racists and known criminals. All from out of town. And now one of them is dead, and it is increasing my workload, and I don't like it. Not even a little bit. Is this connecting for you?"

"Are you suggesting that I have something to do with this man's death?" said Salinger. "If so, then I believe I'm going to have to ask you to leave, or you can talk to my attorneys."

"No need for that," said the sheriff, looking at his watch. "My five minutes are up. You enjoy your stay here, Mr. Salinger. And if my office can be of any assistance, just let me know."

The sheriff stood up, and without another word, left Salinger's trailer.

"Who does he think he is?" said Salinger, after the sheriff left. "Insufferable hillbilly sheriff."

"That hillbilly sheriff, as you call him, just yanked your chain and pulled you all over the room," I said.

"But don't worry," said Chick. "We won't tell anybody."

SEVENTEEN

I left the movie set at five and returned home. My cabin looked as it always did: fifteen hundred square feet of refuge wrapped in oak logs surrounded by timber. The cabin had a wraparound deck with a view that sloped away from one side of my hill and stretched as far as I wanted to see. It was the same view that had been there for the last hundred years. No concrete, no skyscrapers, no shopping malls, no human kennels. Far from the parking lot wars and the electronic hiss of human activity.

I had another cabin I kept up in the Colorado Rockies. I built both cabins myself. Traveled back and forth between them as the mood struck me. I'd bought the land for the Missouri cabin while playing for the Cowboys. I had literally lucked onto the mountain when I'd backed the play of a land speculator down on his markers in Las Vegas. He lost, and I got the deed to the mountain.

I had built the cabins as a kind of therapy. I worked several hours each day on both until they were finished, the Missouri home first, then the Colorado hideaway. I cut the timber for the logs, dug the foundations, laid the carpet, and built the fireplaces with rocks and stones indigenous to both places.

Then one day they were finished, and I didn't have anything else to do. The work had occupied my mind and given my head asylum from thoughts of the gut-ripping loss of my wife and child and the black nightmares of Vietnam. Long enough for time to wedge a barrier and allow me to cope with them.

Playing in the NFL had occupied my thoughts for a while. But at some point, I'd become a guy I didn't know with a star on his helmet, ducking reporters. So, I walked away from it. Sometimes I missed it. And sometimes I didn't. And sometimes I wondered if it was really me up there on the jukebox.

I got the chainsaw out of the shed, checked the oil and gas, started it up, and cut up an oak limb that had broken off during a thunderstorm. The air filled with the aroma of sawdust and exertion as the chainsaw buzzed and sliced through thick limb. I stacked the logs on the pile, selected three cured-out logs from another pile, and built a fire in the stone fireplace. While the fire crackled, I put an old Beatles album on the record player. Sandy had given me a CD player for my birthday.

"People download music from their computers these days," she told me, but once in a while, I liked to pull the black vinyl LPs out of their jackets and watch them spin on the turntable. There was a completeness to it that one didn't get from compact discs or the laptop I rarely used. Call me old-fashioned.

An unambitious man who lives on a hill.

I turned in early, but there was too much on my mind, and I didn't sleep well. I kept thinking about Valeri Darnell and Michael LeBeau and Rance Caraway. I liked all three and did not wish for one of them to be the one threatening Fogarty, whom I didn't like.

Then I started to think about Sandy. I lay on my back and stared at the dark ceiling and missed her. She would get the job. But what would that mean? Would her new job allow her to fly back to Colorado and Missouri to spend her weekends with a reclusive ex-wide receiver, a man who had allowed her to become an essential part of his life? I had been separated from people I loved once before, and though I had learned to cope with the tragedy, I had never fully recovered. Nor would I ever. I had learned to live like a person who had lost a limb, concentrating on learning to use what he had left, strengthening the other parts.

Could I let her go? For her own good? So selfless, Storme, you complete ass. It was for my own good. At least part of it. I loved her...enough to let her go?

I struggled with my thoughts, sleeping in fits and starts, swimming in and out of dreams too real to be dreams, yet too elusive to be reality. I found myself wide-awake at four o'clock. I rolled over on my stomach and was considering the possibility of getting up when I heard the sound. Not a sound associated with the cabin settling on its foundation or wildlife moving around, or any sound natural to the outdoors. One of the advantages of living in a remote setting is that you become tuned into the sounds and movements of your environment. It was the reason wild animals were so alert when you invaded their domain.

The sound I heard was a man sound. A sound that sent pin-pricks of electricity along the back of my neck. It was the sound of someone trying to sneak quietly outside the cabin.

I slid out of bed and moved along the floor on all fours. I opened the lid on a wooden Winchester ammo box and lifted out the Browning Hi Power I kept in there. I had two of them. Twins. One I'd bought and the other I had liberated from a Colorado gun-smuggling ring, a weapon with a fourteen-round clip. This one was loaded. It was always loaded.

As Rooster Cogburn would say, "A gun unloaded and uncocked ain't good for nothin'."

I moved in a crouch through the bedroom door, felt my way through the dining room, careful not to touch anything, my feet cold against the hardwood floor. I was creeping into the living room when the shotgun boomed, followed by the ripping, crashing sound of my bedroom window breaking. A hellish, frantic cascading sound. Then again. And again. I fought down the knot of anxiety gathering in my throat and concentrated on the gun and what I had to do. I hurried across the living-room floor, opening the front door, and I was met by the hard slap of autumn night against my exposed torso and legs. I wore gym shorts to sleep in, nothing else.

I pressed close to the wall of the cabin and moved around the deck to where I had a view of the backyard of the cabin. A dark form ran across my drive. I pointed the Browning, the sights useless in the dark, and walked the bullets at the shadow. I heard a cry of surprise or pain and feet hitting the ground as I continued to blast away with the pistol, spent shell casings pinging off the cabin wall and deck. The running shadow disappeared down the lane, and I heard the sound of an engine being started.

I ran back inside the cabin, grabbed the keys to my Jeep, and hurried outside to give chase. The Browning was empty, but there was a Winchester lever .22 Magnum under the rear seat of the Jeep that I used to shoot coyotes. I ran across the grounds, feeling the terrain, rough and uneven under my bare feet. I stepped on a sharp rock, injuring my foot, and hobbled the last few feet to the truck. I threw open the door and fired up the engine, slamming the transmission into gear.

But the truck lurched and shrieked as if I were riding an angry sea in a small boat, and a metallic scraping sound crunched underneath the wheels. I stopped the truck and got out.

Flat tires. Four of them.

I slapped the hood with the flat of my hand. Heard the vehicle receding in the distance. Too late now to go back to the cabin and get the keys to the Mustang.

I stood in the cold air and ran a hand through my hair. I wondered who my visitor had been. Was it Rory Marchibroda? Had Bobby Frank sent him? Or was it one of Ventura's gorillas? Or maybe someone else.

Maybe the person who wanted to kill Cameron Fogarty.

My foot hurt as I limped back into the cabin.

Damn, I'm getting too old for this.

EIGHTEEN

I limped back into the cabin and called Chick's mobile number, my hands shaking and my heart banging away in my chest. I examined my foot as the phone buzzed in my ear. I grabbed a tea towel off its rack in the kitchen and wrapped it around the foot and watched the blood seep through the thin cloth. My teeth were chattering.

Chick answered on the fifth ring. He didn't sound as if he'd been sleeping, though it was still dark outside. But as I thought about it, I realized for the first time that I'd never seen Chick Easton sleep since I'd known him.

"What do you want, Storme?" he asked.

"How did you know it was me?"

"Either you or Zeta-Jones. She doesn't want Michael to know about us."

"I just had a visitor. Brought a shotgun with him."

"Know who it was?"

"Too dark. Couldn't see him very well. Took a few shots at him, but he got away. Heard him drive off. He blew my bedroom window away and slashed the tires on both my vehicles."

"I'll come out and get you," said Chick.

"No need. I'll have to call someone to come out and fix the tires. Won't be anybody up for a few hours."

"You think it was Ventura?"

"Maybe. One of his goons, or maybe he sent Rory Marchibroda. Maybe Fogarty's stalker. Could even be the skinheads, I guess. Maybe the Washington Redskins hired somebody. They never liked me."

"If he was a pro, he wasn't trying to kill you," Chick said. "A pro shooter doesn't blast away through a window. Why slash your tires if you're going to be dead? No, I don't think it was a hit. Wanted to scare you."

"That part worked," I said.

"Sending you a message."

"Why not use Western Union? Less noise that way."

"This message was 'fuck you.' A little indelicate in a singing telegram."

"Then we can't rule out the Redskins yet."

"You call the police?" he asked.

"No. Haven't decided if that's the most effective response. It it's Ventura, the locals won't have enough juice to go after him. Might be better to discuss this with Bobby Frank in person. Convince him I'm a great guy."

"Whenever you want to go," said Chick. "I'm ready."

"Let me get something done with the tires. We still need to talk to Meagan Ames and maybe Fogarty again. I'll be there later."

Chick said he'd be waiting, and we hung up.

I cleaned up the foot wound, bandaged it, and dressed. I got a flashlight and went outside to check the damage to the Jeep and the Mustang. The only damage was to the tires, which were ruined. He wasn't trying to kill me, but didn't want me to chase him. I went back in the cabin, made coffee, and waited until eight o'clock to call Stallworth, a mechanic friend who was good about taking care of my vehicles and keeping his mouth shut about how they were damaged.

"Eight tires?" he said after I told him what I needed. "How can you have eight tires go flat all at the same time?"

"I've been conducting extensive tests on them," I said, "and discovered you've been selling me defective merchandise."

"Last time it was to repair 'rock dents,' you called them, which looked just like bullet holes to me," he said. "Now it's eight flat tires."

"So hurry up, I've got places to go."

"Twelve-fifty for the tires. Another two hundred bucks for mounting and balancing and seventy-five dollars to come out and tow one in, fix the tires, then drive out and put tires on the other. That's what it's going to cost you."

"Could you wear a bandanna and hold a gun on me while you do the work so I'll feel better?"

"You're getting the tires at cost plus five percent," he said. "Which is a better deal than I give anybody else. Plus, I had to make two trips out to the freakin' booniies. If you lived anywhere close to civilization, you wouldn't have these problems, you know."

"You ever think about giving self-help talks as a career?" I asked. "You have such a soothing tone."

"Naw," he said. "My wife says I'm so natural-born warm-hearted, people'd just take advantage of me."

I hung up, and two hours later Stallworth showed up in his candy-apple red tow truck and hooked it up to the Jeep.

"After I get this one done, I want to put the Mach One on the computer and see how badly you've been abusing it," he said.

"I haven't even been driving it," I said.

"That's what I mean. It's an American road classic, not a yard ornament. You have to drive it once in a while. Does Clapton neglect his guitar?" It was then he looked up at the bedroom window. Then at me. He rubbed his face.

"Remodeling?" he asked.

"How do you like it so far?"

He nodded his head. "Nice. The Beirut look. Trendy." He opened the cab door on his truck, got inside, rolled down the window, and looked down at me.

"I don't want to know, do I?" he said.

"Nope."

"It ain't easy being you, Storme," he said, shaking his head.

NINETEEN

I followed Stallworth to town, telling him I'd give him a bonus if he'd have the Mach I checked out and ready to go in an hour.

"An hour?" Stallworth said. "You think you're the only customer I got?"

"I'll leave the Mach One to you in my will if you'll hurry," I said.

"Make it out quick. I saw your cabin."

An hour later I was back on the road, the sun bright and warm through the windshield as Leon Russell sang "Roll Away the Stone" on the classic rock station on the radio.

I headed for the town square, passing up the new shopping mall along the way. I wanted to pick up a few items: the bottle of scotch I owed Chick, some butterfly bandages for my cut foot, and maybe the odd cigar or two. There was an old drugstore on the square dressed in eighty-year-old brick that I liked to visit. It was one of those antiquated apothecaries with a real soda fountain and red, vinyl, swivel stools, which smelled of candy and waxed floors and vanilla. It also had a small glass humidor where you could buy single cigars. The national franchises were cheaper and more accessible and had a wider selection of goods. And they were less personal and more crowded and had less style, and their owners didn't live around here.

We kill off our local merchants and wonder where America went. America went to Walmart, where the other sheep graze.

I bought a Fonseca 10-10 cigar, a fifth of Glenlivet scotch, and a tin of ouchless bandages. All together it probably cost five dollars more than if I had stopped at the shopping mall. Small price to pay for beauty. The checkout lady placed the items into a paper sack, and I walked out into the autumn sunlight.

He was waiting for me outside. Leaning against the Jeep with a smirk on his five-o'clock shadow face. He was smoking a cigarette and looking around as though enjoying the morning air.

Rory watched the football player walk out of the drugstore. Damn, the guy was big up close. Guy was limping too. Good.

"Wyatt Storme," Rory said. "Nice to see you. You don't care if I lean against your vehicle, do you? I was real careful not to scratch it, you know? These look like new tires. Are these new tires?"

"What do you want, Rory?"

"So, you do remember me?"

"I remember."

"Well, now that's nice. That's real nice. Because we're going to be seeing a lot of each other, you and me." That was pretty cool. Keep the nice chat thing going, like they were next-door neighbors or something. Rory felt on top of this. Feeling good.

"I may faint from joy. What is it you want?"

Rory raised his palms and shoulders in an innocent "not me, I got no problems" gesture. Nice touch, huh?

"Nothing. Nothing. You got a nice place. You know that? I seen it."

"Your night vision that good?" said Superstar, getting right to it. The football player letting him know he knew. Guy was carrying too. Rory could see the slight bulge under the guy's left arm. Could you believe it? The jock was packing heat in the middle of fucking Mayberry. He wondered if it was the cannon he'd been firing away at him last night? Guy was looking at him now in that way he had with those hard blue-gray eyes. Like he was looking inside Rory. Son of a bitch had some nasty eyes.

"Naw. Saw it during the day. Drove out there the other day, but you weren't home. I learned a lot of stuff about you lately. Yeah. You're kind of an interesting guy. I know what you used to do. Know where you like to go. Know who your friends are." Give 'im the smile again. Playing games. Enjoying himself at Superstar's expense. "When would I see it at night, huh?"

I shifted the package to my left arm. Rory was as much admitting he was the guy who had shot through my window earlier this morning. I looked over his shoulder to see if anyone was paying attention.

"What's Ventura want?" I asked.

Rory's reaction was odd. He leaned back and screwed his face up as if he'd swallowed a bug.

A family of four—father, mother, and two boys—got out of their car and walked past us. On their way to buy shoes or toothpaste or rent a video. Meanwhile, I'm standing here talking to a degenerate who extorted and even killed people. A human cockroach whose very existence was an affront to decent society, if there still was such a thing.

"How the fuck I know what that greaseball shithead wants?"

Well, he didn't like that, I thought. Interesting. Maybe bore in a little more.

"Pretty unenlightened of you to refer to him with a racial slur," I said. "Just wanted to know why he sent a sagacious guy like you around to see me. I thought you were his punk."

"His what?" He was getting mad now. Good.

"You know," I said. "His errand boy. He says jump and you ask, 'How high, and where do I land?' He says, 'Rory, go shoot out Storme's windows with a shotgun.' That kind of stuff."

"I don't do nothing for that guinea shit no more. Not ever, see? I'm independent now. Got my own thing going."

"What is it you're doing? You making big money on the market?"

His dark eyes narrowed. He started rubbing the pads of his fingers with his thumbs. Then, as if he remembered something, he smiled again.

This guy has some mouth on him, thought Rory. Busting his chops. "Yeah," he said. "I got something going. Something new. Something I really enjoy." Bugging the shit out of you is what I'm doing.

"Who are you trying to convince?" the guy said. "Me or yourself?" He looked around as if something was funny. Guy was pissing him off. Made Rory wish he still had the insulation sap. "You can't function without Ventura telling you what to do. You're not smart enough. Look at you. Bracing me in broad daylight in the middle of town. I wonder if you know how stupid you are."

Rory started to make a move inside his jacket. Stopped. Don't let him get to you, Rory. That's what he wants. Stay cool. De Niro would be cool, wouldn't he? Yeah. He wouldn't let some jock asshole piss him off while Rory was getting over on him. Keep your shit together, man. Rory rubbed his hands together, then crossed his arms in front of him, hands hidden under his biceps.

"Ya know," he said, composing himself, "had a lot of time to myself in the slam. Thought about a lot of things." Like how it was going to feel to bust a cap on your backward country ass, you smug piece of shit. "You know what I thought about?"

"What it was like in the third grade? Back when your mental processes stagnated?"

No. Don't let him get inside, man. He wants you to get mad. Wants you to make a move. Guy was a fucking bold son of a bitch, that's for sure. Even moved his package to his left arm so he could get at the cannon. What'd he think? That we were going to have a shootout in the town square? Guy was something else. Got to keep the cool rap thing going. Let him know what Rory'd thought about inside. Let the guy sweat that.

"I thought about you. I thought about you a lot."

"I'm touched," Storme said. "I hope this doesn't mean you're going to develop an unnatural romantic interest in me. Sidelong glances during math class. Brushing up against me in gym. That kind of thing."

"No, you smart fucker. What I thought about was how I can't reach up above my head anymore. How my shoulder and knee hurt in the winter. How I lost two years of my life sitting inside with the dipshits and the perverts. How guys like you and Bobby Frank are always fucking with me. And how...," he said, teeth gritting. Drop it down a gear, man. "And how I'm going to turn it around on you. How I'm going to become the most important thing in your fucking, miserable, asshole life."

"Is that a threat?" the guy said.

"No," he said, smiling. Back on top of it again. "I wouldn't do that."

"Get off my truck," the guy said. Just like that outta the clear blue sky, he starts bogarting him.

"Sure, sure. I'm going to."

Rory gave some thought to pulling the knife he had in his pocket, even reaching inside his jacket.

"I see anything metal, I'll kill you right here," Storme said.

"Hey," Rory said. "Getting a little testy here, aren't we? Take some Prozac or something, huh?" Guy wasn't kidding. He meant it. Look at 'im all bulled up. Rory wasn't afraid of him, but he wasn't ready for it to be over yet. Wanted to enjoy it a little while longer.

"Get off my Jeep before I drop-kick you across the town square."

Rory stood away from the car. "There, see? These things can be worked out. I wouldn't hurt your ride for anything." Smiling again. "I gotta go now anyway. Got things to do." He flicked his cigarette butt at the guy's feet. "See you around, Superstar. Nice talkin' to ya."

I watched Rory Marchibroda walk away. He opened the door to a new Cadillac and backed out and drove away. Slowly. I saw him reach up and adjust his rearview mirror to look back at me. Blows up my home, then follows me around town. Talking to him made me feel as if I needed to take a shower.

TWENTY

That didn't go so bad, thought Rory.

He reached up and adjusted the rearview so he could watch the long piece a shit's reaction. Guy was looking at him drive off. Good.

Superstar was a real smartass. You say something, the guy says something back. The kind of guy who made Rory feel stupid. Like those egghead dicks back in high school who used to make fun of him when he couldn't answer the teacher's questions. They always looked different with their heads down the toilet bowl, the water swirling around their ears. But this guy Storme was different. He was a big guy with muscles. It'd take three or four guys just to get him through the bathroom door.

One thing Rory would have to give the guy was that he was cool. Even when he told Rory to get off the truck, he did it without heat. Just "Get off the truck." That was all. Real calm-like but still being badass.

And what did sagacious mean, anyway? He'd have to look it up later.

Bet it was something smartassed.

TWENTY-ONE

Stallworth fixed the Mustang, and I drove it back to Bailey's Crossing, the sunlight bright through the windshield and warm on my shoulders and arms. The creamy blue sky was spotted with white thunderheads imploding and unfolding like shaving cream. Cattle spotted the rolling fields. The two-lane highway was vacant and stretched out in front of me, inviting me. When I hit the long *S* curve on 27 Highway, I pushed down on the pedal, and the Mach I growled and sat down, the wide radials hugging the curve. The powerful thrust sent a sensation through my shoulders and neck, pushed me deeper into the seat.

I powered out of the curve and dropped the transmission into third, buried the pedal, and the pride of the Ford stable fishtailed, roaring and bellowing, then straightened. The RPMs and speed odometer climbed in concert. I shifted to fourth, and the tach dropped, and the speedometer continued to climb. Fence posts clicked by the windows. The Mustang snarled.

Cheap thrills.

I backed off the throttle and thought about Rory Marchibroda and his relationship to Bobby Frank Ventura and Ventura's relationship to Geoffrey Salinger. And Cameron Fogarty's lack of a relationship with nearly everyone. The whole bunch was unlikable enough to be in the United Nations.

How did I get involved in this?

I parked the Mach I under a huge oak tree to keep the sun off the paint job. Stallworth would have been so proud. I got out of the car and found Chick lounging outside Fogarty's trailer dressed in regular clothes: jeans, polo shirt, and jacket, leaning against a prop rain barrel and smoking a cigarette.

"What are you doing hanging around?" I said. I handed the bottle of scotch to him. "I expect to find you beating a path through the tangled web of intrigue. Instead, you're sitting around contracting lung cancer. What kind of sidekick are you? Roy Rogers wouldn't tolerate this crap from Gabby Hayes for even one second."

"I kept waiting for somebody to swing by and confess," Chick said. "Nobody did. Nobody showed up with a telegram from Western Union telling me who was sending the death threats. I drank coffee for a while. That didn't seem to help either, so I switched to cigarettes. It was starting to work too, then you broke the mood."

"I think we need to talk to Fogarty," I said. "Salinger and Ames too."

"Wait 'til you talk to Ames. You're going to enjoy that. She's Stella Starbanger."

"There's too much we don't know."

"That could be construed as a semigeneric statement regarding us," Chick said. "Fogarty's got a break coming up. Tell me about what happened last night while we're waiting."

I told him, including my conversation with Rory in town.

"Pretty ballsy," said Chick, "coming up on a strange cabin in the middle of the night, slashing tires, then blasting away at a window and leaving. Then following you around town so he could catch your reaction. Shit, this guy's got some 'nads."

"Rory reacted funny when I mentioned him working for Ventura. I ask myself, why Ventura anyway?"

"Because he doesn't like people disarming his apes and making him look weak," said Chick. "Because he's a genetic mutant dipshit. How's that for motivation?"

"The last thing Ventura wants is trouble while he's trying to get a piece of a Hollywood production. It's too sloppy. He'd have to balance the result against me involving the police. Guys like Ventura can't afford personal vendettas. The people downtown don't like it."

"You're talking about a guy whose head is lashed together with barbed wire. He's a fucking deviate. His thought processes are short-circuited by his twisted way of seeing things."

"Something doesn't feel right," I said.

"Maybe your underwear's on backward," said Chick. "Thanks for bringing the whiskey. I was low on provisions." He swirled the bottle, popped the bottom with the heel of his hand, and cracked the seal with a quick twist, which left a slice in the seal as clean as if he'd cut it with a razor blade. He took a sip, leaned forward at the waist, and looked around the corner of the trailer.

"Here comes Fogarty now."

Fogarty was walking our direction. Kerry Kane and Peter Braithwaite were with him. Volts was missing. Maybe he was at the library. Maybe he was at a UFO convention. Maybe he was hanging upside down in a closet. Interesting he wasn't around, though.

"We need to talk to you," I said to Fogarty.

"I don't have time," Fogarty said. "I want a drink and get my head on straight, then I got a call in thirty minutes."

"Just take a couple of minutes," I said.

"You hear what he said?" said Braithwaite. "He don't wanna talk to you."

"Stay clear of this," I said, looking briefly at Braithwaite. "It doesn't involve you."

"Everything with Cam involves me," said Braithwaite.

Fogarty smiled like a sadist with a sackful of kittens.

"Look, Peter Breath," said Chick, "this is between the adults, so take your little sister here and go get an ice-cream cone or something."

"It's Braithwaite," said the heavy man, his face reddening.

"I was close," said Chick.

"You think you're a badass, dontcha?" said Braithwaite.

"No," said Chick, smiling his smile. The smile that demonstrates he thinks the world was created for his personal entertainment. "I'm for sure a badass. You want to talk to me, you look under *B* in the yellow pages."

"It's important that I ask you some questions," I said to Fogarty. "Somebody took a shot at me last night. Just a couple of minutes, then you can go back to regaling the lapdogs."

"See if you can find any tequila, Pete," said Fogarty. Braithwaite took a deep breath and looked at everybody, then stomped off.

"You too," Fogarty said to Kerry Kane. "Get lost."

"But—" began Kane, then closed his mouth and walked off.

"Two minutes," Fogarty told me. "All you get."

I stifled an impulse to cuff him upside the head. "You didn't tell us about the troubles you've had with your costars," I said.

"What trouble?"

"Stop being the typical Hollywood jerk-off," said Chick. "I'm trying to protect you, and you're not helping. Wyatt found out you had an affair with Caraway's ex-wife, you sued LeBeau for punching you out, and you abused Darnell's sister. Those would've been nice things for me to know in case I had to wrestle Darnell to the ground."

He chuckled. "That the way they tell it?"

I nodded.

"Did Valeri give you her girl-next-door routine?" he said. He looked at me and smiled. "Yeah, I'll bet she did. Just a little old girl in a mean old world."

"What about LeBeau and Caraway?"

"Patty Caraway wakes up horny every day of her life," he said. "I couldn't keep her off me. Can I help it if Chance can't take care of her? And LeBeau? That's old news. Fuck him, fuck them, and fuck you. You're talking about a bunch of bit players and hangers-on. I'm going places. Me. All by myself." He chewed at the corner of his lip. "Yeah, so they all fucking hate me. Doesn't stop them from jumping at the chance to be in one of my pictures, does it?"

"Who wouldn't?" I said. "I'm all atwitter just standing close to you."

Fogarty laughed and scratched his head. "Like I give a shit what a fucking has-been thinks."

Chick chuckled to himself.

"Are the death threats for real?" I asked. "Or something you and Salinger cooked up for publicity?"

"I don't know what the fuck you're talking about. Your time's up, hero." He pushed by me and disappeared into his trailer.

Chick unscrewed the cap on the bourbon bottle and took a swallow. He chuckled. "Has-been."

I looked at Chick. "Shut up."

"He-ro," he said, laughing again.

TWENTY-TWO

Rory watched Superstar's Mustang pull away from him. The Caddy was powerful, but it couldn't keep up with the muscle car.

But what the hell, he thought. He'd accomplished what he'd wanted already, though he wished he hadn't let Superstar get to him. The guy had a way of getting under your skin, looking at you like you were a sewer rat or something. Rory didn't like guys who thought they were better than him. Bobby Frank was like that.

Bobby Frank, with his fancy fucking clothes. He was still a Wop with tomato sauce on his face. That's all he'd ever be. A smartassed half Wop whose mother was a Jew. Yeah, Bobby Frank was just another mongrel with a big mouth.

It was like those asshole kids who picked on Rory's landlady's boy...Gene, that was the kid's name. They messed with Gene all the time, following him home from school and slapping him around and calling him names. And the kid just took it. Gene let them mess with him. It made Rory angry at the kid, but at the same time it made him feel sorry for him. Rory tried to tell the kid to stand up for himself, but the kid would just look at him with those sad eyes, and it made Rory feel weird inside. Like him and the kid had something in common.

But they were nothing alike. Kid was a sissy who let people push him around. Rory didn't let nobody push him around. They both had shithead dads who ran off on them. Gene's mom drank all the time too. Kid was all alone. Rory knew about being alone.

Then yesterday, when Rory was getting ready to go out, he happened to look out his window and saw some bigger kid push Gene down on the sidewalk. Gene lay on the ground, and Rory could see he was crying.

And something snapped inside Rory. It had felt like a stick breaking inside his head, and the next thing Rory knew, he was down the stairs and outside and picking up Gene and wiping away the kid's tears.

"Why you fucking take that, huh?" Rory had said to Gene. "What's the matter with you?"

Gene continued sobbing.

Rory shook the kid. "You can't put up with that shit, kid. Goddammit, they'll run you over if you do."

The other kid was still standing there. Some punk kid about fifteen, wearing his baseball cap backward, an earring in one ear.

Rory stood up and looked at the punk.

"What's the matter with you, mister?" said the kid. Yeah, that's the way they talk to you nowadays. They talk to their parents that way. And they let 'em do it. But Rory wasn't this kid's parent. It was time this kid got a hardball lesson.

Rory reached out and grabbed a handful of the punk's sweatshirt, pulling the kid up close.

"Hey, you can't do this, you—"

Rory interrupted the punk by shaking the kid by the hair.

"Yeah?" said Rory, jerking the kid's head like a toy. "Well, can I do this, tough guy? Huh?"

Then Rory put the kid on the ground, pinning the punk with one knee. "Listen, jerk-off. You leave Gene alone. Understand? I'm talking to you, you little fuck. You listening?"

"I'm gonna tell my dad," the punk said, but the tears had started, and he was scared. Rory could smell his fear, and that was when Rory was best.

"Yeah," said Rory. "You tell your dad. And if he says one word to me"—Rory opened his jacket, letting the kid see the

Taurus—"I'll drop him in a fucking rock quarry. You with him. You follow me?"

The kid nodded his head up-and-down. His lip was quivering like Jell-O. Yeah, that was better.

He told the punk, "I better never see you or any of your buddies around here again. 'Cause I got something for all of ya, if I see you. You got that?"

The punk nodded his head up-and-down, again, as if there were an invisible wire jerking on it. Then Rory picked him up and shoved him up the sidewalk.

But that was yesterday. That's what had given him the idea to shoot up Superstar's house. Scare him. Then he followed him to town to see if it had worked. But it hadn't. The guy still had a mouth on him. Time to shake him up some.

Show Superstar what life was really all about.

But first he had to take care of the two kids who he'd bought the beer from. And like always, Rory was able to find them.

Yeah, he always found them. Like the Canadian Mounties. That's what he was thinking about as he turned off on the road that led to Gilmore, where the two kids lived.

TWENTY-THREE

"You must tell no one what I'm about to tell you," said Salinger.

"Come on, Geoffrey," Chick said. "We'll be too old to remember it if you don't hurry up. I'm still keeping it a secret that I took Mary Sue Jennings's virginity when we were sixteen. Whoops. Guess I let it out."

"We're not going to tell anyone, Geoffrey," I said. "You have my word."

Salinger pressed his lips together in a thin, straight line. "Four years ago," he began, "I was skiing in Colorado. I'm not going to say where, and I'm not going to give you names. In the bungalow next to mine was the wife of...of a high-ranking government official."

"A senator or a congressman?" I asked.

"I don't wish to divulge even that much."

"Higher than that," said Chick. It was a statement, not a question.

Salinger's eyes widened. "What?" He looked at Chick as if Chick had suddenly turned purple and grown tentacles.

"Heartbeat away from the big desk," said Chick, smiling.

"How—" Salinger was stammering. "How do you...I mean, what makes—"

"Relax, Geoffrey," Chick said. "Your secret is safe. Besides me, only a CIA operative and her secret service agents know. And regardless of what you may think, those guys would rather have their kneecaps removed than divulge it. They take their jobs seriously."

"But how did you know about it?"

"I'm Captain Midnight," said Chick. "My feet don't touch the ground. Surprised you hadn't noticed. You got any scotch?"

"In the cabinet," said Salinger, shaken. His eyes were opaque and round.

"Hey, fellas," I said. "Remember me? The guy who doesn't know this story."

"Geoffrey had himself a fling with the vice-presidential nominee's wife," said Chick, lifting a green bottle of Glenlivet scotch out of the cabinet. "Lots of heavy breathing and enough body heat to melt the slopes."

"It wasn't quite like that," said Salinger, leaning forward with his elbows on his knees, his fingertips touching together, his arms forming a triangle. "It was quite tender, actually."

"You crazy kids," said Chick. "Shit. Jumps the VP hopeful's wife. You're my hero, Geoffrey."

"How did you manage to get involved with her?" I asked Geoffrey.

"It was at a fund-raiser."

"The beautiful people," said Chick, pouring scotch into a lowball glass. Salinger frowned at him. "It's okay," said Chick. "I owe you guys a lot. Really." The scar next to the apostrophe eyebrow, the one that had been burned off by shrapnel, turned purple, though Chick kept smiling. "People like the vice president and his lovely wife sent me to off to war, and I got to visit a foreign land where they were trying to kill me and my brothers. And you never invite me to your parties." He drank off the scotch and poured more.

"I was against the war," said Geoffrey. "Many of my friends also. But no one blames you or any soldier who served. I don't why you're upset with me."

"Because you're close by."

"I'm one hundred percent behind veterans like yourself," said Geoffrey. "But we shouldn't have been there, and I—"

"Watched people die," said Chick, interrupting. "When was the last time you thanked one of them?" He didn't wait for an answer. He wasn't looking for one. He drank more scotch, swallowed it. Poured more. His eyes were dark and charged with an internal electricity.

"I don't mean the *last* time you thanked one, man. I mean the last fucking time it was *cool* to thank one of those guys. When was that? Do you know, Geoffrey? Do you? And when did the last guy die? I mean the last fucking guy. We all talked about not being the last guy to die, but who was it? What was that guy's name? Nobody knows. That guy didn't get shit. So, just fuck you, Geoffrey. Fuck you and your I-feel-so-bad-now posturing. That poor mother died, and you're punching the vice president's wife, and you don't really give a shit. So, spare me the angst."

It was very quiet in the trailer. Chick took a cigarette out of the package and lit it. Salinger didn't say anything. I didn't say anything. The dragons that slept inside Chick's head were awake and flapping their wings and dragging nailed claws across his soul. Who knew what triggered it? Maybe it was the booze and the pain-killers. But you never knew. It was just there, and you coped as best you could. Nobody who wasn't there will ever know what it's like. You just lived with it.

I'd never seen Chick like this.

"Okay," I said. "Tell me the rest."

"Anyway," said Salinger, subdued now, "the vice presidential nominee got called back to Washington—he was a congressman—and she and I had lunch together. One thing led to another, and we ended up sleeping together."

"What's the connection to Fogarty?" I asked.

"Chick was only partly correct," said Salinger. "The CIA and the secret service agents assigned to"—he started to say her name, then checked himself—"the…ah…woman in question aren't the only one who knew of our relationship."

"Who else?" I asked.

"Cameron Fogarty was staying at the same resort," he said. "We skied together. Drank together while we were there. We became friends. That's what I thought anyway. He knows about the…ah…the affair. I told him. Then he parlayed the information into a friendly sort of extortion. I helped him get a part in a movie he wanted. That's why he has this part. And"—he chewed his lower lip—"he may have told Ventura about the affair."

I looked at Chick.

"That's pretty fucked up, Geoffrey," said Chick, blowing a cloud of smoke over Salinger's head. "Even for you."

We left Salinger's and walked back to Chick's trailer. Chick got a bottle of Budweiser beer out of the refrigerator and handed me a red can of Coca-Cola. We opened them and sat at the veneer-topped table. A clutter of magazines and two weapons holsters were strewn over the backs of the chairs. Chick was cleaning the .380 Colt with solvent, running a cleaning brush through the stripped-down breech. I sipped the Coke and looked at him, searching his eyes.

"You okay?" I asked.

"Sure," Chick said. "Why wouldn't I be all right?"

"You were a little rough on Geoffrey. He's not a bad guy."

"Guys like Salinger need to get brushed back once in a while. What do you want to do about Rory?" His way of saying the matter was closed.

"Nothing, I guess."

"It can be fixed." He reassembled the pistol and slammed the breech shut with a metallic finality.

"No," I said, understanding his meaning. "Not that way."

"What're you going to do then? Wait around for him to get a clean shot at you?"

I looked out the window of the trailer. "I don't know yet."

"Either take him out or turn him into the sheriff."

"For what?" I said. "Felonious following me around with intent to lean against my truck?"

"How about shooting up your cabin?" Chick picked up the Thompson single-shot pistol and began to clean it.

"What if it wasn't him?"

Chick looked up from cleaning the weapon.

"Okay," I said. "We know he did it. Can't prove it, though."

"You just don't want the sheriff and his deputies poking around up at your cabin."

"That's a factor."

"You know what has to be done," said Chick, oiling the barrel of the Thompson, then wiping it off.

"I can't do that," I said. "You know that. Not like that."

"I can," said Chick. His eyes were flat. Something was simmering inside him.

"I know. Just don't."

"I'll wait some," said Chick. "But if it becomes necessary, I'm going to do it. We need to be clear on that."

I knew he meant it. I understood why. There was no bluff in Chick Easton. I didn't want to take Rory like that. It wasn't my way, but there would be no point talking about it with Chick just now.

"How'd you know about Salinger's affair?" I asked.

"I read it in the *National Enquirer*."

I waited for him to get to it.

"Dirk Donovan told me," said Chick. Donovan was a CIA operative Chick had known since the war. I'd met Donovan in Colorado years before when I'd tripped over a gunrunning operation.

"Why'd he tell you?"

"We were drinking beer in a bar up in Aspen. We started talking about old times. This was right after I'd met you. He told me about something funny he'd come across up in Vail. He'd been sent by somebody high up to watch over the nominee's wife, keep her off the evening news. She's kind of known for similar escapades, and they were afraid the opposition was looking to catch her at it. He said Salinger and the lady went to elaborate lengths to hide it from the secret service guys. Even thought they were getting away with it, but those guys didn't let her out of their sight for a second. She wore a wig, and Salinger wore a hooded parka and a ski mask. She even crawled out a window one night. Not conspicuous at all. Dirk said Salinger looked like a cross between the Unabomber and Jason. Dirk had to accidentally break a camera or two." He took a pull off the beer bottle.

"How many times did she and Salinger sneak off?"

"That's classified," said Chick. "I tell you that, I'd have to kill you. Let me ask you a personal question. She doesn't look all that good to me. Does she look good to you?"

"What kind of personal question is that?"

"I've seen how you perk up when she comes on the evening news."

"I don't know why I even talk to you," I said.

"Let's go talk to Meagan Ames. There's a little light left. You need to see her in the daylight."

I finished my Coke and pulled on my jacket, and we left the trailer.

TWENTY-FOUR

Meagan Ames's personal secretary was a big, blond, beachboy type who looked like an extra from a Frankie and Annette flick. He answered the knock at her trailer door wearing a pair of gym shorts, no shoes, and no shirt. He smelled of Stetson and sex.

"Yeah," he said when he saw us.

Chick and I looked at each other. Yeah?

"We'd like to speak with Ms. Ames," said Chick.

The blond stared at us, then said, "Wait a minute. I'll ask her."

"He didn't ask our names," I said.

"No need to confuse him," said Chick.

Inside a minute he returned.

"Who are you guys?" he asked.

We told him. He left again. Chick and I looked at each other again. Beachboy returned and opened the door, and we walked inside the trailer. "She'll be in in a couple minutes," he said. "She said go ahead and sit down."

We sat in chairs. He sat at a desk. I gathered that it was his desk by the way he sat at it. On the desk was a laptop computer. Maybe he was smarter than he let on. His bronze pectorals glistened with the smooth sheen of workout. Where one might expect to find the kitchen table, there was one of those workout machines that used thick rubber bands instead of weights and dumbbells of various sizes. There were huge pictures of Meagan Ames on the wall in various poses and positions. One was nude.

I tried not to look at it. Beachboy watched me not look at it. Chick looked at Beachboy. Beachboy looked at Chick. Chick looked at him some more and began to smile.

"What?" said Beachboy after several seconds of this.

"What?" said Chick.

"What do you mean, 'what'?"

"I asked you second," said Chick.

"Are you messing with me, man?"

Chick turned to me. "Am I messing with him?"

"You are," I said. "So knock it off."

Meagan Ames breezed into the living room, wearing an electric-blue bodysuit and some kind of designer top with a strange pattern of whorls and lines over the bodysuit. It looked like Picasso threw up on it. Probably cost her three hundred dollars. I wouldn't wax my car with it. High up on the inside of her left thigh was a tattoo of a butterfly. The bodysuit was barely more than a covering. A white toy poodle followed her into the room. When the dog saw Chick, it began yipping angrily.

"Dogs naturally dig me," said Chick.

"Desdemona," said Meagan, talking to the dog. She used a singsong baby-talk voice to speak to the animal. "Is that any way to treat guests? Now you be nice." Meagan patted the dog's head. "I'm sorry, but she's been going through some depression lately. I feel so sorry for her, but you just can't find a good pet psychiatrist here."

The dog stopped yipping and growled low in its throat, looking at Chick. It sounded like an angry hamster.

"We wanted to ask you a few questions," I said. "If that's all right with you, Ms. Ames."

"Call me Meagan," she said. She had a way of speaking that sounded as if she practiced it in front of a mirror. Breathy and husky. A habit. "You're the football player, aren't you?"

I admitted I was.

"They say you hunt things," she said. "Little deer and other mammals. I could never eat another living thing."

"You know there have been threats made against Cameron Fogarty?"

"Can you believe it?" she said. "It's just incredible, isn't it? Cam told me all about it. He's been so brave through the whole thing."

"The show must go on," said Chick. He bared his teeth at Desdemona, and the little dog jumped back and began the low growling thing again.

"How well do you know Fogarty?"

"We had sex a couple of times," she said.

Chick and I looked at each other again.

"Oh. Excuse me," she said, her head lolling to one side. "Does it bother you when I talk like that?"

"Naw," said Chick. "Grandma used to talk like that all the time."

She shrugged. "Well, we did." Beachboy was rubbing his hands together. Tightly. It caused his pectorals to ripple and roll. Meagan noticed he was agitated.

"You knew about that, Chester," she said. "We've already talked about this."

Chick looked at me and lipped the word *Chester*, then smiled.

"Doesn't mean I like it," said Chester.

"Darling, you are my favorite. Don't get all pissy." She looked away from him, effectively dismissing him. "He is very pretty, isn't he?" she asked us, meaning Chester.

I ignored her. I looked at the electronic equipment in front of Chester. "You know how to use that computer?" I asked.

"Why, you looking to hire me?" Chester said. "I've got a degree in secretarial skills and business machines. Why is that any of your business?"

"One of the threats was a letter," I said.

"Yeah, like I'm the only guy in America's got a computer."

I shrugged. "Somebody sent it. How do you get along with Fogarty?"

"We get along all right," Chester said.

"Ha," said Meagan.

"Well, I didn't try to kill him, Meagan," Chester said.

"But it wouldn't break your heart if he was killed."

Chester's lips pursed together, and he looked down at his hands.

"Ms. Ames," I began. "Have you ever—"

"Meagan," she said.

"Meagan," I said, "have you ever had any trouble with Cameron Fogarty?" She made a face, as if she didn't understand. "You know, any conflicts, arguments, any problems of any kind."

She made a show of thinking about it. She placed a finger alongside her face in thought. "Can't think of a thing. We get along *famously*." She emphasized the word *famously*, looking at Chester when she said it. Chester's face colored, and his jaw muscles bunched into a walnut-shaped knot.

"You get along with Geoffrey Salinger?"

"I slept with him once," she said. Theatrically, she put a hand to her mouth. "Oh, I forgot, that upsets you."

"I'm sure you're very serviceable," I said. "I have a washing machine like that. It'll wash about anything you throw in it."

"Now, look here, you son of a bitch," she said, placing a balled fist against a cantilevered hip. "I didn't invite you here. What's your problem? Don't you like it when the girls talk about sex like you boys do?"

"I don't know anybody talks like that," I said. "Of either sex. And I don't hang around with boys."

"Cameron said you were kind of an uptight asshole."

I turned to Chick. "See, he's telling everybody," I said. "Pretty soon everybody's going to know."

"You mean, besides people who already know you?" Chick said.

Meagan's face flushed, and her lips pursed, causing her delicate chin to dimple. "Are you two finished?"

"Almost," I said. "One more question. Who do you think has the most reason to wish Fogarty dead?"

"That's easy," she said, tracing a wisp of hair on her forehead back on top of her head. "I think Valeri does. The old cow doesn't like him. Doesn't like me either."

"Hard to imagine," I said. Innocently, I thought. But her eyes narrowed, and her mouth turned into a hard line. "You seem to be the only person around here who gets along with Fogarty."

"I'm carrying his baby too," she said. There was a challenge in her voice.

Chester stood up quickly.

"Oh, sit down," said Meagan.

"How long have you known you were pregnant?" Chester asked.

"None of your business. I just know I am, and I know it belongs to Cam."

Chick looked perplexed. "How'd you determine that? The way you talk, it could be anybody south of the Canadian border."

"You're a smartass bastard," she said.

"Aw shucks, it's nothing," said Chick.

"Look, Meagan," I said, feeling the situation slipping out of control, "what we're trying to do here is gain information that will help us protect Fogarty. Which is what you want too, isn't it?"

"Of course," she said.

"So, is there anything you could tell us that might help us do that?"

"Valeri hates Cameron because he used to be married to her sister, Darla. Darla is mental, you know. She's at the funny farm."

"Yes, Valeri told me that also," I said. "Not quite so colorfully, though. What about you, Chester? You had any problems with Fogarty?"

Chester looked at Meagan, who said, "You don't have to answer that, Chester."

"Why shouldn't he answer?" I asked.

"Because it's none of your fucking business, that's why," she said.

"She do your talking for you, Chester?" asked Chick. "'Cause if she does, it doesn't look too good for you. A guy built like you. Tsk, tsk."

Chester rubbed a bicep with his other hand. "Cameron shoots his mouth off at me," said Chester. "I don't like it. But Meagan says I can't touch him, so I don't."

"What's he say that you don't like?" I asked.

"Calls me cuckold boy."

Chick started chuckling.

"You think that's funny?" asked Chester.

"Aw c'mon, Chester, I know Fogarty's an asshole. It's not a secret."

"I think it's time for you two to leave," said Meagan. "Chester, show these two men to the door."

Chester stepped from behind the desk, muscles rippling like wind across sand. He was glad to be restored as the main brood stud. I wondered if I should rip off my shirt and have a pose-down with him. With my luck the shirt wouldn't rip. The white rodent began yipping again, bouncing back and forth on the floor like a windup toy.

I stood. I wasn't going to learn anything else here. And though I didn't like being told what to do and where to go, there was nothing to be gained by dancing with Chester. There were few things less productive than fighting with a man trying to impress a woman. Chick was less inclined to move along.

"You're going to have to do better than Chester," Chick said.

"I can bench four hundred pounds," said Chester.

"That's nice, Chester," said Chick. "I'm sure it's awe-inspiring." The angry rodent began snarling. Chick stamped his foot and snarled back at it. The dog ran from the room, then came skittering back.

"Don't do that to Desdemona," said Meagan.

"I wouldn't hurt the little doggie," said Chick. He stuck his tongue out at the dog. "Might eat her, though."

"Get going," said Chester. "While you can still do it upright."

Chick laughed. "Chester, you nut, you. You say the craziest things. Have you got a book of clichés or what?"

"Let it go, Chick," I said. "Chester's got enough trouble. He's stuck here, you know."

"Hadn't thought of that," said Chick. He looked down at the floor, then raised his head and nodded. "It's cruel to think about."

"What does that mean?" Meagan asked.

We opened the door and left.

The dog yipped spasmodically as I shut the door from the outside. Something thumped against the door. Throwing things at us.

"I think she figured it out," I said.

"Well," said Chick. "That was pleasant. Maybe she'll name the kid after one of us."

"Probably too much to hope for," I said.

TWENTY-FIVE

Sandy got the job with the network.

While I was frittering away my time being shot at, cursed, confronted, stalked, and run around the bushes like a clown by the movie community, Sandy had been dealing with the guys with the big desks.

I wanted to be happy for her when she told me, but it was a stretch. The distance between us, which had seemed like a gap, was beginning to yaw and swell like a dry canyon.

"I've only got a second," she said on the phone that evening when she called to give me the good news. "But I wanted you to be the first to know."

"That's great, San," I said.

"They're sending the contract over today," she said. "You won't believe the obscene amount of money they're offering."

"At least they won't be wasting it for a change."

"I'll be flying in Saturday night or Sunday morning."

"Let me know which," I said.

"You don't sound happy."

"Well, I am." Liar.

"Nothing's changed."

"Of course it hasn't."

"Why don't you sound happy then?"

"I'm just tired," I said.

"Get some rest then, because we're going to celebrate this weekend," she said. "I've got a couple of things to do. I'll call you back in the morning."

When we hung up, I put on Otis Redding, lit up a cigar, sat at the bay window in the dark, and felt sorry for myself because nobody else could do it so well.

At six thirty Thursday morning, I was sitting in a tree stand overlooking a deer trail. The air was chill, and I was into the coffee thermos. Fifteen minutes later the sun rose up over the forest and became a golden-orange globe in the eastern horizon, pushing purple shadows ahead of it. An owl sounded in the deep woods, a haunting, ominous tone.

The interview with Meagan Ames hadn't gone well, and although it might not mean a thing, Meagan Ames's pregnancy and Chester's dislike of Fogarty added a couple of warped pieces to the puzzle. Everybody disliked, or had to a reason to dislike, Cameron Fogarty. But as yet, nobody seemed the type to kill him. The only violent person of the bunch was Volts, and he liked Fogarty.

And as yet, there had been no attempts made or even any new threats. It seemed like a cold trail. So I went hunting. Probably wouldn't help anything, but for a few hours, no one knew where I was.

Years ago I had retreated to the solitary life. Saved my money, invested it, and squirreled away enough to drop out of society's neon glare. But I had waited too long to make the jump. I was tucked away in too many computers. I was too many numbers on too many files to make the break a clean one. One hundred years ago, a man could disappear without a trace. He could escape the cities and the people and even the tax collector. Nineteenth-century man didn't have to dodge the shopping mall lemmings and the celebrity worshipers who lived their lives vicariously through television personalities they would never meet.

All the frontiers had been boxed and stamped and catalogued. They could find me if they wanted to, no matter how well I tried to hide. Freedom is just a word in the dictionary now. On the same page with *frenzy*, just across from *frustration*.

I had chosen my life. Chosen the solitude, the isolation.

But I hadn't chosen the loneliness. Somehow it had just found me.

Two does walked by my stand. A minute later a six-point buck followed their trail. I let him pass without raising my bow. Later I shimmied down the tree and walked home.

Back at the cabin, I loaded the Remington 1100 pump shotgun with number four buckshot, backed with a three-inch slug in case Rory decided to drop by to borrow a cup of sugar. Then I made a fresh pot of coffee and called Sandy's New York apartment. I wanted to hear her voice again.

"Hello," she said, her voice thick with sleep. "This is Sandy."

"Really? I was hoping for Gretchen Carlson."

"What time is it?"

"Ten thirty. Eleven thirty where you are."

"I suppose you've already been up and bothering the wildlife."

"Sounds like you stayed up and bothered the wildlife there," I said.

"I went out with some friends," she admitted. "Stayed out late."

"Well, you're a big star now and need to circulate."

"Don't get sarcastic."

"I'm not sarcastic, I'm jealous."

"No need," she said. "You're my sweetheart. My one and only. How are things going there?"

"Everybody still hates Cameron Fogarty."

"I interviewed him once. He kept trying to put his hand on my leg."

"Hmmm," I said into the phone.

"But," she said, "once the camera was on, he morphed into this personality, this charming character, the one the public can't get enough of." I heard the faint whisper of a yawn, which had a kittenish quality. "He's a different person when he's on."

"Tried to touch your leg, huh?"

"Don't get any misguided male notions. I took care of him."

"I won't," I said. I was more thinking along the lines of breaking his fingers, one by one, and stuffing them in his mouth.

I told her about the conversations I'd had with the cast. She listened without speaking. I left out Rory Marchibroda shooting up the cabin and slashing my tires and then following me to town. I also left out the part about Salinger's confession. National security considerations, of course. I was, after all, talking to a reporter.

"Let's see if I've got this straight," she said when I finished. "Michael LeBeau, Valeri Darnell, and Rance Caraway all dislike Cameron Fogarty. Geoffrey Salinger also might wish him to disappear and was eager to let you know he would never do such a thing."

"He was anxious about it anyway," I said. "Probably doesn't mean anything. It doesn't make sense that Salinger would threaten Fogarty, then hire Chick. Meagan Ames likes Fogarty, though. She thinks he's brave and courageous. Probably why she's carrying his child."

"The thought of a child possessing their collective characteristics is a load."

"Then there is Chester, the overmuscled secretary and blow-up sex doll," I said. "He probably wouldn't wear a black G-string if Fogarty bought it."

What about Bobby Frank Ventura and Rory Marchibroda, a pair of bottom-feeders who might have their own twisted reasons for whacking him out? Or doing the same to me? Maybe if I put them all in a room and forced them to watch an endless loop of Madonna videos, one of them would crack.

"As yet, though," Sandy said, "there haven't been any attempts made on Fogarty?"

"Nope. Not one. Chick suspects it might all be a publicity scam to create interest in the movie."

"Surely not."

"These are some squirrely people," I said.

"The industry's full of them."

"Which makes me wonder why you chose a job that puts you in close proximity to them."

"Or why I chose to love a man who is so adverse to them."

Another good question.

Thirty minutes after talking to Sandy, I was sitting on the deck drinking coffee when a charcoal-gray Infiniti sedan pulled up to the cabin. The driver got out, smoothed the line of his suit, and looked around as if he expected Tarzan to swing out of the trees at any moment. I recognized him as the accountant-lawyer type who had been with Ventura and his bodyguards. His suit was the same color as the car. His briefcase was the same color as the interior of the car.

He started to speak, but I stood and said, "Get back in the car and point it at the highway."

He stopped walking and looked up to where I was standing on the deck. "My name is Yancey Carlisle. I'm an attorney. I represent Robert Ventura. If you have a few moments, I would like to talk to you."

I shook my head. "Huh-uh."

"It will just take a moment."

"Moments are precious. I don't want to waste them on anyone who would associate with Bobby Frank Ventura."

"Please, Mr. Storme," said Yancey Carlisle, attorney-at-law. "I'm just doing my job. I mean you no harm."

"So talk."

He started toward my steps. "If I could just come inside—"

"No. You stay down there. I can hear you fine."

He put a hand to his forehead and looked around nervously. "This is rather awkward," he said. He reached into the inside of his coat.

"Too bad," I said, reaching down to pull up the shotgun. "And keep your hands where I can see them. First time I don't see them, I'm going to cut you off at the knees."

"Good God, what are you doing? There is no need for weapons," said Carlisle, his eyes large. "I'm not a violent man."

"Why does that sound so funny coming from an employee of Ventura's?"

"Mr. Ventura sent me to assure you that there is no reason for animus between yourself and him. That what has happened in the past is in the past."

"His assurances are worthless," I said.

"He asked me to give you this." He opened the leather briefcase and produced a fat manila envelope that he held up for me to see.

"What's in it?" I asked.

"Five thousand dollars."

"I don't want anything from him."

"It is a peace offering. A token, as it were. To cover the cost of your irritation. He regrets the incident the other day."

"Take it back to him."

"I...I can't do that," said Carlisle. "His instructions were most explicit. I was to come here and—"

"Talk's over," I said. "Go."

"But...but this money. I'm supposed to give it to you."

"Money from Ventura stinks of prostitution and blood."

"I'll just lay it here," said Carlisle, bending over to lay the envelope on my step.

"Pick it up," I said.

"You may do as you wish with it."

"If you don't pick it up," I said. "I'm going to make you eat it."

"You wouldn't...do that," said Carlisle, hesitating.

"Sure I would. Pick up the envelope and back away from my house."

"Yes sir," said the lawyer. "I'm doing so." He picked up the envelope. "Mr. Ventura is going to be very upset."

"I don't care."

"Very upset. I must caution you, Mr. Storme, Robert Ventura is a man of much influence. People who defy his wishes seldom prosper." The last part sounded like a threat. Maybe I'm just sensitive.

"Set the envelope down on the ground," I said.

Carlisle smiled and nodded. "I think this is much better." He placed the envelope on the ground, then stood. "This is a wise decision."

"Now, move away from it," I said.

"What?" said the lawyer, confused.

I shuffled a three-inch shell into the shotgun's breech, took aim, and squeezed off a shot. The air erupted with the blast of the shotgun. The envelope jumped as the pellets tore through the cover, tearing the pouch and shredding the contents. Little scraps of green pushed through the torn mailer and danced in the air.

At the sound of the shot, Carlisle had jumped back, dropping his briefcase and spilling the contents. "My God, what is wrong with you? Are you insane?"

"Probably. Pick up the envelope," I said. "And take it back to Ventura. Tell him if he's serious about making peace, he can start by not sending Rory Marchibroda around anymore."

"I'm afraid I don't know whom you're talking about."

"Then we don't have anything to talk about, do we? Have a nice day, counselor. But have it somewhere else."

TWENTY-SIX

Yancey Carlisle, attorney-at-law, gathered up the ruptured money pouch, jumped back into his matching car, and departed in record time. After he left, I called Chick.

"Listen," said Chick. "Guys like Ventura don't run out and buy a box of chocolates and start putting on weight when they experience frustration. That's twice you've spit in his eye. He won't like that. Makes him look bad, and since he's a moral dimwit, he won't have developed many coping strategies. At this moment he is probably considering interfering with your Karma. You need to get over here where I can watch your back."

I didn't argue with him. But I preferred to stay close to the cabin for a couple of days. If Sandy called with her flight plans, I wanted to be able to head her off. I couldn't have her around if somebody from the big city came visiting. Besides, when they did come, and they would, I wanted home field advantage. I told Chick my intentions.

"Better if you're over here with me," he said. "But there is something to knowing the terrain. Get yourself heeled and stay loose. And no moral dilemmas. They won't have any. You understand that?"

I said I did and hung up.

Then I got the second call. Cryptic. Terse.

"Ventura's gonna put some guys on you. Soon."

"Who is this?" I asked. I knew.

"Never mind that. I don't want you dead. Yet." Then he hung up.

Rory Marchibroda. A guy who wanted to kill me called to keep me from being killed by someone else. What a life.

I reloaded the Remington pump with double-aught buckshot and loaded a Browning autoloading rifle with soft-nosed .30-06 bullets. I loaded four fourteen-round clips for the twin Browning nines and strapped on a shoulder holster, hanging one of the pistols in it. I placed the other pistol in a clip-on at the small of my back. The only thing more uncomfortable than carrying a concealed large-frame handgun was carrying two concealed large-frame handguns. I was also carrying a Puma knife strapped to my leg.

Had a nine-mill gun in my pocket for fun and a razor in my shoe.

I didn't like toting that much firepower, but Chick was right. An off-the-charts lowlife like Bobby Frank could not allow reclusive wide receivers to disparage his name and refuse his gifts in front of the help. It might give them ideas, and before you knew it, they would start slacking up on their extortions and beatings. Ask for better hours. Form a union or something. He'd send somebody.

Maybe I'd get lucky when they made their move.

They drove out the next afternoon. A couple of slender guys dressed like locals—John Deere caps and flannel shirts and work boots—in a Chevrolet pickup truck they'd probably stolen. Pretended to ask for directions like they were lost.

I was walking back from the woods when I saw them bounce up the lane. I put down the compound bow, moved the clip-on holster to the front, and unsnapped the hammer strap on the shoulder holster. I cocked both pistols and set the safeties.

Wyatt the pirate. Locked and loaded.

The driver got out of the truck all smiles and gee-whiz-how'd-we-end-up-here and stood behind the front fender of his truck. The passenger opened his door but stayed in the cab, one foot on the ground. Just a couple of good old boys lost on the road to the American Dream.

"Howdy," said the driver, raising his left hand to wave, his right hand hidden behind the truck fender. "This is kind of embarrassing, but we were out drinking a few cold ones and looking for a place to maybe hunt some deer, and what the hell happens?" He looked at his buddy. His buddy rolled down his window and smiled at me. I smiled back.

Everybody was happy.

"We're lost," said the passenger. "Can you beat that?"

I moved behind a pile of ricked-up oak logs. I stood behind the four-foot-high pile, arms crossed in front of me, right hand tucked under my jacket and resting on the butt of the shoulder-holstered Browning. I thumbed off the safety.

"I'm sorry," I said, turning my head to one side. I gave them my best country-boy accent. "I don't hear so well. Come on over closer where I can hear y'all better."

The pair looked at each other. The passenger nodded at the driver, and the driver walked around the truck to my side. I watched the passenger rearrange himself.

"Nice pickup," I said. "Chevy Silverado? Got the four-oh-nine high rise and the dual quad rear end?" There was, of course no such thing as a dual quad rear end, not to mention they didn't make the four-oh-nine engine anymore, which was a pity.

The driver hesitated, then said, "Yeah. It can really haul ass."

"What?" I said.

"I said you're right." There was irritation in his voice. He moved closer now as he reached up and scratched his neck. The door creaked as the passenger eased open his door and put both feet on the ground. My advantage would be that they didn't expect much from some guy who would live this far from a liquor store. I had surprise on my side. I had protection behind a barrier of oak logs, and I had the angle and the high ground. Now all I had to do was keep from getting killed.

The driver's hand strayed down his shirt and along the line of his jacket. Slowly I inched my left hand up and along my belt until it touched the clip-on Browning. I would have to take out the driver since he was the closest before I could concentrate on the passenger. I could not afford to divide my attention when it started happening.

"You know," the driver said, nearing the woodpile. He reached deeper inside his jacket. "It's a hell of a thing when a guy's an unappreciative fuckup. Disrespectful not to accept gifts. I've got a message for you from Bobby Frank—"

I pulled both pistols and shot the driver twice in the chest as he cleared his weapon. His arms flapped out as if broken, and the pistol flew from his hand. I moved left after the second shot as a section of the woodpile was splintered by a shotgun blast. I felt something sharp strike my face and neck as if someone had thrown gravel at me. I knelt down behind the pile and duck walked three quick steps back to my right.

I came up over the woodpile with both Brownings pointed at the second shooter. He had made the mistake of shooting through the open window of the truck's door, which limited the arc with which he could swing the scatter-gun. I started pulling triggers. First one, then the other, concentrating on keeping the front blade of each gun trained on the truck door. The shotgunner tried to swing my direction, but the door prevented it. I heard the clink of brass against wood and the slap of lead against the metal truck door. But louder than anything was the bellow and snarl of the twin pistols.

Finally, after what seemed several minutes, I saw the truck passenger's shotgun on the ground, his legs buckling as his body slithered lifelessly out of the cab.

Then silence. Tons of it.

I stepped from behind the woodpile, keeping the Browning trained on the closest guy, the driver. He had two black holes in the new flannel shirt and his body twitched spasmodically like a smashed cockroach before he stopped moving forever, his mouth open, eyes staring at the sky.

There was a heavy aroma of burnt cordite and a high-pitched ringing in my ears. Heavy cardiac thump in my chest. I felt the first wave of hyperventilation. Still holding the pistols, I placed the palms of my hands on my knees and tried to breath, slowly and deeply. Slowly and deeply.

Perspiration beaded cold on my forehead. My face felt clammy and numb. Mouth dry. At the back of my throat was the sickly sweet tickle of nausea. With my palms still on my knees, I vomited into the dirt, some of it splashing on my boots. I hacked dryly. Tears formed at the corners of my eyes.

I stood, swaying slightly, and wiped my mouth with a sleeve. As I did, I felt a sharp stinging sensation in my cheek. I looked at my sleeve and saw a reddish-brown stain. Blood. I holstered the Browning and reached up and pulled a tiny wood splinter from my cheek. There was another sliver of wood in the skin of my neck. The shotgun blast had barked the woodpile, driving splinters into my face like a tornado drives wood beams into the side of a barn.

I washed my mouth out under the outdoor hydrant. The colors of the day, which had seemed brown and gray, had now bled into the vibrant colors of autumn, and through the tangle of trees, I looked into the deep shadows of the forest.

From the shed I got a pair of leather work gloves and a pair of faded gray coveralls. I put them on and went to work. The door of the truck was pocked with dark silver-ringed holes the size of quarters. The shotgun-toting passenger was riddled with torn cloth and blood, and his nose had disappeared, pushed into the recesses of his face. I tried to lift him, but the slackness of death had caused one leg to fold under him, effectively wedging him under the truck.

I couldn't get him out. I decided I would have to drive over him until his body turned, freeing the corpse. Or call the sheriff. But calling the authorities would mean questions and hours downtown and the media and all the other official entanglements. Possible arrest, making bail, court appearances, lawyers chipping away at my savings account, cops and cop technicians tromping around my place, killing the grass, taking pictures, measuring distances. Yellow restraining tape and more questions and more cops with badges and judges with grave features and me fidgeting in the courtroom. People telling me where to go and when to be there. No. I couldn't have that. I'd gone to too much trouble to avoid such things to give it up over two paid killers.

I looked at the dead hit men and wondered what kind of savagely perverted man accepted money to murder someone he never met. I had killed in a war and hated every minute of it. No, that was disingenuous. I hadn't hated all of it. I had despised the killing and the fear. But there was a tingling blood rush of adrenaline to battle. A sensation that I had felt in smaller measure in the NFL. I had felt it when I had shot the two killers. The sensation that was replaced by realization of what could have happened. My shoulders and arms trembled at the thought of what could have happened.

I opened the pickup door, and shards of glass rattled and chunked inside the door. Curiously, like the aftermath of a natural disaster, there was no glass in the interior of the vehicle. Both windows had been rolled down, and the windshield had not been struck. There were tufts of foam rubber sticking from the punctured seats, and the automatic gear stick had been sheared off by a bullet. I retrieved a pair of locking pliers from my garage and clipped them onto the nub of the gearshift. I started the truck, using the pliers to engage the transmission, set my jaw, and eased the truck forward.

I heard a groaning sound as trapped gases escaped from the wedged corpse, followed by a crunching sound as the pickup lurched over the body, then settled on its springs. Peristaltic juices burned in my throat, and I suppressed the whimper forming at the back of my throat.

Shutting off the truck, I got out and picked up the broken shotgun passenger, tugging and lifting and trundling him into the pickup bed. His leg flopped obscenely, then lay at an extreme angle, like a branch of a tree that had been broken and twisted by a high wind. I threw his shotgun in with him.

I started the truck again and drove it to where the driver lay in the dust. I was a lazy assassin who didn't want to have to drag his victim. After I got both bodies in the truck bed, I connected a garden hose to the hydrant and washed the blood off the truck. Then I turned the hose on a dusty patch, made a mudhole, and smeared the mud from the mudhole over the sides and passenger door to camouflage the bullet holes. That done, I took off the coveralls and gloves, soaked both in gasoline, and set them on fire. While they burned, I dug a hole. When the clothing had burned down, I raked the ashes into a pile and buried them, smoothing the filled-in hole with the rake, then soaking that with water so it would settle and smooth out.

I took an old musty tarp from the shed and covered the bodies. I picked up the spent shell casings, then went into the house, washed the blood off my face and neck, and dabbed peroxide on the splinter wounds. After I put on a pair of latex gloves, I broke down both pistols, wiped them down, cleaned them with WD-40, and reassembled the weapons. I filled a canteen with water, then made a sandwich and wrapped it in plastic wrap. I found an old baseball cap with the word "Caterpillar" across the crown and placed it on my head. I went back outside, taking the canteen, the sandwich, a Mini Mag flashlight, and a walking stick I had fashioned from a hickory limb.

Then I went about my dirty business.

It was early evening now, and the shadows lengthened and stretched away from the hills and trees. I heard the clear, melancholy yipping of coyotes in the distance. I started the truck and drove five miles of back roads before I stopped on a rust-pitted bridge spanning Fletcher's Creek. I got out of the truck, the engine idling, and dropped one of the Browning pistols into the rolling waters. My luck was holding. I had not met another vehicle.

I drove two more miles, jumped a fence, and tossed the other Browning into a cattle pond. I returned to the truck, drove across the county line, and abandoned the Chevrolet on an old logging road grown over with saw grass and weeds. I began the long, dark walk back across pasture and field and hill and forest.

And tried hard not to think about what I had done.

TWENTY-SEVEN

arrived back at the cabin around midnight, tired and dirty and scraped and scratched by branches that seemed to reach out at me in the dark. My boots and jeans were soaked from crossing two creeks; both would have to be burned and discarded along with any clothing I was wearing, and the foot I'd injured chasing Marchibroda hurt. My knee ached as if there were broken glass inside it. I had limped the last mile, feeling worn-out, no longer the young wide receiver fresh off the draft. Each misplaced step made me suck in my breath. I peeled off the creek-soaked jeans and looked at the bad knee. It was swollen up like a water balloon. The knee was a souvenir of the traffic jams of the NFL: some cartilage damage and a touch of arthritis to keep me humble. A doctor once told me the knee would eventually require surgery. I fooled him. I just let it hurt all the time.

I hobbled into the bathroom and took a couple of Percocet tablets for the pain. My last two. The end of my supply. But that was okay. I didn't need it anymore. During my playing days, I'd used anything and everything—Butazolidin, Darvocet, Percodan, ibuprofen, injections of vitamin B, Xylocaine, Cortizone, and other substances unavailable by prescription—just so I could get up off the trainer's table and walk back out into the Sunday-afternoon sun and pull footballs out of the sky.

Generally, I was crazy, with moments of clarity where I was only stupid.

It had seemed important at the time.

I slept on top of the unturned bed in my dirty clothing and awoke at seven thirty the next morning, groggy from guilt, pain, and the residual shadow of the Percocet.

While eating breakfast I examined the small box-shaped handgun I'd retrieved from one of the shooters. It was a Glock 27, one of the ultra-compact pistols. It was shaped like the guns we used to carve from scrap wood when I was a kid—square-barreled with a space-gun grip. It was the size of my hand and weighed little more than a couple of Zippo lighters. Forty caliber. A lot of firepower in a small package with a composite frame. I didn't like the way it looked or felt. I shouldn't have kept it. Maybe I'd give it to Chick.

I wished I still had the Brownings, but knew I couldn't keep them. I thought there was little threat of tracing the dead shooters back to me, but it was better not to take chances. I hefted the Glock. Pointed it. Still didn't like it. Forty caliber was interesting, though. I picked up the phone and dialed a man I knew who collected and sold guns. I asked him if he could get me a forty-caliber Browning Hi Power.

"Sure," he said. "Just get a permit from the sheriff's office and come by sometime."

"I prefer a gun with a lower profile," I said. "Can you swing it?"

He was quiet for a moment. "Let me make a couple of calls," he said and hung up.

He called back twenty minutes later. "Got one," he said. "Guy bought it at a gun show a couple years ago, shot it once, and put it away. It's still in the box. He wants nine hundred for it. Fifty more for me. You want it?"

"Yeah."

"You can probably get a new one for less if you check out the gun shows and pawnshops."

I said I'd rather give him the money and save the time and that I'd come by after lunch to get it. We hung up.

I put on some sweats and a pair of tennis shoes and did thirty push-ups and fifty sit-ups to prove to myself I still could. Take that, middle age. From experience I knew better than to allow myself to get stiff. The swelling had gone down in the knee, but it was still tender. I went outside to try to get a little running in. The sun was high in the azure sky, and the air smelled of evergreen and wildflowers. It felt good to get up a sweat, but after about a quarter mile, little electric waves of pain knifed through the lateral side of my left knee. I hobbled back to the cabin.

There was a message on my phone recorder. I punched the button, and Sandy's voice said, "Hello, Wyatt. My producer gave me a couple of days off to think about my decision with FOX. They're wanting to make a counter offer. Pick me up at KCI Airport. I love you, you big dummy. Don't give up on us."

I took a long shower, allowing the hot water to wash over and relax me. After lunch I got twelve hundred dollars out of the floor safe under the kitchen sink, drove to my gun-collector friend's house, and picked up the new weapon. The barrel on the forty caliber was thicker than my nines had been. The weapon was a dark matte black with hard rubber grips, and it felt good in my hand. I handed money to my friend for the weapon, adding a little extra.

"What's this?" he said. "A tip? It's a grand."

"That's for not having to fill out papers," I said and left.

I listened to an old Ry Cooder CD as I drove the Jeep to Bailey's Crossing. The sun was high and bright yellow, and rabbits darted across the road in front of me while Ry Cooder sawed at his guitar. Sandy was coming, so I needed to do something about Bobby Frank Ventura before she returned. It was early afternoon when I arrived on the movie set, once again intrigued by the resurrection of the old ghost town.

I found Chick watching the crew setting up to film a scene. A movie set is one of the most boring places on earth. Worse than the marines. Always setting something up or waiting around to set something up. Chick took note of the cuts on my neck and cheek and my uneven gait.

"What happened to you?" asked Chick. "You look like you tried to shave on horseback, jumped off, and sprained your ankle."

I told him about the two killers and my walk back after dumping them. When I was done, he said, "You shouldn't have taken a chance like that. Should've come back here or had me come over."

"They wouldn't do it here because of Ventura's connection to the movie. Then I would have had it hanging over me. Besides, you have a job to do."

"Watching over the world's only talking hemorrhoid." Chick's jaw worked, and he looked off in the direction of where the crew was setting up. "No more solos, Wyatt. Okay? Life wouldn't be worth laughing at if you weren't around."

A serious Chick Easton was always a novelty.

The scene being shot portrayed Rance Caraway and Michael LeBeau as sheriff and deputy confronting Fogarty as Jesse James on the streets of Bailey's Crossing. Fogarty was seated on a horse while Caraway, double-barreled shotgun cradled across his chest, stood on the porch of the Broken Horseshoe Saloon. Sheriff Caraway was warning the outlaw James against any raids on his town.

"I know your reputation, Mr. James," said Caraway, one eye squinted, his western accent perfectly cadenced. "I don't want any trouble. But if I hafta, I'll arrest you. Even kill you." He paused. "If I hafta."

"Why, hell, Sheriff," said Fogarty, tipping back the brim of his hat. "No need for all that. Me'n the boys're just here to get the road dust out of our throats, maybe get a beefsteak and lose a few dollars playin' cards. All that desperado talk is just horseshit."

"Just the same," said Deputy LeBeau, a palm resting on a low-cut holster, "you just do as the sheriff here tells you."

Fogarty leaned forward in his saddle and said, "I don't know as I like colored boys with badges getting uppity with me."

LeBeau's face hardened. "That's not your line, Fogarty."

"It's an ad lib," said Fogarty.

"Cut!" yelled Salinger. "What the hell is going on now?"

Fogarty turned in his saddle to speak to Salinger. "Just inserting a little realism into the scene, and LeBeau here gets all hypersensitive."

"I don't wish to portray Jesse James as a racist," said Salinger. "Just read the line as written."

Fogarty smiled. "What are you getting all worked up over? You think Jesse James, who rode with Quantrill and fought for the Confederacy, would allow himself to be talked down to by some cotton field slave? Mikey just needs to relax."

"Don't call me Mikey anymore," said LeBeau. He said it without emotion, as if he'd just told the quarterback he thought he could get open on a swing pattern.

"Give it up, LeBeau," said Fogarty. "There aren't all that many parts available for punchy halfbacks."

"Why don't you shut that hole under your nose, boy," said Rance Caraway.

"Bite me, old man," said Fogarty. "Don't tell me what to do."

"You'd be too stupid to listen if I did."

"Anytime you want to discuss this like a man," said LeBeau to Fogarty, "I'm ready. That is, if you got enough heart to do it without hiding behind your lawyer."

"How about right now," said Fogarty, sliding down off his horse. He lighted on his feet and took a step toward LeBeau. Then abruptly, Fogarty shoved LeBeau and quickly jumped back. The shove barely moved LeBeau. It did manage, however, to make LeBeau mad. LeBeau advanced toward Fogarty.

"Your client seems in danger of physical injury," I said.

"Yeah," said Chick, scratching his cheek with a finger.

Fogarty jumped into his martial arts pose while LeBeau continued toward him. If I were a betting man, I'd say Fogarty was counting on someone stopping the fight. It was pure theatrics. Only a masochist or a fool would jump in Michael LeBeau's face. Fogarty was in luck, because a pair of stunt men stepped up and grabbed Michael.

"Why is this happening to me?" said Salinger, jumping down from his boom seat and running across the lot, yelling for security.

Fogarty was hopping and shuffling around like an amateur boxer. "Let him go. Come on, Mikey," he said to LeBeau. "You want some of this, bitch?"

LeBeau said nothing. The stunt men held LeBeau, yet he dragged them along one step at a time in Fogarty's direction. He had experience dragging guys.

"You realize that Michael will put your client in traction," I said.

"Probably should do something, shouldn't I?" said Chick. He struck a match and lit a cigarette.

"I'd think that's what a bodyguard would do."

"Hmm," said Chick. "Maybe I'll send LeBeau a strident e-mail, warning him off such activity."

"That ought to work," I said. "It's a moving experience to watch a pro in action."

Chick nodded. "All part of being the best." He took a languid draw on his cigarette. LeBeau was still moving in Fogarty's direction. Fogarty was still dancing around like a windup toy. LeBeau was working free of the stunt men holding him.

"Aw hell," Chick said, throwing his cigarette to the ground. "Guess I better do something."

I nodded. "Yep."

"Well, here I go." He sauntered over John Wayne-style, and I followed.

LeBeau had managed to free himself from the men restraining him. Fogarty's buddy Volts rushed to aid Fogarty, and LeBeau stiff-armed him as if he were a second-string high school defensive back. Volts sat down hard on the turf.

Two stunt men took advantage of the moment and grabbed LeBeau again. "Get out of here, Fogarty," said one of the men holding LeBeau. "We can't hold him forever."

"So let 'im go," said Fogarty.

Chick stepped in front of LeBeau. "Let it go, Michael," Chick said. "What have you got, you kick his ass? Sure, everybody'll wanna buy you drinks and slap you on the back, but what the hell, huh?"

LeBeau nodded. He looked at Chick, then smiled and relaxed. "You're right," said LeBeau. The stunt men released him. LeBeau turned and walked away.

"Everybody take a fifteen-minute break!" said Salinger. "Take a break, dammit."

"What the hell did you mean by that?" Fogarty asked Chick as LeBeau walked away. "That shit you were telling LeBeau?"

Chick looked at Fogarty, rubbed his chin. "Cooling him down. He'd have put you in an ambulance."

"You don't have to cool anybody down for me."

"Just protecting you," said Chick.

"Some protection. Volts got here before you did."

"He was pretty effective too," said Chick, watching Volts knock the dust off the seat of his pants.

"I'm getting real tired of the way you do your job."

"You're still in one piece, aren't you?"

"No thanks to you."

Chick shrugged. "I might be able to keep you from getting killed. I'll even take a bullet for you if I have to. Not because I'm brave or because I like you, but because it's the job. But I'm not going to come running every time your over amped mouth runs away with your miniature brain. Might do you some good you get your wig twisted, anyway. Hell, I know it'd do me some good to see it."

"Maybe you'd like to give it a try?" said Fogarty.

Chick laughed. It was genuine laughter, as if he were watching a great slapstick movie. "It's a nice thought, but quit trying to cheer me up."

"I ought to fire you."

"You didn't hire me, junior," said Chick. "Try to keep that in mind. But when this is all over, I'll be glad to accommodate you."

Fogarty muttered an obscenity and walked away. As he walked away, I saw Rory Marchibroda's Cadillac sitting up on the access road again.

Salinger came up to us. "That was almost a disaster," he said. "Thanks for getting between them. The last thing I need is a fistfight between two of my actors."

"There wasn't going to be any fight," said Chick. "Fogarty's stupid, but he isn't suicidal. It was all a big show on his part."

Rory was standing outside the car. I pointed him out to Chick.

"Who is that?" asked Salinger. "I've seen him around here before."

"Somebody who doesn't belong here," said Chick. He looked at me. "I believe it's time to get his attention."

TWENTY-EIGHT

Rory saw Superstar and his buddy coming up the hill. Getting closer now. That's right, assholes, come right on up here. Superstar had a serious look on his face. Superstar's badass buddy had a different look on his face.

Things were starting to go Rory's way. He'd had a talk with that fancy-pants lawyer of Bobby Frank's, Yancey what's-his-face. Carlisle, that's his name. Ventura would pay Rory two grand to pop Superstar. Another grand for the badass. Three grand to do what he wanted to do anyway. The lawyer had been kind of upset when Rory'd talked to him—something had him spooked, and there had been some kind of foul-up. Guy didn't say what it was, just got uppity and asked him if he wanted the deal or not.

Superstar and the badass stopped and were talking now. Rory crossed his arms and leaned against the Caddy. I got all day, guys, but you ain't got any time left. Just whatever I allow. Needed to be ready when they got here, though. Give them the big smile like in town. That's the ticket. If thing's got hot, there was always the Taurus under the back of his jacket.

What were they talking about?

Rory was leaning against the Cadillac with his arms crossed, a big stupid grin on his big stupid face, like he was glad to see us. I hated to admit it, but he was beginning to irritate me. I knew that's what he wanted.

Chick grabbed my elbow and said, "Let me talk to him."

"No," I said. "I'll take care of it."

"You've already talked to him."

"It's my problem."

"If he's messing with you, he's messing with me," said Chick. "If he's messing with me, then he's screwing ol' Shep. He knows you're too virtuous to take him out without provocation. He knows it the way all the recidivist imbeciles know it. You're the good, he's the bad, and I'm the ugly. Let me try ugly. Doubt he's ready for that."

I wasn't convinced. Chick read it in my face.

"Five minutes," said Chick. "Let me rearrange his priorities. You can give me that. I need the outlet after talking to Fogarty."

I nodded. "All right. No broken bones or lacerations, though."

Chick turned his head sideways. "Have a little faith, huh? Wait here."

I watched Chick walk ahead.

What's this? Rory asked himself. The badass was coming on alone. Superstar was hanging back. That chickenshit. Maybe he'd finally scared the guy, and he was letting the badass fight his battles for him. Who gives a shit, though? Both going down the same slide.

"What's up?" asked the badass, smiling. Guy had a weird kind of smile, like he was laughing at you on the inside. Rory didn't like that.

"Nothing," said Rory. "Enjoying the weather, ya know? Nice day, huh?"

The guy was still smiling at Rory. Not saying anything, just standing there with this annoying grin on his face, like Rory had food stuck between his teeth or something.

"What the fuck you want?" Rory asked.

"My buddy, Storme, you know Storme, has this problem."

"Oh yeah?" Rory's turn to smile big this time. He *was* getting to Superstar. "What's his problem? Me?" Rory laughed. "I'm just hanging around. Not hurting nothing."

"No," said the badass. "That's not his problem. His problem is he has this weird moral code. He's kind of a slave to it, you know? Like the code of the West. You know about the code of the West, don't you?"

Rory screwed up his face and looked at this crazy guy. "I don't know about no code of the West. What the hell are you talking about, huh?"

"It's his way of doing things. No back-shooting. Tries to shoot the gun out of the bad guy's hand. Doesn't throw the first punch. Real Lone Ranger shit."

"Yeah? What's that got to do with anything?"

"I'm enlightening you," said the badass. Guy was starting to piss Rory off the way he kept staring at him and smiling. What a dick head.

"You're enlightening me?" said Rory, turning his hands toward his chest.

"Yeah. I'm enlightening you, you dumb shit. I'm letting you know why Storme hasn't stuffed you in a drainage ditch with broken arms. It's because he's a nice guy."

"Hey, do me a favor, huh, and go fuck yourself," said Rory.

"I'm not finished." Guy smiling at him again. Who'd he think he was, Paul fucking Newman? "See, Storme's a nice guy. Then we have me, Chick D. Easton. The *D* stands for 'Don't-fuck-with-my-friends.'"

"You seeing somebody here gives a shit? I don't care if you hump each other." Rory could feel the heat rising up around his ears. He was tired of gabbing with this smartass. "In fact," said Rory. He badly wanted to clear the Taurus from behind him and stick it in this guy's face, watch the smile disappear. "You guys got people angry with you. I got a feeling you might not be around so long, ya know?"

"Means nothing to me," said the badass. "You can tell Bobby Frank and the other mutants to come get me. But what I want you to plug into is that anything happens to Storme, anything at all, then I'm going to drive a shit train right through your life-span. Could happen preemptively, in fact, if I see your dumb ass around here anymore."

Then Rory watched the guy's smile blink off for less than a second, and in that time Rory saw something else. Something cold and hard. And cruel. Nothing like the smile. Who was this guy?

"Now, get in your car," said the guy, "and disappear over the horizon and don't come back." Then he started smiling again.

Rory thought about spitting in the guy's face, but got the feeling the guy was on the edge of something. Guy was maintaining, holding something back. He was almost vibrating with it. Guy wanted Rory to make a move. The guy smelled of something Rory recognized from somewhere else. What was it? The way it was in prison? Rory decided to get in the car. Every dog had his day, and Rory'd have his, and this guy and Superstar would catch the brunt of it. Then he'd wipe that smile off his face.

As Rory opened the door to get in the car, Rory felt something at the small of his back. Trapped between the door and the car, Rory couldn't move in time to stop the guy from lifting his piece.

"Well, lookee here," said the badass. Rory turned, and the guy was hefting the Taurus. "This loaded?" the guy asked, pointing the gun between Rory's eyes.

"Let's see if it's loaded," said the badass. "Make a wish, dog ass."

Rory sucked his breath in and waited.

I saw that Chick had a gun in his hands and pointed at Rory's face. Like always, with Chick, it happened faster than I thought possible.

I had watched Rory turn and open his door, thinking the exchange was over. Suddenly Chick reached behind Rory and pulled a gun from under the back of the thug's jacket. I started running toward them.

When I got closer, I heard Chick say, "Let's see if it's loaded."

"Don't shoot him," I said, yelling at Chick.

"See?" Chick said to Rory. "Code of the West." Then Chick lowered the weapon, shoved it into his own waistband, and stepped back from the car. "Thanks for the gun. You have a nice day now. And don't be such a stranger, huh? Always good to see you."

Rory glared over Chick's shoulder at me, then at Chick.

"You guys're coupla circus clowns," said Rory. "But somebody wants to close you out."

"It won't be you, shit-for-brains," said Chick.

"I'll be around, assholes." Rory got into the car and left in a spray of rocks.

"I'll give the guy credit," said Chick as we watched Rory leave. "He doesn't scare easy."

"This isn't getting us anywhere."

"Nope."

"Any suggestions?"

"Rory mentioned that somebody is after us."

"Ventura."

"Yep," said Chick. "He probably needs a personal visit. Time to cancel his act."

This time I didn't argue.

TWENTY-NINE

From Chick's cell phone, I called a Kansas City private investigator I knew. He told me where I could find Ventura late on a Saturday afternoon.

"Cost you a hundred bucks for the info," he said.

"For an address?" I asked.

"For that one."

I agreed to the extortion terms, and he gave me the address. Told me Ventura kept an office in a side building at Ventura Trucking out on Highway 40.

"He goes in every Wednesday and Saturday afternoon to look at the books," said the PI. "No illegal stuff comes through the dock at those times, so Bobby Frank can deny knowledge. The drugs and black market stuff come in at other times. He's on the way up. The bosses got their eye on him, but he ain't inside the inner circle yet. He's too unpredictable and emotional. Likes to do enemies without permission. Got him in trouble a few times. Besides, his mother was a Jew. Not all those guys downtown are enlightened, you know? What do you need Ventura's address for, anyway? If you look up 'homicidal pukes' in the yellow pages, there's a picture of Ventura underneath it."

"I want to pay him a social call."

"Yeah? Could you send the money in advance then?"

Two hours and forty-five minutes, later we were on the outskirts of Kansas City, rolling through Independence on I-70 Highway. Ventura Trucking set back off old Highway 40—a strip of urban decay dotted with businesses dealing in raw materials, surrounded by chain link fences, adult motels with Eisenhower-era marquees, and "We Finance Everyone" used car lots—which cut through the east side like a running sore. There was a perpetual film of grit covering the crumbling blacktop parking lots, which crunched under your shoes and under the tires of your car.

Ventura's office was located in a building on the west side of the main warehouse. Pulling into the parking lot, we were nearly crushed by an eighteen-wheeler that roared out of the lot, dual horns braying like some metal dinosaur. I swerved from its path, and the driver gave us the finger as he lumbered by.

"Good start, huh?" said Chick.

I drove the Jeep to the rear of the lot and parked between a pair of maroon Peterbilt tractor trailers with "Ventura Trucking Lines" printed in gold letters on the doors. We got out.

"You go on in," said Chick. "And I'll recon the layout and arrive, as always, in the nick of time. Give me your weapon. They'll just pat you down and take it anyway."

I handed it to him, and he stuck it in his waistband. "How are you going to get inside?" I asked.

"I haven't decided whether to turn myself into a vapor and float in through the ventilation system or just swing in through a side window. Watch your topknot, pilgrim." He winked and walked away in fully visible three-dimensional form.

But they would not see Chick Easton coming.

I walked across the lot to the side building, opened the door, and walked inside. A guy in a gray suit with a faint blue glen plaid pattern, blue-and-gray striped tie, sat at a metal desk eating Chinese food from paper takeout cartons. There was a bottle of Chinese beer on the desk. He looked up as I walked in.

"What do you want?"

"I'm here to see Ventura," I said.

"Yeah?" he said, dusting egg roll crumbs from his jacket with the back of his hand. "Who're you?"

"Bob Dylan."

"Yeah," the hood said, "and I'm fucking Axl Rose."

"Then you've got a lot of nerve," I said, not singing it, "to say you are my friend."

"You think smart talk is funny?"

I shrugged. "I think it's a waste on you."

He thought about that for a moment, didn't know what to do with it. "Tell me who you are and what you want, or you're on the fucking pavement. Got it?"

"Wyatt Storme," I said. "He'll talk to me."

"Maybe he's busy."

"I'm not coming back."

He gestured with his arms extended, palms up. "Big fucking deal."

"Bobby Frank won't like it," I said, "he finds out I was here, and you wouldn't let me see him."

With an index finger, he reached back inside his mouth to free some chow mein from a molar. A Harvard man. He stood and pointed at me.

"I'll check with Mr. Ventura, but first I gotta frisk you. Raise your arms."

I did as he asked, and he checked me, finding nothing.

"Okay, bright boy," he said, stepping back. "I'm gonna tell Mr. Ventura you're here. Turns out he don't wanna see you, I'm gonna do a polka on your head."

"I feel a smart answer coming on," I said.

"Wise ass," he muttered, and opened the door to the next room. As the door closed, Chick slipped through the front door behind me.

"Couldn't find the ventilation system?" I asked.

"You can see me?" Chick asked in mock horror. He handed me the Browning, and I placed it in the small of my back under the waistband of my jeans. "Back door's locked with a dead bolt on the inside."

"Superman foiled."

"There's Kryptonite all over this place."

Chinese-food guy returned. "The boss says—" he began, before he saw Chick. "Who the fuck're you?"

"This cloak of invisibility stuff isn't working at all," Chick said to me.

"Nope," I said.

"Guess I'll just have to reach into my bag of tricks," Chick said, pulling out the Glock I'd recovered, "and surprise!"

"What the fuck's going on?" asked the hood.

"He talks like that all the time," I said.

"Maybe he needs diction lessons," said Chick. He looked at the hood and said, "Can you say, 'forty-caliber bullet up the ass'?"

"Another funny fucker."

"Were you trying to be funny again?" Chick asked me.

I shrugged.

"Take us to your leader, dick head," said Chick, gesturing at the door with the Glock. "And don't entertain any foolish notions, or I'll ventilate ya."

The hood pursed his lips, one corner of his mouth curling up in resignation, and he opened the door to the inner sanctum. We followed him in.

The interior office was a marked contrast from the outer one. Thick charcoal-gray carpet set off smartly by burgundy, leather, Mediterranean-style furniture. There was a print of Romano's *Fall of the Titans* on the wall and a reproduction of Cellini's *Salt Cellar of Francis I* on a marble pedestal. Against one wall was Easton's "hood with fractured patella," which was Haywood with a knee brace over his pants leg. Seated behind a mahogany desk in a dark-blue suit with an understated powder-blue pinstripe was Bobby Frank Ventura, art lover, snappy dresser, and prince of thugs.

When Ventura saw Chick, his jaw tightened, his eyes closed briefly, and he shook his head in disgust. "The fuck do you guys want?"

"They all talk like that," said Chick.

"It's epidemic," I said.

"Good thing we're here. If I'd known it was this bad, I would've brought a tape of *My Fair Lady*."

Haywood glared at Chick.

"Where in hell did this other guy come from, Dom?" Ventura asked Chinese-food guy. "And what's he doing with a piece? Nobody's supposed to come in here with a gun, you dumb shit."

Dom hunched his shoulders and showed his palms. "I don't know. He wasn't out there when I come in here. When I go back out, he's standing there, pulls the gun."

Ventura looked at us as if appealing to our sense of fair play and understanding. "He's not a nuclear scientist, is he? This is what I put up with. What is it you guys want, huh?"

"You sent two shooters after me," I said.

"Could he put the piece away?" Ventura said. "It's fucking disrespectful to come into a man's office and pull a gun on him in front of his employees. Makes it hard to relax, ya know?"

Chick shrugged. "No problem," he said. "I hate being 'fucking disrespectful' above all things." He ejected the clip from the handle, jacked the chambered bullet into the air, and caught it one-handed almost without looking at it.

"How's that?" Chick asked.

"Better," said Ventura. "So, you got a visit from a couple guys. I notice, with some despair, that you're still around. So, I'll guess I can take those guys' names out of my Rolodex."

"If you don't call off Rory," Chick said, "same thing's going to happen to him."

Ventura looked around the room, as if wearied by trying to make us understand something. "You guys keep bringing up Marchibroda. But that dumb Polack don't work for me no more. How am I gonna make that clear to you?"

"Marchibroda hinted around that somebody wanted us killed."

"I think you'd be used to that," said Ventura. "Neither one of you goes out of your way to be likable. Carlisle, my attorney, was pretty upset about you shooting up his briefcase. Even talking about whacking you, but he's just a yuppie lawyer. Maybe he's shooting his mouth off. But it's not me."

"Why should I believe you?" I said.

"Why lie? I already admitted to the other two."

I looked at Chick, who shrugged.

Ventura leaned back in his chair. "I'm going to have to quit underestimating you, cowboy. You aren't the dumb-shit hick you look like."

Chick smiled at that.

"But don't get the idea that you can fuck around in my orbit. There's a whole bunch more where those two came from." He gestured by making a tent of the fingers and thumb of one hand. "*Capisce?*"

"I love it when he talks Italian," I said.

Ventura pointed a finger at me. "You need a geography lesson, Storme," he said, his face hard and angry. "You need to learn how the world turns. You get in my way one more time, and I'm going to rotate it back over you."

Reacting to Ventura's threatening tone, Chick pulled his jacket up over his ears and head like an elementary school kid caught in a rainstorm.

"What the fuck is this guy doing?" said Ventura. "I want him and you to get outta here, or you're both hanging meat. You understand what I'm telling you?"

The jacket dropped from Chick's head, and in his hand he had the .380 Colt pistol.

"Look what I found," said Chick, pointing the gun at Ventura.

"How many guns he got?" Ventura asked.

"They were having a sale," said Chick.

"You two assholes are shitting in your nest."

"You know, Bobby Frank," said Chick, "I am sick to death of hearing your tough talk. You want to throw down? I'm ready. You, Dom, the gimp, all three of you before you can get a shot off."

"What's he doing, Storme?" Ventura asked. "You better get him under control. What're you, crazy? Put that thing away, huh? What do you think this is, the Wild West or something?"

"You can't take all of us," said Haywood.

"Sure I can. It's what I do. Some people are good at word games, some are good at golf or tennis. Me? I can find people and kill them. No matter where they are, no matter how well protected. I just show up like a bad dream and turn their lights out. And it doesn't even bother me to do it. Like, right now. I don't want to kill you, Ventura"—Chick shrugged—"and I don't *not* want to kill you. Pretty blasé about it, actually. But Storme getting dead? That's different. I won't like that. He dies, then who'll I hang out with? Drive the car while I drink?"

"We can take 'em, boss," said Haywood.

"Shut up, Marty," said Ventura. "Can't you see we got us a situation here?"

"Next time anyone comes near Storme, I'm coming after you, Ventura."

"I'll send people for you."

Chick shrugged. "I'll still get you."

"Yeah?" said Ventura. "You take me out, and somebody'll send people after you. Eventually, they'll get you."

"Life near the bone's more interesting. Besides, I'll get some of them, and I'll for sure get you. You don't have a chance. You just need to know that the next person who even remotely threatens Storme gets his ticket canceled."

"He's a fucking dead man," said Haywood. "Soon as—"

Haywood was interrupted by a loud bang. I jumped, startled by the noise. Haywood's leg kicked out from under him like he'd been hit by a baseball bat. A smear of blood appeared on Haywood's shoe. The shoe on his remaining good leg.

Ventura came up out of his chair. "What the hell are you doing?" said Ventura, his voice high-pitched, his eyes wide as he looked at Haywood, writhing on the floor, then back at Chick. "Are you crazy? Are you fucking nuts?"

"See," Chick said, "how easy that was? I warned you. I warned him, but he didn't listen. Are you listening now?" Chick pointed the gun at Dom. "Don't have any momentary lapses, Dom. I've already taken my warning shot. I'll park the next one in the middle of your ugly face."

"You fucking shot him," said Ventura, the whites of his eyes like fried eggs.

Chick leaned over and looked down at Haywood, who was grimacing and groaning. "Yeah, guess I did."

Ventura was breathing hard, mouth open. "This ain't done this way."

"So call the police," said Chick.

"You know that ain't happening."

Chick nodded. "I know."

Ventura's mouth worked. He pinched his bridge of his nose with thumb and forefinger as if he had a headache. Then he said, "So now what?"

"Let's say we believe you about Marchibroda," said Chick. "You sent two guys after Storme, and now they're gone. Haywood's got two bad legs now, but I shot him through the meat, not the bone, so he'll heal up. All of it unnecessary. Let's call it a bad misunderstanding for a group of people who have other things to do and call a truce. You say it, and I'll believe you. Although you remain a piece of shit, Wyatt says you'll keep your word."

Ventura thought about it. "I won't send nobody else if he stays out of my business."

"What happens on my property is my business."

"What?" said Ventura. "You gotta have everything your way, huh?"

"Just that. Nothing else."

Ventura took a deep breath and let it out. He lifted his hands out in front of him, palms showing. "I got nothing to gain from this anyway," said Ventura.

"What's your connection with Salinger?" I asked, fighting down the uneasy feeling I had about carrying on a discussion while Haywood was bleeding on the carpet. "Why would someone like him do business with you?"

"Like I got bad breath or something, right?"

"Let's strip away the superfluous posturing. We know each other."

"Where does a guy used to play football learn to talk like that? You two are a pair." He shook his head, said, "It's a business opportunity, that's all. Not everything I do is illegal, no matter what you think."

"Sorry, I'm not buying that. You've got some hold on Salinger, don't you?"

"Why do you say that?"

"Because you never get involved in things you can't control. Besides, I may know what you have on Geoffrey."

"I'm not saying nothing," said Ventura.

"What's your attitude about Haywood going to be?" I asked.

"I told him to shut up," said Ventura, looking at the thug on the floor, who was doing his best not to scream out in pain. Had to give the guy credit. He was tough. "He didn't do like I told him. Not the first time. This is what he gets. You hear that, Haywood? Next time, shut the hell up." Ventura looked back up at us. "There's no problem."

"Everything's cool, then?" asked Chick.

Ventura nodded. "Yeah," he said tersely. "Look at this, Haywood, you're bleeding all over my carpet. Dom, get a couple guys and do something with Haywood, then get somebody in here to clean up. See if you can do it without screwing it up or letting anybody else in, okay?" Then Ventura looked up at us as if suddenly remembering we were there. "You still here? Get the fuck out, huh?"

"Been a pleasure doing business with you," said Chick.

"Yeah, yeah," said Ventura. "Storme, you gotta know this guy you're hanging with has got shit loose in his head, don't you?"

THIRTY

After we left Ventura Trucking, Chick and I stopped to eat in Blue Springs. Chick ate heartily, devouring his steak with relish while I picked at my chef's salad like a swimsuit model who was ten pounds overweight.

"You believe Ventura?" Chick said. "What he said about Marchibroda?"

"Who knows?" I said. "I doubt he'd let me know he'd given Rory the green light."

"Kinda what I thought too."

"But getting Marchibroda to kill me after I'd accused him of bringing him in would be sloppy. He has no way of knowing if I've told the authorities about it. Besides, he wouldn't have Rory stalking me like some kind of B movie thug."

"You shotgunned the lawyer's briefcase?" said Chick.

"And five thousand dollars that belonged to Ventura."

Chick laughed. "That's nice work. Wish I could've seen it." He cut his steak with his knife. "You get kind of creative when I'm not around. That's pretty deliberate the way you waited on those two shooters and took them out."

"I guess."

"Didn't like it, did you?"

"No."

"Well, it was the only way," said Chick, forking a piece of steak and placing it in his mouth. He chewed then swallowed the meat. "Once it's done, that's the end of it. Can't second-guess it."

I took Chick back to the movie set, then drove home. The Jeep's headlights pushed through the starless night like a flashlight in an underwater tunnel—a match for my mood, thinking of the two men I had killed and the events that led to their deaths. Chick said it was necessary. I thought shooting Haywood was excessive. But a man who could shoot two men, cover up the evidence, then proceed as if it had never happened, just so people wouldn't interrupt his retreat from society, had limited moral ground from which to launch a protest.

Chick had done what he felt he had to do in order to protect me.

I slept until eight the next morning. I made and ate a breakfast of venison steak and eggs over easy, juice, and coffee, then showered, shaved, and attended church service at the little country church five miles from my cabin. The church had an old-style steeple with a real bell, and its members were farm families who sat politely and dutifully in the wooden pews, respecting the preacher's message and anticipating the fried chicken dinners and the afternoon drowsiness awaiting them.

And in their midst sat a man who had witnessed a shooting and killed two men. A man they smiled at and knew by his first name. I kept telling myself there was no other way. *But I had lain in wait for them*, the same way a predator waits for its prey to walk into its trap. I had *wanted* them to come by. I had enjoyed the hot glow of firefight and the sick satisfaction of victory. And as the hymns were sung and the Bible read, I felt the unsmiling eyes of God looking deep inside me and peeling back my tortured rationalizations like the summer sun burning through a morning fog.

After church I drove to KCI to pick up Sandy, stopping along the way to eat a solitary lunch at a chain restaurant as ironically stark and lonely as a rural Kansas highway in its familiar resemblance to a thousand other restaurants in a thousand other franchises. They sprang up like aggressive weeds along the edges of towns stripped of individuality and personality by the disease called change. Change disguised as progress. A progress without conscience or opposition, driven by greed and political gain.

I felt cynical and disenfranchised. A cultural refugee, ostracized and alone.

At 2:37 p.m. United Flight 76 from New York City taxied and docked at the walkway that stretched like an umbilical cord from the terminal to the jet airliner. Sandy emerged from the tunnel all blond, smiling, freckled woman, incognito in sunglasses and blue jeans, a Yale sweatshirt over her slender frame, honey-gold hair under a Yankees baseball cap and pulled back into a ponytail. She turned her head side to side looking for me through the tangle of people, ponytail flying like a schoolgirl's, as I waited for her to find me, enjoying the moment of watching her.

And when she did find me and smiled at me, suddenly I didn't feel like something unsanitary that had washed ashore, soiled and rancid, after a hard rain.

We stopped at Crown Center, where I bought a couple of cigars and Sandy bought some kind of weird cheese and a bottle of champagne, which, I tried to point out, might be lost on my plebian palette.

"Might as well be Boone's Farm and Velveeta," I said.

"You try too hard to be a reverse snob," Sandy said.

"A reverse snob?" I said. "What is a reverse snob?"

"It's a pigheaded doof who won't drink champagne with his true love because he's afraid someone will think he's being self-absorbed and who is going to miss out later if he keeps it up."

I looked at her, raising my chin slightly and closing one eye as I did. "Okay then," I said. "I was afraid it was going to be something I wouldn't understand."

She yawned.

"Tired?" I asked.

"Air travel wears me out."

"See?"

She shook her head. "How about just enjoy the time we have?"

"Okay."

Leaving Crown Center, we dined at the Peppercorn Duck Club so I could prove I wasn't a reverse snob and also so I could sit down and watch the reflection of candlelight in Sandy's eyes. I was a closet romantic in addition to the reverse snob thing. She ordered lamb for herself and prime rib for me.

Over coffee we small talked, updating each other on recent developments before she hit me with it.

"They say I have to live in New York," she said. "Full time. It's a requirement of the job."

I sipped my coffee, set the cup down, and tried not to look disquieted and devastated. Instead I settled for dumbfounded by staring into my coffee cup, as if a solution might swirl up out of its black depths.

"I have to take this opportunity, Wyatt," she said.

"I know."

"So, say something."

"I don't know what to say. I think you have to do this. You're good at it. It's one of the things I like about you."

"But I know you," she said. "And you're holding something back."

"I just have trouble with change."

"Nothing's changed."

"The time we have is already limited," I said. "This will further restrict that time."

"We can work that out."

"You're probably too young for me anyway."

"Oh pooh," she said, a wry expression on her face. "That doesn't matter at all, and you know it. Come with me to New York, Wyatt."

"I can't."

"Give it a chance."

"I can visit."

"You won't visit," she said.

"You don't know that for sure."

"I know you."

"You can't hold that against me."

"Marry me and come with me to New York, Wyatt." I watched the candlelight dance and flicker in her eyes. The offer was sincere.

I smiled and took her hand. "You're something special," I said. "And nothing would make me happier than to be with you. But I can't live in New York, and I won't be responsible for ruining your dream. I think you should take the job."

"Then I'll marry you and stay here," she said.

"Can't do that either."

"Why not?" There was heat in her eyes when she said it.

"Because sooner or later, you'll resent it," I said. She started to say something but was too honest to argue the point. Sandy was the most honest person I knew. One of the many things I loved about her. "And not only that, I'll resent myself for diminishing what you are, and I don't want to change that. It'll make us both unhappy. Eventually, maybe things will change, and we can work something out."

"You're an impossible asshole sometimes," Sandy said. "Who are you to tell me I can't marry you and live here with you if I want to?"

"I'm the guy who loves a woman who's going to anchor a national news program. And that's where I like you best. Up there on my television screen showing up Brian Williams for the stuffed shirt he is."

She smiled. "I love you and want to be with you."

"Same here."

"But you won't move to New York, and you won't let me move in with you. Why is that?"

"We've gone over this."

"Not to my satisfaction." Her blue eyes were incandescent, glowing.

We were quiet for a long moment. Her eyes bored in on me while I picked out a spot on the table and looked at it.

"You've got to let her go, Wyatt."

I looked up at her. "What does that mean?"

"You know what it means," she said. "It's why you won't leave your cabin. It's why you won't marry me."

"I don't know what you're talking about."

"I'm talking about Heather Storme."

I shook my head, to myself more than anything. "That's not it."

"It is *exactly* it," she said, boring in. "Her death still tears at you, and your memory of her is standing between us. You can't leave because of her, and you can't give yourself totally to me because of her memory."

"I think we need to talk about something else," I said.

"Do you love her more than you love me?" she asked.

"I love you both."

"You're being evasive."

"Who do you love more?" I asked. "Your mother or your father?"

"That's not a fair question," she said.

"Maybe not," I said. "But it's a hard one, isn't it?"

She put an elbow on the table and leaned her cheek against a hand. She was so beautiful, it made my eyes hurt to look at her. Why she chose me, I'll never know.

We drove back to the cabin and listened to Tchaikovsky. She loved the Russian composer. I built a fire in the fireplace, opened the champagne, and even poured some for myself. I only drank with Sandy and then only rarely. I didn't need it and had given it up long ago for no other reason than that. I didn't object to

Sandy's drinking, which was moderate, and she didn't object to my cigars, which were not. We sipped champagne, and I smoked a cigar and enjoyed the moment.

Then I thought about Rory Marchibroda and our present situation and predawn shotgun blasts. One of the problems of a long-distance relationship was that so much could happen between visits. I hadn't mentioned the danger before and knew it would irritate her if I brought it up now, but it was time to be straight with her. She objected to edited conversation, particularly when I wouldn't tell her I might be in danger. But I didn't want anything to happen to her. Didn't want anything to happen to me either.

"It's dangerous here now," I said. "I've got a guy, a leg-breaker with a grudge, following me around."

She sat forward, holding her champagne glass out in front of her. "What? When were you going to tell me about that?"

"Must've slipped my mind."

"Don't give me that crap, Wyatt. You didn't want me to know."

"That's another possibility."

"What kind of person is he?"

"The worst."

"Have you called the police?"

"No."

"Why not?"

"What do I tell them? That this guy is following me around, and my girlfriend doesn't like it?" She looked at me with her truth-serum eyes. "Look, San, he hasn't done anything yet." Once again I fudged on the shooting incident. Also on the shoot-out with the hit men.

"Then what does he want?"

"My autograph?"

She was silent for several seconds. Sipped her drink. Swallowed it, actually. She was quiet long enough that I started to feel uncomfortable.

I cupped her elbow in my hand. "Look, Sandy, I can handle this."

"How nice for you," she said. "What am I supposed to do, sit around and wonder if someone is going to hurt you? Maybe kill you? Now if I go back to New York, I'll worry about you, and if I stay here, you'll worry about me."

"Just a pair of worriers, that's us."

"Don't kid about this."

"Yes ma'am."

"Don't patronize me either."

"There's no pleasing you women," I said. "My theory is that it has something to do with hormones or latent guilt associated with making us eat that apple in the garden."

"Nobody forced you to eat the apple," she said, smiling now. "You *wanted* to eat it. You've just been using us for an excuse ever since. But you're not going to sidetrack me with that crap. We need to deal with this problem."

"Chick's here," I said.

"But he's preoccupied with guarding Fogarty."

"What do you want me to do?"

"You could leave the area for a while."

"That's a temporary solution," I said. "He'll show up again. Somewhere else."

"God," she said, putting a hand to her face and shaking her head. "How do you get involved in these things?"

"It'll be all right. You need to believe that."

She brushed the hair back from my forehead and shook her head again. "Unfortunately, to borrow from Kesey, I'm in love with the bull goose loony"—she paused to let out a breath—"and I'm afraid I don't know what to do about it."

"Well," I said, pulling her closer, "I'm sure if you put your mind to it, you'll come up with something."

"That doesn't solve everything."

"It's a start, though."

THIRTY-ONE

andy returned to New York. Started missing her the moment she disappeared past the TSA check. How long could we do this? I would see her, knowing I could not hold on to her, and then at her departures, I was left with the sting of her absence.

But, we *could* make it work and I was set on doing just that. The relationship was worth it.

I could not sit around and think about it right now. Since I had nothing better to do than miss her, I returned to the set of *The Night Riders* to hang around with Chick. My head had too many things in it to stay at the cabin.

Cameron Fogarty didn't show for the run-through of the big shoot-out scene Tuesday morning. He had received another threatening letter, which had resulted in him and Volts and Braithwaite getting drunk and stoned Monday night. Kane had stayed in town with the lucky girl he had picked up.

Odd that suddenly Fogarty was more upset than previously. Filed it away.

The threatening communique came in a regular envelope with a local postmark. It read:

TO: the soon-to-exit movie star, Cameron Fogarty

FROM: Wouldn't you like to know?

Dear Mr. Fogarty:

When the curtain comes down on your final act, that's what it will be—your final act. You're number one with a bullet. Good-bye.

There was no signature.

Even Chick was unable to stir Fogarty.

"They're hammered," said Chick to a distraught Geoffrey Salinger. "Lying around like clocks in a Salvador Dali painting."

"We have only one scene left to film after the shoot-out scene," said Salinger. "I must get something done today. The light is perfect, and we're running out of time, and we're over budget. I want it. I have to have it. It has to be today at noon, when there is the least amount of shadow."

"Go ahead and shoot it," suggested the assistant director, a short, hard-muscled man with dark hair who looked like he could be Richard Jaeckel's brother.

"Cameron is too hung over," said Salinger.

"Then have the bodyguard do the action stuff," said the assistant. "He's been doing the double work anyway, and you've seen the way this guy can move. We can edit the close shots later."

"You realize Cameron likes to do his own action scenes."

"So where is he?" asked the assistant.

Salinger nodded, then looked at Chick. "Can you do it?"

Chick looked at me, his head lolled to one side, arched his eyebrow-and-a-half, and said, "A star is born."

Chick read the script, which didn't call for any dialogue, and went over the scene with the action choreographer. Chick had the whole thing down in his head in fifteen minutes. The plan was to shoot the whole scene as if Fogarty were in it, then shoot close-ups with Fogarty after he woke up. The preliminary walk-through went smoothly, and Chick hit every mark.

"Talk about a quick study," said the assistant director. "Guy's a natural. How's he able to get that so quickly?" he asked me.

What to tell him? That every day years ago, Chick had slipped into enemy territory, into areas he had only seen on a map or an aerial photograph, without backup, alone, and then had shot, knifed, garroted, or blown-up target or human being—all with a hairsbreadth of allowable error—then melted into jungle, desert, or countryside and returned to base to do the whole thing again another day. All for a government that would react to his being caught or killed or tortured with the collective coolness of inmates at an apathy clinic watching a checkers game. And this guy wanted to know how Chick could memorize a three-minute scene in a movie. What would his reaction be if I told him the truth?

So I shrugged. Wasn't a great shrug. "I don't know either," I said.

"He certainly knows how to handle a six-shooter," he said.

"We'll see how he does when we speed things up," Salinger said, unconvinced.

"Put live ammunition in the weapons," I said. "And watch what happens."

Salinger gave me a strange look. So, I shrugged again. I was getting better at it.

The scene called for Chick as Fogarty as Jesse James to run from the Wells Fargo office, along with the other gang members. He would leap from the boardwalk onto the bed of a buckboard, shoot down a deputy, jump down from the wagon, run, and jump up on his horse to make his getaway. Meanwhile, Sheriff Rance Caraway and several townspeople would blaze away at the escaping James Gang. They already had the interior shots of the robbery in the can.

Salinger yelled, "Action!" and Chick, along with the gang of outlaws, burst from the double doors of the Wells Fargo office, pistols drawn and flashing in the midday sunlight like flaming brands. Now I knew why Salinger wanted this time of day for the shot. Chick jumped into the back of the wagon and shot an actor-deputy. I shivered when I recalled the cold manner in which Chick had dispatched Haywood.

Following was a cacophony of gunshots as a dozen weapons—Colt revolvers and Winchester rifles and double-barreled shotguns loaded with blanks—opened up in a burst of muzzle flash and powder smoke. Chick jumped down from the buckboard, hit the ground lightly, and spun. From the hip he fanned off two shots, and two stunt men fell. The sound from the guns was deafening. Many more gunshots rang out, and more stunt men bit the dust.

Chick ran and mounted the horse, clutching the reins in one hand while continuing to shoot. He jerked the reins, turning the horse, then shot again, looking every inch the legendary outlaw. Then I saw him flinch, just before he tumbled from the horse. I hadn't read the script, so I wasn't able to ascertain if that was part of the script.

But it didn't feel right.

Chick fell to the ground as if he were a sack of feed, taking the brunt of the fall with the back of his shoulder blades. I watched him struggle to get to his feet before he was thrown down again by some invisible force.

"That's not in the script," said the assistant. "What's he doing?"

Someone was using live ammunition.

I started running.

"What are you doing?" yelled Salinger.

The shooting continued as I ran through the middle of the scene, ripping the Browning from its holster. I yelled for them to stop shooting, but my voice was lost in the volley of gunfire. Reaching Chick, I skidded onto my knees, covering Chick's body with my own. Little plumes of dirt flew up close by, the spray of dirt stinging my face. In that brief moment, I recognized the sick irony of possibly being killed by an unseen assassin while several men pretended to shoot one another. I panned the area as the guns continued to crack and pop around me, searching to see which of the actors had their guns pointed our direction. I yelled again but the shooting continued.

I pointed my weapon at the huge window on the saloon facade, double-tapped the Browning, and the saloon window exploded into a shower of glass shards.

The shooting stopped. Good. I heard Chick moan.

Salinger was yelling. "What the hell is going on?"

Chick moaned again.

"You okay?" I asked, body tense, ears and eyes straining to hear the sizzle of bullet or the flash of gun barrel. Nothing.

Chick didn't answer.

The set, loud and filled with the sounds of shouting and gunfire, was suddenly still.

Cameron Fogarty staggered onto the set, dressed in cowboy garb, his shirttail hanging out like an unmade bed, dark half-moons under his eyes, skin dull with alcohol saturation. Rocky Raccoon as Jesse James.

"I'm ready," he said, absently shoving the shirttail into his jeans. The stunt men and other actors had stunned looks on their faces.

"Chick?" I said, my mind running away with possibilities. "Come on, Chick."

"It's...about time you came to my rescue," Chick said, his voice croaking dryly. He coughed.

I pushed myself off the ground and looked at him. His left sleeve was soaked in blood. He rolled over, wincing as he did. There was another bloodstain on his right thigh.

"Get a doctor here," I said. "Now!"

I cut away his sleeve with my pocketknife. There was a nasty puncture above the bicep, which was bleeding freely. I removed my jacket and shirt, tearing the shirt into strips to bind Chick's wounds.

"Tell the doctor," said Chick, "that...that I'll need some serious drugs." He grimaced as I moved his arm to wrap a strip around it. Chick growled between clenched teeth as I cinched up the makeshift bandage. I cut away his pants leg to reveal a similar wound in his right thigh. Actors and extras crowded around like watering cattle watching a snake wriggle across a murky pond.

"Wha's goin' down?" asked Fogarty, his words thick and slurred with sleep and drug fog. He was fifteen feet from where Chick lay. I finished binding the leg wound.

"You okay?" I asked Chick.

"I'll...feel better," said Chick, "when it quits hurting."

"Is he all right?" asked Salinger, kneeling beside me. His voice was anxious and fearful. Chick tugged at my sleeve.

"And I'll need...a nurse," Chick said. "One with big lungs. Really big ones."

"Shut up," I said. Chick was going to be all right. I was relieved. "Every time you say something, you bleed more."

"You big...galoot," said Chick, growling with pain again. "Didn't know you cared. Kiss me, right now."

"Why's he dressed like me?" asked Fogarty. "Geoffrey, you asshole. Did you have him playing my scene? That's my scene. Nobody plays it but me."

I felt heat snake up the back of my neck. "Somebody better shut him up," I said, between clenched teeth. "Before I do."

"Take it easy, Storme," said Salinger, who turned to face Fogarty. "Can't you see this man has been shot?"

Fogarty leaned forward and looked at Chick. His bloodshot eyes widened with realization as he saw the blood. Movie people see much ersatz violence and imitation blood but seldom the real thing. It is vastly different.

"Hey," said Fogarty, wide-awake now. "They thought it was me. They shot him thinking it was me."

I hadn't thought about that. By this time the set doctor had shown up and was tending to Chick. I rocked back on my heels, knees on the ground. The sun was straight up in the sky.

"My God!" said Fogarty, pointing at Chick. There was panic in his voice. "Look at that. They thought Easton was me."

I stood up and faced him. "Shut up, Fogarty," I said.

"I'm sorry about your friend. Really, I am. Shit. But don't you see? That could've been me. It was supposed to be me."

I nodded. "Yeah. I'm pretty broke up about that too."

Chick tugged on my pants leg. "Hold still," the doctor told him.

"Whiskey," Chick said. "They always give whiskey to the hero when he's shot."

One of the stunt men handed Chick a flask. Salinger glared at the man questioningly. The stunt man shrugged.

Chick tugged on my pants leg again. I looked down at him.

"You're my...hero," he said.

"Shut up and quit milking it," I told him. "Or *I'll* shoot you."

Chick actually chuckled.

THIRTY-TWO

Rory looked through the scope of the rifle. He could see the entire movie set from this ridge. He hated to shoot long-distance, because he liked to see the victim's face, but this Easton guy was something different. He wouldn't be easy to do in person. And he had to take him out to get to Storme.

Storme. Yeah, he'd do Superstar up close, where the guy could see it was Rory closing him out.

It was like the two kids. He had had to do them or give up on Storme. All they had to do was drive the car to the airport and leave it. Sure, they woulda found it, but the kids would never make the connection, and by the time the airport security turned it, Rory would be done with the business here. Was it his fault the kids had dumbed up and gotten tanked and had been pulled over by the state bull?

Just good business practice, but he hadn't gotten much enjoyment out of it. The second one didn't die right away. Whined and cried until Rory parked one at the base of his throat.

Dumb fucking kids, anyway. It was their fault.

Rory put the rifle down, picked up the binoculars, and watched Easton run out of one of the buildings and jump into the back of a wagon. Guy was moving too fast to take a shot at this distance. He picked up the rifle again and tracked the badass. Now the guy was up on his horse. This was a good time. He flipped off the safety and put the cross hairs on the guy. Rory took a breath and let part of it out like they taught him in the service before they kicked him out. All over some ready-mix ROTC lieutenant.

Almost ready now. Finger on the trigger. Ready. Squeeze…

Rory backed off the trigger.

What the hell was this? Something had knocked the guy right out of the saddle.

Rory dropped the rifle and grabbed at the binos again. Through the glasses he saw the badass lying on the ground. Maybe it was a stunt or something. He watched the guy jerk again, lying on the ground.

Then he saw the football player run into the field of view. This couldn't be part of it. Superstar was wearing civvies. Then it came to him.

Somebody was trying to do Rory's job for him.

He watched Superstar run across the street and lie on top of his buddy. Crazy mother was willing to take a bullet for the guy. Guy made Rory sick. He'd be doing the world a favor getting rid of this Dudley Do-Right cocksucker.

Rory scanned the location with the binoculars down. There! He saw something. Somebody sneaking behind the trailers. Was that a rifle he had with him? Rory brought the glasses up to get a good luck at his face. It was somebody Rory didn't know, but Rory would remember the face. You never knew what might come in handy later.

Who was this trying to kill Superstar's buddy?

And why now? This was messing things up. The cops'd be all over this. Make it difficult to get close to Storme.

Dammit! It had to be soon. This was going to bring heat. What with the two kids, and then that asshole Ventura calling and changing his mind about busting a cap on Superstar, everything was going into the shitter fast. First Bobby Frank's tossing money around to hit the guy, then the next thing you know, he sends the lawyer to call the whole thing off. The people downtown don't want no trouble. Sends the lizard lawyer around again. The lawyer looking all nervous and scared. Bobby Frank was pissed at him or something. Things need to cool off, he says.

What next?

At least the Easton guy was out of the way.

And who give a shit if Bobby Frank was mad at the lawyer? Or if the guys downtown were mad at Bobby Frank? Yeah. Take out Superstar and let it fall on Bobby Frank. Maybe the big bosses would cool out Bobby's action. No more expensive clothes and big cars. Storme and Ventura both with one shot.

Not bad, Rory, he thought. This may work out yet.

THIRTY-THREE

An ambulance took Chick to the county hospital, where they treated his wounds and released him. They didn't have much choice about releasing him.

"I'm not laying around here," he said. "They keep the bar closed, and I can't smoke." The leg wound was clean, but the shoulder wound was another story. The X-rays showed a tiny lump lodged behind the scapula.

"Looks like the bullet fragmented, and some of it stayed behind," said the doctor. "The entry wound indicates a small-caliber bullet like a twenty-two." The doctor told Chick he could operate, but it was better to leave it alone unless it began to move.

"That's okay," said Chick. "It's got company in there."

"I'm required by law to report all gunshot wounds," said the doctor. "So someone from the sheriff's office is coming by. Also, I'm not pleased with your plans to leave the hospital. You need rest and quiet so you don't open up those wounds again. I'd like you to get bed rest," he said, "but at least please sit quietly. You were fortunate. I don't think there will be any long-term damage, but you should not stress those wounds."

A sheriff's deputy showed up soon after that. He asked the usual questions and told us that the sheriff would have more questions later. We left the hospital, picked up the antibiotic and the pain-killer the doctor had prescribed, and returned to the movie site.

Sheriff Carney Statler showed up on the set that afternoon, and he didn't smile once when he saw me. He didn't show up alone either. Besides the two deputies he brought with him, there were two uniformed state troopers and a state patrol investigator in a suit and tie. The deputies and troopers were searching for the weapon that had shot Chick. They found a spent bullet lodged in the wood of the saloon boardwalk.

The sheriff showed me the small misshapen lump of lead.

"It's a twenty-two or a twenty-five," he said. "But it hit hard enough to knock Easton out of the saddle. Maybe a wildcat load like a twenty-two Hornet."

Looking at the disfigured projectile, I had a sickening thought. "How about a twenty-two Magnum?" I asked the sheriff.

"Maybe," he said.

"I know where there is one."

"Where?"

"In my Jeep."

We walked to the truck, and I opened the door to look under the seat. The lever-action Winchester was missing, along with the flexible gun boot I kept it in.

"Who knew it was in there?"

"Just me," I said.

"Why was it in there?"

"For coyotes."

"Was it loaded?"

I nodded.

"You realize it's against the law to carry a loaded weapon in a vehicle?"

"Don't lecture me, Carney. Not with Chick shot."

He turned his head and spat. "That's not the only thing happening around here," he said. "They found two bodies in a stolen truck. The truck and the guys had been shot up. Nine-millimeter bullets. Turns out they were a couple of bad actors with long sheets. Looked like a mob hit. Payback of some kind. But why around here, and why were the guys dressed like locals?"

I shrugged.

"They found the truck abandoned just across the county line. It looks like they had been killed somewhere else, then driven to that spot. Sure would like to thank whoever it was that got it out of my county."

"I'm sure they'd want you to know you're welcome."

He stared at me for a long, hard moment while he removed the wrapper on a cigar and shoved it his teeth.

"You own a nine-millimeter?" he asked.

"Used to." There was no record of the gun I'd found in Colorado, but the other was registered. "Somebody stole it."

"You report it?" the sheriff asked, one eye partly closed as he lit his cigar.

"Why? When would you have time to look for it?"

"When was it stolen?"

"Couple months ago."

"Uh-huh. They tell me you shot out a window to get the actors to quit shooting. What were you using then?"

"Browning Hi Power," I said. I reached under the jacket and handed the Browning to him. "It's a forty caliber."

He looked at it and handed it back. He pushed back the brim of his Stetson hat and scratched his forehead with a thumb.

"You're carrying a concealed weapon with all these law enforcement types running around here?"

"I'm on my own property. Besides, people are shooting each other around here."

"Also hear you bought eight tires from Stallworth."

I nodded.

"You want to tell me why?"

"Needed tires."

"Did somebody slash your tires?"

I shrugged.

"Dammit, Storme," said Statler. "Help me out some here. I've got one killing already with that convenience store guy and another shooting today and two dead hit men just across the county line. Not to mention those two kids over in Gilmore have disappeared."

"What?"

"They're gone. Paradise County sheriff thinks they might be running because they're scared about being arraigned on the DWI. Really like to talk to them too. I need a description of the guy they say they got the car from. Supposedly, they got it from a guy at the same convenience store where the clerk was killed. All this stuff is linked somehow, and I need you to be a little more forthcoming with me."

"What kind of car was it?" I asked. "Was it a light-colored Cadillac?"

"I don't know," Statler said. "We could ask one of the troopers." Statler turned and hollered at one of his deputies, "Hey, Jerry. Ask one of those state guys if they can tell you what kind of vehicle those two kids were joyriding in when they picked them up. Ask if it was a light-colored Cadillac."

The deputy nodded and left to find a trooper.

"What are you thinking?" Statler asked me.

"Maybe nothing," I said. I told him about Rory Marchibroda. Told him how unpopular Fogarty was with the other actors. I left out several items, such as Chick bracing Marchibroda and me shooting at him the night he shot my window out.

"Why didn't you tell me this before?" Statler asked when I was done. "I wish you would not take it upon yourself to determine what pertinent knowledge is. It might've helped me out some if you'd have told me about some of this. Particularly about this Marchibroda fella."

"What could you do about it? He hasn't broken any laws."

"He's a felon."

"Ex-felon."

"That's a charitable attitude. Maybe this ex-*felon* shot your friend. You ever think of that? Maybe this ex-felon has something to do with the death of the store clerk. Maybe he's gone on a rampage. This guy sounds like your garden variety bucket of shit, the kind not likely to maintain predictable behavior patterns."

I gave that some consideration. Rory was capable of doing about anything, including murdering the two boys from Gilmore. He had slashed the tires on my Jeep, which hadn't been locked, and perhaps he had found the rifle under the seat. I hadn't checked the rifle in several days. It might appeal to some sick, ironic impulse of Rory's to shoot Chick with my gun.

"We still have the problem of the threats against Cameron Fogarty," I said. "The shooter may have mistaken Chick for Fogarty." Or maybe not. Maybe Chick was the target. I didn't bring up Ventura's name. I hoped Ventura was a man of his word, but despaired of my romantic notions about covenants between enemies. Chick's pragmatic approach to conflict—remove all adversaries from the board—might have possibly spared him this injury.

"Why would Marchibroda use a strange gun?" I said. Just now thinking Rory didn't shoot Chick. A twenty-two wouldn't have the necessary range. "He's a pro and not the kind to miss."

"Missed you the night he was shooting at you at your cabin."

"I never said anyone shot at my cabin." Statler was trying to ambush me.

"Aw hell, Wyatt," said Statler, throwing his cigar on the ground. "Cut this shit out and play me straight."

"I'm not trying to be oblique," I said. "It's just that I don't think there's anything to be done about it."

"File a complaint and let me come out and look around."

"You know I don't like public officials on official business out at my place," I said. "You're welcome anytime, long as you don't bring a badge and a business purpose when you come."

"You may not have much choice this time," he said, his dark eyebrows moving closer together like thunderclouds.

Jerry, the deputy, returned. "Yeah, Carney. It was a white Cadillac."

Carney Statler looked at me. "Well?"

"Rory Marchibroda was driving a light-colored Cadillac the first day I saw him. He's still driving a caddy, but it's red, and it's new."

"That's interesting," said Statler. "Where can I find this guy?"

"I don't have any idea."

"I'll assign a guy to you," said Statler. "Sooner or later he'll show up."

"Nobody's following me around."

"This guy is."

"The answer's still no."

"Maybe I'll make you accept it."

"You do, and I'll have a lawyer out here, today. I like you, Carney, but I like my privacy too."

"You're a stubborn son of a bitch."

I nodded. "What I hear."

Another deputy showed up just then. "They found the weapon, Sheriff," said the deputy.

"Was it a Winchester lever action?"

The deputy looked perplexed. "Yeah," he said. "How'd you know?"

Statler looked at me. "You think this Marchibroda guy did it?"

"I don't know," I said.

"Who do you think is threatening Fogarty?"

"I don't know that either."

"You're a storehouse of information. You know that?"

"Always glad to help," I said.

Statler took his hat off and ran fingers through dark hair snowed with gray. Shook his head. "This Marchibroda fella may've done all this," he said. "Next time, stick to football."

"Next time."

"Well, I got other people to talk with," said Statler. "If they're as cooperative as you, we should be able to wrap this up in a decade or two. We're going to keep the rifle for a while. I hope your refusal to keep me informed hasn't cost those two kids over in Gilmore their lives."

I couldn't think of anything to say to that.

He muttered an obscenity and walked off.

The law enforcement people stayed the rest of the afternoon and into the evening. When I ran into Geoffrey Salinger later in the day, he looked as if he'd swallowed a roll of toilet paper.

"Everything is ruined," Salinger said. "My timetable is shot to hell. The police are interviewing everyone on the set and demanding a list of people we are unable to account for at the time of the shooting. But the worst thing," he said, "is that Easton has been shot." He looked at the floor and shook his head. "He could've been killed. I'm sorry."

"I appreciate that," I said. "Chick will too. It's not your fault, Geoffrey. Chick knows the risk. The police will find out who did this, and we'll know who was sending the threats."

Salinger gave me a strange look.

I looked at him and read it. "The threats were phony," I said. "Weren't they?"

His eyes avoided mine. He stared at the floor and slowly nodded his head.

"Yes," he said.

"Well, that's great, Geoffrey," I said. "Just perfect."

THIRTY-FOUR

I made Salinger go with me to Chick's trailer so Chick could hear the director's true confessions. I wasn't ready to let the police in on this until I had the information myself. Once the police were clued in, Chick and I would be locked out.

"It was what you suspected," said Salinger. "It was a publicity ploy. Cameron is in on it. He knows the threats aren't real. We agreed it would provide us a measure of media exposure not otherwise available."

"What about the skinheads?" I asked. "The sheriff mentioned you talking to one of them, the one killed in the robbery."

Salinger pursed his lips, then said, "I hired him and his friends to create a disturbance on the set and call attention to the love scene between Michael LeBeau and Meagan Ames." He was quiet for a moment while I looked at him. "Okay," he said. "So, it was stupid."

"Not to mention insensitive," I said. "And dangerous."

"I didn't know Easton would start shooting. They made me pay double because of that." He looked at Chick. "You broke the man's nose."

"Good," said Chick.

"Why do you need any more publicity?" I asked. "You're well-known and have a celebrity cast."

"Rural Missouri is not exactly a media hotbed," said Salinger. He was drinking vodka over ice. Chick was drinking scotch in violation of the doctor's orders and smoking cigarettes in spite of Salinger's. But Salinger wasn't in the mood to protest. He was slumped in his chair gulping vodka and aggressively wiping his hands on his pants leg as if they had come into contact with something unsanitary. As for Chick, he looked like a flu victim, with his complexion pale, left arm in a sling, and his right leg bandaged and lumpy and stretched out stiffly in front of him. The worst thing was his eyes, which were dark-rimmed and blood-shot with fatigue and pain-killers. "It seemed so…so harmless."

I sat back in my chair. "If no one was trying to kill Fogarty, then everything we've done has been a waste of time."

"Maybe not," said Chick. "We discovered motives for several people to kill Fogarty. Now somebody has decided to take advantage of the situation."

"Take advantage of what situation?" asked Salinger.

"No one was shooting at me. No reason."

I knew Chick was right. I said, "Anybody know about your publicity stunt besides you and Fogarty?"

"No."

Chick smiled, but his eyes weren't up to it, leaving his lips to carry the load. "So you got several people around here who don't just dislike Fogarty, they despise him. Then you've got this secret publicity stunt brewing they don't know about, so they pop Fogarty and wait for the police to find the person responsible for the threats."

"Why not wait until they get it done?" I asked.

Chick shrugged, wincing as he did so. "Who knows? Maybe they couldn't stand to wait any longer."

"Or couldn't afford to," I said. "Or just wanted the satisfaction of doing it themselves."

Chick nodded. "See? You got a nose for this detective stuff."

"So," Salinger said. "What you are saying is that someone on the set decided to kill Fogarty and allow the blame to fall to the person they assumed was making the threats?"

"It could've gone that way," I said.

"Except they didn't know the threats were bogus," Chick said.

"If I wrote this into a script, it wouldn't be believable," Salinger said.

"I think it's a beauty," said Chick. "Besides, who'd want to harm lovable old me?"

"Besides Rory Marchibroda?" I said.

"And my old girlfriends, of course," said Chick.

"And Bobby Frank Ventura," I said.

At Ventura's name Salinger sat up straight. "Are you going to insist Robert might have something to do with this?"

Chick and I looked at each other.

"Boy, Geoffrey," said Chick. "For a sophisticated guy, you are naive."

"It's not Ventura's style, though," I said. "He would do it quietly, not on the set of a motion picture he's invested in. Costs him money, so can't see him doing that. And he wouldn't steal a gun out of my truck to do it. No, someone thought Chick was Fogarty. Bet on it. So, who does that eliminate?"

"Caraway was on the set," said Chick. "So he's off the list. What about the rest of the cast?"

"Why wasn't LeBeau in the shoot-out scene?"

"His character is killed before the shoot-out scene," said Salinger.

"Did Valeri Darnell and Meagan Ames know Chick was standing in?" I asked.

"No," said Salinger. "Valeri complained of a headache, and Meagan was not required on the set until later. But they wouldn't shoot a man."

"I don't think LeBeau would either," I said.

"That's what they thought about O.J. Simpson," said Salinger.

"Don't forget Meagan's secretary, Chester the molester," said Chick.

"Wait," said Salinger, as if talking to himself. "But that's too horrible to think about. She wouldn't...at least I don't think she would."

"Get it said, Geoffrey," said Chick, rubbing his face with a hand. His eyes were frosted with a medicated glaze.

"Valeri can shoot a rifle," said Salinger. "And she's good at it. She was in a dinner-theatre production of *Annie Get Your Gun*. In order to make her character more realistic, she took lessons at a gun club in Beverly Hills. Anything Valeri does, she does well."

Another factor to add to the problem. Plus this marked the second time Salinger had mentioned Valeri Darnell as a possible suspect. I couldn't tell if Salinger was legitimately interested in finding the killer or making sure the outcome was to his liking.

Chick, worn down and weakened by blood loss and bullet shock, decided to rest while I headed back to my cabin. He still wasn't sleeping, though. At least not where anyone could see it. A sheriff's deputy was staying on the set in case the killer took another shot at Chick, which I didn't think was going to happen, as I was convinced the target had been Fogarty. Besides, even in his weakened state, Chick Easton could take care of anything that might come his way.

Only now, it would fall to me to help out.

During the drive back to my house, I took the opportunity to reflect upon what we had just discovered, laying it alongside what we already knew.

Fact number one. Many people dislike Cameron Fogarty.

Fact two. The death threats were contrived.

Fact three. Despite fact two, we were still looking for a would-be killer and still hadn't narrowed the field much, except we could eliminate Rance Caraway. Perhaps I was looking at it the wrong way. Maybe revenge wasn't a factor.

Maybe I needed to take a look at who might benefit directly from Fogarty's death.

I drove out to the convenience store that had been robbed. The store where the clerk was killed and where the two missing teenagers said they'd met the man who gave them the Cadillac that had belonged to a couple of guys who were also dead. Maybe it didn't have anything to do with Chick being shot. But it was something to do.

The store wasn't all that far out of the way, so it wasn't long before I was pumping gas, premium, from the self-service pump into the Mustang's tank. Nothing seemed significant about the place. No spirits of the dead appeared. No significance in the faint tread marks crisscrossing the pavement. No clues in the soft-drink cooler. No insights borne in on the heavy aroma of raw gasoline. I was stumped. I bought a Coca-Cola, regular, paid for my gas, and headed for my cabin.

If Rory Marchibroda wasn't working for Ventura like they both insisted, then what was Rory's motivation for stalking me? Revenge? Pure unadulterated hatred? Sure, I'd busted him up back in Denver, but for a guy like Rory, that was an occupational hazard. Chick was right. There was something flawed in the thought processes of guys like Marchibroda and Ventura. Something feral and unsound, as if the impulses along the synapses had stalled before careening off in erratic directions. Something that all the social programs and school curricula would never overcome. Somewhere along the line, whether by event or design, they had veered off the main trail and headed down a path laid by paranoia and aberration.

My path lay home.

About a mile from the turnoff onto a two-lane blacktop, I picked up a tail. A shark-gray Lincoln Continental turned off the road behind me and followed me onto the two-lane blacktop. I watched them in the mirror as they followed me onto a gravel side road. There was nothing down the old road that would attract such a vehicle. They were interested in me.

I turned down an old logging road and parked the Jeep.

I opened the glove box and pulled out the Browning. After I shuffled the action, I set the safety, stuck the pistol in my waistband, and buttoned the bottom three buttons on my jacket to cover the pistol.

Then I got out of the Mustang to see what they wanted.

THIRTY-FIVE

The shark-gray Lincoln pulled up behind me, dust swirling up around its wheel wells in small, angry clouds. Two well-dressed men, the size and thickness of draft horses, got out of the vehicle and walked my way. They had slicked-back hair, unblinking eyes, and the confident manner born of getting their way. Probably due to their size. Bet I could outrun them.

"Mr. Giovanni wants to see you," said the dark-haired gorilla in the gray suit. He said it as if it were a foregone conclusion that I would comply. "He's back in the car, if you'll step this way."

"No," I said, then waited for their reaction, which I knew would be nothing if not interesting.

They looked at each other briefly before Gray Suit turned back to me and said, "No?"

I smiled and nodded helpfully. "Yes," I said. "No."

His eyebrows knit together. "Gus said you were kind of smartass. He told us to ignore it."

"Hard to do, isn't it?"

He nodded. I looked at the other hood, another dark-haired thug in a blue suit, who looked as excited as a world-champion mattress tester and less tolerant of clever conversation. He had a wad of scar tissue at the corner of his left eye.

"A lot easier if you go talk to him," said Gray Suit.

"For you," said Scar-Eye.

"Nobody's going to hassle you," said Gray Suit, his tone even and cordial. "Just talk."

"How about I take off running and you guys chase me?" I said.

Gray Suit shook his head. His neck was so thick that his chin only traveled half the normal radius. "Noticed you're limping," he said. "Probably wouldn't take long to catch up."

"And it would piss us off," said Scar-Eye.

"Maybe I don't want to talk with whoever it is you represent."

"You sure it's not 'whomever'?" said Gray Suit.

"Nobody likes an intelligent thug," I said.

Gray Suit smiled.

Scar-Eye pulled out an auto loading pistol, which looked small in his huge paw. He held it down at the side of his leg.

"Oh," I said. "That Gus Giovanni. Sure, be glad to talk to him."

They escorted me back to the Lincoln, the windows of which were heavily tinted. Gray Suit opened the door to reveal a man in his late sixties, white hair on top, with a face that looked like the side of a cliff. He wore a charcoal topcoat over a gray suit, a blood-red tie with an understated blue print neatly knotted and set off by the snow-white silk shirt. He was drinking coffee from a service tray that sat on the transmission hump. Roughing it. The two gorillas stood behind me.

"Come in, Mr. Storme," said the man in the car, waving his hand in a welcoming gesture without looking at me. "Sit down."

"My mom said not to accept rides from strangers."

He stopped sipping his coffee and looked at me with a pained expression, as if someone had farted at his daughter's wedding.

"Do you know who I am?" he asked.

"Adolfo Celi?" I said. Scar-Eye stiff-armed me from behind, knocking me against the car.

I turned around and looked at Scar-Eye. "Don't do that again," I said. He looked at me with dull predator eyes.

"Hey," said Giovanni, his voice calm and conversational. "Lay off that, Mike. We don't need that here."

"Have some respect," said scar-eyed Mike.

"No thanks," I said. "Already have some."

Nick stared at me some more, then Giovanni said, "Phil, you 'n Mike take a walk so I can talk with this guy."

"We haven't patted him down, Gus," said Phil, the gray-suited thug. "He's got his jacket buttoned down in front. I think he's carrying."

"I'm sure he is," said Giovanni. "And we know he can shoot, but he's no killer. You two go on ahead. I'm not concerned about Storme."

"All right, Gus," said Phil. "Nice to meet you," he said to me. Phil and Nick walked off.

"You're giving me a stiff neck," said Giovanni as his bodyguards walked away, "from looking up at you. Come on. Sit down. Please. I want to talk to you."

I sat and sank into the burgundy leather. The interior of the car smelled of coffee, expensive cologne, and the singular aroma new cars possess.

"That's better," he said. "Would you like some coffee?"

"What do you want?"

"No need to be uncivil," said Giovanni. "This is unusual, don't you think? Gus Giovanni taking the time to come out here and talk to you."

"I can hardly control my bladder, I'm so excited."

"You should have more appreciation for this situation."

"I didn't request an audience."

He looked perplexed, as if he couldn't comprehend what was wrong with this child before him.

"Why you always come on so hard-ass?"

I shrugged. "I thought I was being incredibly restrained."

"I'm told you had a run-in with a couple of people we have used in the past to conduct business. Is that right?"

"What's your point?"

"They're dead."

"I've been wearing a black armband for days." I made a show of checking my arms. "Now, where is it? I just had it on."

"You go to a lot of trouble to be a wise ass. You know that?"

"It's not really all that much trouble."

"There is no need for it here," he said. He took a long, slender, black cigar from a leather cigar case and put it in his mouth. He offered the case to me, and I shook my head. He lit the cigar with a silver lighter and took the smoke into his lungs; the electric window slid down with a soft hum, and Giovanni blew smoke out the window.

"My wife," he said, holding the cigar up for me to see, "she doesn't like it that I smell up the car with these things. Bad for my health, she says." He chuckled to himself. "Women? What do you do with them?"

I waited.

"We know a lot about you, Storme," said Giovanni. "War hero. Silver Star, Bronze Star. Even understand you might've been a candidate for the Medal of Honor, but you don't take orders so good. Is that right?"

"I was also a hall monitor in the third grade."

"You have earned a fair amount of consideration within certain circles," he said, ignoring me. "Among people I do business with. You have even made money for people within our organization."

I looked at him questioningly. He responded to the look by smiling.

"It was inadvertent, of course. You didn't know you were doing it. There was money riding on games you played in. There's money on everything. I know guys who'll bet on the number of passes each team will make in a quarter. Two games you played in come to mind. Both times we had key members of the other team paid off. Both times it appeared as if we had thrown the money away and would have to visit these people. It's not easy to fix a pro football game. The league office is better at it than we are. You made big catches at the end of those games and saved our money."

"Hooray," I said.

He gave me a hard look. "You also saved a couple a guys some distress. Now, listen to me, Storme. I'm trying to get along here. I even forgive you for that incident a few years back when you killed my nephew."

"He didn't give me any choice," I said.

"That's what my information says also. They told me you gave him a way out, but he didn't take it. He chose the hard way." He leaned back against the seat, which made a pleasant leather sound. "Still," he said, "that's an unusual thing. A fed standing right there, and you give Tony a chance to walk away. You're an interesting man, Storme."

"I was voted most interesting by my graduating class."

He waved his cigar in the air as if there were a slow moving fly buzzing overhead. "But don't misunderstand," he said. "I'm not here to entertain you with stories from the past."

"What are you here for?"

"You and Bobby Frank have had difficulties."

"I don't like him," I said. "And I don't want him around."

"He has assured me that he will not allow his personal feelings to interfere with business decisions."

"That why he sent the two shooters?"

"As it turns out, that was an unfortunate decision for the two guys he sent. They were reliable. A shame to lose them. Bobby Frank should've informed us before taking such action. That is in the past now and has no future significance. It is a fact this friend of yours shot Haywood."

I looked at him.

"Relax," he said. "Your generation is too suspicious. Too many movies. You did what you had to do. I understand that. Twice now you have killed some of our people. Not many people get away with that. But they left you no other options, and I have no problem with it. Sometimes that's the way things are. Mistakes are made. But"—he let the interjection hang in the air while he took another draw on the cigar, then leaned toward me—"your friend made threats."

"They weren't threats."

He nodded and leaned back again. "I will agree with you on that. We had him checked out, though we didn't get much information. I do know he has the ability to do what he says he'll do. Not even our organization would be able to completely protect Bobby Frank from this assassin, this..." He waved a hand as if searching for the right word. "This ghost, for want of a better word. I made Bobby Frank aware of this. I wouldn't mind having a guy like this Easton on my payroll."

"He wouldn't work for you," I said.

"What?" he said, his hands held up in front of him, the backs of his wrists toward me. "Because I'm such a bad man? Is that it?" He leaned forward again, eyes narrowing. "You're right. I'm a very bad man. Don't forget that. Ever. And you're also right when you say he wouldn't work for us. That was part of the profile on your dangerous friend. Which makes no sense to me, y'understand? This guy's got more blood on his hands than any of my employees. No. You're stubborn, the both of you. Stubborn, stupid men who think you have some kind of moral imperative that sets you apart from everything and everybody.

"But make no mistake about it. We would get Easton. You need to accept that as a reality. Eventually we would find him and remove him. And you. But by that time, I would've lost Bobby Frank and some others and would have expended energy and money better spent. And although I don't like Bobby Frank much better than you do, he makes money for me. Sure, he's got a hot head and thinks he's Al Pacino or something, but he produces good numbers."

"So what does this mean to me?" I asked.

"Somebody shot your friend," he said. "I'm here to assure myself that you realize Bobby Frank had nothing to do with that. He wouldn't risk it, you know what I'm saying?"

"You came here to tell me that Ventura wouldn't kill someone who threatened to take him out?"

"Not only wouldn't," said Giovanni, measuring out the words so they had the finality of a metal door clanging shut, "he knows he better damned well not. That would be the end of his…ah… employment with our organization. We don't want any misunderstandings that might bring unnecessary publicity to this situation. We have an interest in becoming more involved with the movie people. Bobby Frank had nothing to do with your friend getting shot. We had nothing to do with it. Had we done it, you would know."

"I didn't think you did," I said. "Doesn't fit you or Bobby Frank. Besides, I have an understanding with Ventura."

Giovanni tilted his chin and considered me. "Yes," he said, nodding. "Bobby Frank will do what he says. He has no choice. I will ensure that. You are a man of your word, I'm told. I'm told that by many. That is as things should be. That is the way things used to be. Not so much anymore. It's a good thing to see, though."

He looked at me some more, like a jeweler might consider a rough stone, trying to read my face. There was force in the look. Probably many men had wilted under the force of that look.

"So," he said. "We understand one another. You don't want to end up dead, and I don't want the aggravation and time spent getting it done. I see no reason we should ever talk again."

"I have a question," I said. "Who were the guys that were supposed to throw the games? The games you mentioned."

"One of the names escapes me at this time," he said. "The other one comes to mind more readily. He is acting in the movie on your property. That smart nigger with the French-sounding name."

"His name is Michael LeBeau," I said. "And he's not a nigger. He's a man. A better one than any of the deviates you associate with."

Giovanni's face clouded up. "I see. LeBeau is a friend of yours, huh? But you are in danger of pushing things too far here, Storme." His teeth were clenched together. "Don't keep picking at it."

"I don't believe Michael would throw a game. Not for money, not for you, not for anybody."

Giovanni leaned back an inch and considered me. "So, that's it. He's a friend. Why don't you ask him whether or not he was paid to throw the game? It would be interesting to know if he was also a liar." He waved the back of his hand at me in a dismissive gesture. "Tell Nick and Phil I wish to leave now."

I got out of the car and headed back to the Jeep. I didn't tell Nick and Phil anything. That'd teach Giovanni to mess with me.

THIRTY-SIX

L eaving Giovanni and his bodyguards, I drove to my cabin, thinking about what Giovanni said about Michael LeBeau. Wondered if it meant anything. I had trouble believing Michael would throw a game. He had too much inner pride. But I had been wrong before. It was still a long throw from shaving points to murder.

Back inside my fortress of solitude, I got out an album of newspaper clippings and photos from my playing days. We had played the Rams several times during my career, but I was looking for a game where I would have caught a touchdown pass late in the game. After thirty minutes of leafing through laminated newspaper and *Sports Illustrated* articles, I found the game I was looking for. The clipping was from 1982. I caught a thirty-five-yard touchdown pass from Murphy Chandler with twenty-five seconds to go in regulation. I checked the statistics from the game and found a weird stat. Michael LeBeau had scored two touchdowns and gained a hundred and five yards rushing. One of the touchdowns was the go-ahead score, with one forty-seven left to play.

Didn't sound like a man trying to throw a game.

Something to ask him about, though.

———

Back at the set the next morning, things were in an uproar. The media, having scented the aroma of a story—or even better from their point of view, a scandal—had descended upon the production in full battle array: minicams, reporters, sound trucks, and photographers. As usual, their information was sketchy and in many cases, inaccurate. None of which really mattered since they were after a story, not the facts. The rumor winds had given them the idea that it was Cameron Fogarty who had been shot, and they were disappointed when Salinger disabused them of that delicious notion.

Still, they had movie stars and a famous director and danger and intrigue. There was blood in the water, and the media was snapping at anything that swam by. Unfortunately, that also put a media-shy former wide receiver at risk.

As I walked across the lot, I was set upon by a member of the fourth estate, a young guy with rimless glasses and wavy hair clipped neatly above his ears, long in front and parted in the middle.

"Hey, aren't you Wyatt Storme?"

"No," I said. "He's much older. I think I saw him over by the stables. If you hurry, you can catch him." I continued walking.

He reached out and grabbed my arm, something I always enjoy. "Yeah," the reporter said. "You're him. What do you know about this shooting?"

I looked down at his hand, then up at his face. He removed his hand, and I continued on my way. As I walked away, the reporter said, "Hey, I'm not through talking to you yet."

"Sure you are," I said, without looking back. "Just nobody told you."

I found Michael LeBeau surrounded by media types trying to talk over one another. I lit up a cigar, leaned against an oak tree, and waited for them to finish with him. The interview was largely your standard-stupid questions session. "Who do you think shot the stunt double?" "Why do you think he was shot?" "Do you think it was an accident?" Then there were the answers, with "no comment" topping the list.

Two of the questions, however, caught my attention. "Is there any truth to the rumor of a relationship between yourself and Valeri Darnell?" and "Do you think this will hurt the movie?" I thought about the last question. Not only would it not hurt the movie, I thought, but it also would probably pique the interest of more popcorn purchasers than it would have had the shooting not happened.

Finally, they finished with LeBeau and drifted off to assail another principal player with their relentless and penetrating questions.

"This is crazy," Michael said after the reporters left. "We're never going to finish this movie the way things are going. What's up?"

No use waiting. The sharpest knife cuts cleanest. "I talked to somebody who said you were paid to throw a game against us back in the early eighties. Any truth to that?"

He turned his head to one side and looked at me. "You been smoking something?"

I shook my head. "You try to throw the game?"

He put up a hand, showing me his palm. "I don't have to listen to this bullshit, man."

"I looked it up," I said. "We won. You had a good game. Over a hundred yards rushing."

"But you ask anyway, right?"

"The source was reliable."

"Where are you coming from?"

"I'm not sure. There are mob connections to Geoffrey Salinger. You don't like Fogarty. Chick is shot because somebody thought he was Fogarty. You weren't around. Then, the king of the KC rackets tells me you were paid to throw a game. I'm not articulate enough to devise a diplomatic way to say these things, so this is the way I ask. Don't read anything into it."

He stared at me with hard, flat eyes.

"I didn't throw that game, man."

"But you were approached."

LeBeau looked around, then said. "I can't talk about this. I'm eligible for the Hall next year. You can't even whisper this kind of shit. Do you understand that? Do you know what the Hall would mean for me? For my career and my family?" I didn't say anything, which seemed to make him mad. "No, you don't, do you, white boy? You don't understand nothing. Everything goes good for you, right? You don't need Canton, do you? Easy enough to blow it off when you're the right color. That it?"

"Don't hand me that racist dodge, Michael," I said. "It's beneath you, and you know better."

"Well, you're pissing me off," he said.

"Okay, that's fair. I'm not trying to do that either, but I have to know. Did they approach you about throwing the game?"

"You aren't listening to *anything* I'm saying, are you? I'm not going to talk about this."

"I'm not accusing you of anything," I said. "Just asking. What you say stays between us. Did they approach you about shaving points?"

He pursed his lips and shook his head slowly side to side. It was not meant to be an answer to my question. "Damn, you're a persistent bastard," he said.

I nodded.

He put his hands on his upper thighs and looked down at the ground, his mouth in a thin, tight line.

"I was going out with an actress in LA," he said, still looking down. "A white girl named Whitney. She was a doper. Ludes, coke, whatever." He looked up at me. "Yeah, I know, but she was beautiful, and I was young, and I was crazy about her. She told them she'd get me to throw the game if they gave her a year's supply of blow. She loved that shit more than she loved me. I told her she shouldn't have promised that."

His lower jaw worked as he struggled to control his emotion. "They sliced her nose with a razor so she couldn't snort any coke. There isn't any work for actresses who don't have noses, you know? So she couldn't work. They would've killed her if we'd have won. I paid to get her nose fixed, but our relationship was over after that. She thought I should've compromised my honor for her habit. I didn't."

I nodded. "You didn't have any good options," I said.

"Am I supposed to feel better because you think that? You have that kind of effect on people? Dammit, Wyatt. I don't need this shit. Not from you or anybody." He turned and walked away from me.

He was twenty feet away when he turned around and said, "I wouldn't throw a game, Wyatt." His eyes burned into mine. "I need you to believe that."

I nodded. "I believe you, Michael." I did.

He nodded his head, eyes glistening with emotion. "I appreciate it. You are a straight-ahead dude, Storme. Nobody can say you're not."

Yeah, it's won me a lot of prizes, I thought.

THIRTY-SEVEN

With the media and police tripping over each other, production slowed to a crawl. Geoffrey Salinger considered packing up and heading for the coast and going with what he had in the can, but Sheriff Statler vetoed that idea.

"Are you telling me I'm not allowed to leave?" said Salinger.

"For the present," said Statler.

"That is not going to happen," said Salinger. "The governor of this state is a friend of mine, and we'll see what he has to say about this."

Statler shrugged. "He's state, I'm county. We don't socialize much. We're not from the same party, so I don't much care what he says. The patrol and I agree that this is the best course of action for now. So you're here for a while. I apologize for the inconvenience, but that's the way things are."

Salinger stormed off, the back of his neck redder than a crop farmer's.

"You forgot to say, 'you're in a heap of trouble, boy,'" Chick said to Statler.

"Yeah," said Statler, rubbing his chin and watching Salinger walk away. "Guess I did."

Chick, weakened by his wounds and struggling with his lack of mobility, had settled into a melancholy state exacerbated by prescription drugs, alcohol, and some exotic pain-killers he had scored from the stunt men. He was drinking Jack Daniels from a quart bottle and chasing it with Budweiser. Also, for whatever reason, Valeri Darnell had decided to serve as his Florence

Nightingale. She had spent the day with him, tending to his wounds, running errands, and who knew what else.

"Slow down on that stuff," I said to Chick. "You need to rest and heal up."

"Thank you, Carrie Nation," he said, taking another slash from the whiskey.

"Wyatt's right, Chick," said Valeri.

"Wyatt's always right. Wyatt's my guardian angel." The way he said it had a residual tone of bitterness. Like the other day, Chick's eyes looked different. They glowed with an inner light, as if reflected through broken glass.

"Just telling you it's not a good idea to mix alcohol and pain-killers," I said.

"Wyatt Storme," said Chick. "The fairest of the fair. The squarest of the square. A straight-shooting, horse-kissing, honest-to-Randolph Scott American hero. Always ready with advice for the chemically impaired."

"What is he talking about?" Valeri asked.

"He's just talking," I said, looking at him. "He drinks too much sometimes and gets stupid."

Chick lifted the whiskey bottle. "I salute you. You and all who have tried to square away my fucked-up existence, which is God's joke on all of you."

"You're drunk," I said. "I'll talk to you some other time when you haven't pasted your head shut with whiskey."

"I'll be drunk then too," Chick said. "I plan to persevere and remain drunk. Where're my cigarettes? What kind of room service is this if there are no cigarettes? I must chain-smoke if I am to maintain this pace."

"I don't think you want to talk that way in front of Valeri, do you?"

"Talk which way?" he said. "I'm an incredibly sensitive man. Just ask any of my bitches."

I walked away, and Valeri followed me. Out of earshot.

"He doesn't mean any of that," I said.

She looked at me questioningly, with her knock-'em-dead-at-the-box-office eyes. "What do I do with him when he's like this?" she asked.

"It always passes," I said.

"What is he upset about?" she asked.

"Something that happened a long time ago, and he can't forgive himself," I said. "But, taking the present situation, did the police ask where you were when Chick was shot?"

"Yes," she said, appraising me questioningly.

"What was your answer?"

"I told them I had a headache and was at my trailer." Her voice picked up a slight edge of indignation. "Alone."

"Did you tell them you were an expert shot with a rifle?"

Her eyes narrowed, and her lips parted slightly. "So you know about that? How were you able to learn that? Who do you think you are that you can go around prying into people's lives?"

"I'm the guy whose best friend just got shot," I said. "I always get this way when that happens."

"Well, I didn't shoot him."

"Why the sudden interest in his well-being?"

"Are you jealous?"

"Of course. That's why I asked."

"You can really be an asshole, you know that?"

"I've heard it," I said, shrugging. "You know, around."

She smiled ever so slightly. "You enjoy being irritating, don't you?"

"Passes the time."

"Do you think I shot Chick?"

"I don't think you would shoot Chick. I think whoever shot Chick thought it was Fogarty."

"Which makes me suspect?"

"Yes."

"And you think I could do that?"

"I think you have reason, and I think you have the ability."

"You haven't answered the question," she said. "Do you think I did it?"

I shook my head. "No. I don't think you're capable of shooting anyone, even Fogarty. But I'm not always right and I'm not the police." My feelings were rapidly exhausting the supply of likely suspects.

She smiled. "Thank you for that," she said, eyes glistening. "I like Chick."

"He's easy to like."

"I think I'm starting to like him more than a little."

"It happens," I said. "He's habit-forming."

"There is a tenderness inside him. And something else. Like a deep secret, or an injury or something that he tries to hide. I don't know how to describe it."

"That's pretty close. Part of that is what's bothering him now."

"What did he do?" she asked. "Before he became a bodyguard?"

"You'll have to ask him," I said, avoiding the question.

"Why does he get like that?"

"You mean the drinking and the sarcasm?"

"Yes," she said. "The bitterness. It seems so out of character. What causes it?"

"A long time ago," I said. "He allowed himself to get in the way."

"Of what?"

"Of the ambitions of men of less honor," I said.

"I don't understand."

"That's okay," I said. "Neither did he."

THIRTY-EIGHT

Cameron Fogarty was a changed man.

After seeing Chick bloody in the dirt, Fogarty began to reassess his situation. The fearless braggadocio had disappeared. Easier to be brave when the threats weren't real.

"Man, that coulda been me," he said more than once. And each time he said it, I had to smother the impulse to punch him in the mouth.

I was more or less standing in for Chick as Fogarty's bodyguard while they flew in a new bodyguard from the coast. Who do you call for something like that? It wasn't like ordering a pizza.

"Shit, man," said Fogarty, in between gulps of Southern Comfort and Coke. "Somebody's trying to kill me. Me," he said, incredulous. "Why's anybody wanna kill me?"

I was amazed at my restraint.

"It could be anybody around here. You understand that? Somebody working on this set right at this moment is trying to kill me. It ain't right. Dammit, Kerry, I thought I told you to keep that curtain shut."

Fogarty ran a hand through his thick hair and looked around the trailer. "Shit," he said. "Just when I need that fucking Eastwood, he gets himself shot."

"Pretty inconsiderate of him," I said.

"Hey, I don't mean anything by it. I'm not glad he got shot up. He was better at the protecting thing than I gave him credit for. I need him. Especially now. I could use him now."

"Hey, Cam." Volts was lounging on the sofa and playing one of those martial arts video games where the loser dies a gory death on the TV set. "Why don't you smoke a number? Settle you right down."

"Yeah," said Fogarty. "Yeah, that's a good idea."

"I rolled a couple last night," said Volts. "They're in that cigarette box by the recliner."

"You light that up," I said, "and I'm out of here."

"What?"

"I'm not going to stand around here and watch you get hammered," I said. "I don't want to smell like marijuana."

"Man, you're getting paid to protect me."

"No, I'm not. You couldn't pay me enough. I'm doing it as a favor to Chick."

Fogarty walked over and lifted the lid on a mahogany box. "There's nothing in here but cigarettes. Where's the roach, man?"

"I smoked them," said Kerry Kane. "Last night after everybody went to sleep."

"You stupid asshole!" said Fogarty. "What the hell're you doing smoking my shit without permission?"

"I'm sorry, Cam," said Kane. He looked like he might cry.

"Yeah, that's great. Your sorrow means so much to me. Get me some more and roll a couple up."

Kane left the living room to fulfill his master's command. He returned, hastily rolling a paper around the illegal substance.

"Don't get in a hurry," said Fogarty. "Look out, you're spilling it all over the place. Give me that." He reached out and snatched the partially rolled cigarette from Kane's hand. "You can't do anything right."

"You light that, and I walk," I said.

"Go stand outside if you don't like it. This is for my mental health."

"It's not strong enough for that," I said.

I went outside.

Peter Braithwaite was outside, sitting in a lawn chair next to a plastic picnic table. On the table was a plate with three hot dogs in buns and a twelve pack of beer.

"I don't know why Cam's getting a new bodyguard," said Peter Braithwaite, eating a hot dog and washing it down with beer. "Or why he needs you either," he said to me. "We can take care of him."

"Probably wanted someone who would be sober most of the time."

"Like your buddy, right?"

"Shot to pieces, stone-drunk, and crippled, Chick Easton is more help than the three of you put together. You cannot imagine how much man he is."

"Yeah," said Braithwaite, his mouth full of soggy bread and red meat. "You're a couple of hot-shit motherfuckers, aren't you? How're you going to keep Cam from getting shot?"

"May not be able to. If somebody wants him bad enough, they'll get him. Might be different if Chick were still able to protect him."

"How's that?"

"Chick would take a bullet for him," I said.

"And you won't?"

"Nope."

"So what good are you?"

I shrugged. "Maybe none. Would you stop a bullet for him?"

Braithwaite stopped chewing. "Huh? Sure. Sure, I'd take a bullet for him."

I smiled.

"What're you smiling at?" Braithwaite said.

"You ever been shot at?"

"What difference does that make?"

"All the difference in the world."

"Anybody ever shoot at you?"

I nodded. "Yeah. And you don't feel brave while it's happening either. You just want it to stop. You want to shrink up and disappear where they can't see you. It's not like television or video games."

"Were you in a war?" Braithwaite asked, his tone changing, suddenly interested.

"Yeah."

"So was my dad," said Braithwaite. "He lost a leg."

"Sorry to hear that. I was lucky."

"He started drinking a lot when I was in junior high. Taking pain-killers. It messed him up. I've been thinking about him ever since your friend got shot."

The combination of pain-killers and booze reminded me of someone. More than one someone, if the truth were known. "How's he doing now?"

"Not so good. He shot himself in the head," said Braithwaite. There was a silence in the air that had nothing to do with the atmosphere. Braithwaite blinked his eyes rapidly. Took a big swig off the bottle of beer. "The night I graduated from high school."

"I'm sorry, Peter," I said. "I had no idea."

"I don't want your sympathy, man."

"I'm not offering it," I said. "I'm offering shared sorrow for a brother who lost his leg and couldn't recover from it."

"He was a chickenshit," said Braithwaite.

"No," I said. "You have no right. You have no idea what he went through."

"Yeah. Well, what about what he put a seventeen-year-old kid through? What about that? Shit, man." His voice was starting to break as he looked up at me. "He left me alone. I loved him, and he fucking left me. On the happiest night of my life, he chickened out."

His chest was heaving, and his eyes were translucent and dead set on my face, defying me to doubt what he said. I didn't.

"I can't excuse him for that," I said. "Nobody can. It was wrong. He should've given some thought about how it was going to affect you. How it would affect your life. It was a selfish act on his part. There is probably no act more selfish. But sooner or later, we all screw up. I do, Chick does, and your dad did. We feel sorry for ourselves and forget about everyone else. We're selfish people at times. But it's not too late to forgive him. I promise you, he wants that. It's not too late to forgive him and remember him for all he was and not just his final act. Not too late to remember that you love him."

Braithwaite looked down at the ground at a point between his feet. "I used to wheel him out on this back porch we had. Mom died when I was seven. He'd sit on the porch and play his harmonica and talk about California back when he was a kid. He told me he was proud of me. I was an honor roll student. An all-city defensive tackle. Dad loved football. He'd sit on the porch and play his harmonica." Braithwaite raised his head and looked across the lot, his eyes seeing something no one else could. "He'd talk to me and then sometimes…sometimes he would sit there and cry and get so drunk, he would pass out and fall out of his chair, and I had to carry him to bed. He'd always feel bad about that."

Braithwaite looked up at me. "I never minded carrying him," he said. A huge tear formed and trailed from his right eye. "I wish I was still carrying him to bed. I didn't mind." He looked away. "I shoulda told him I didn't mind."

It was quiet again. A breeze rustled the trees, shaking loose orange and gold leaves that fell to the ground like feathers.

"He won the Silver Star," said Braithwaite, looking at me now.

"They didn't give those away," I said. "He must've been a very brave man."

"I still have it," he said. "The harmonica too. I take them with me when I go places."

"I think he'd like that."

It was quiet. I heard a quail whistle across the harvested field. There was an answering whistle from the draw bordering the field.

"I'm hanging with losers, aren't I?" Peter said.

I nodded. "Yeah, kid. You are."

He nodded his head. He looked at the trailer, then back. "I know," he said. "I just...I just don't have anybody else. Got nowhere else to go."

"Sure you do. It seems like that when you're young. Sometimes when you're older too. You got a lot ahead of you."

"This wasn't where I was heading when I started out," he said. "I was going to college, play some football, get a degree in graphic arts."

"Yeah, well, I'd think the son of a harmonica playing war hero would be able to change directions whenever he chose."

He smiled. I don't think I'd seen him smile before.

"Thanks, Mr. Storme," he said.

"Wyatt," I said, correcting him.

He nodded his head, eyes glistening. "You're all right, Wyatt."

"Don't let it get around."

The trailer door burst open, and Kerry Kane came tumbling down the steps. In the doorway stood Cameron Fogarty, a doobie hanging from his upper lip, a la James Dean. He laughed a marijuana laugh as Kane picked himself up off the ground.

"Kinda clumsy, aren't you, double K?" said Fogarty.

Braithwaite stood and helped Kane up. "Why don't you lay off him for a while?" said Braithwaite.

"Who the fuck you think you are, Petey?"

"I'm sick and tired of you, Cam," said Braithwaite, pointing at Fogarty. "You're an asshole."

Fogarty looked shocked at the statement. As shocked as someone can look under the hazy influence of cannabis.

"What's the matter with you?" said Fogarty, his arms out.

"I'm packing my shit and leaving," said Braithwaite. "I had enough of this. I had enough of you. I'll be back later to get my stuff."

"Hey, Peter. You owe me, man."

"I don't owe you shit, Cam. I don't owe anybody anything." He looked at Kane. "You want to go with me, Kerry?"

Kane looked at the big man for a moment. Then he looked at Fogarty. He dropped his eyes and shook his head.

"No, Pete," he said, "you go on without me."

Braithwaite looked at me and nodded. I returned the nod. Then he walked away in the direction of the road. I didn't know where he was going—maybe he didn't either, but it was somewhere else. And it was a start.

"Is everybody crazy?" asked Fogarty.

"Maybe just the opposite," I said.

THIRTY-NINE

Peter Braithwaite, after hitching a ride to town with one of the stunt men, spent the night at a motel. Maybe he was going to make it.

We can't always do what is right. We try to. We fumble around trapped in a psychic cocoon formed by experience, and it's hard to see out of it. And it seems safe in there because it is what we're accustomed to. But sometimes safety lulls us into inaction. So, even though we can't always do what is right, sometimes we just have to do what we can.

I wasn't idealistic enough to imagine that Peter Braithwaite's life would now be filled with happiness and success, but getting himself free from Cameron Fogarty's influence and decadent lifestyle was a good start. When he arrived at the point where he could forgive his father, then he would be free.

Had to start somewhere.

At six o'clock the next morning, I was sitting outside Chick's trailer drinking coffee, the dawn bleeding through a horizon spattered with purple-black clouds and the air thick with the smell of impending rain. Chick's eyes were bloodshot, and his manner was more subdued than normal, but otherwise he showed little of the effects of yesterday's drinking bout. The new bodyguard hired to replace Chick had arrived to relieve me of that duty.

We sat in molded plastic chairs at a folding table drinking coffee that we poured from a steel-lined thermos bottle. Chick was smoking cigarettes, occasionally rubbing his eyes. The coffee mug warmed my hands, and the vapors rose from the hot liquid to dissipate in the cool morning air. The nights were getting cooler, the days shorter, and the afternoon sun would glow with a diminished luminescence in the quiet blue sky. But at this moment, the morning sky was not in the mood to promise sunshine.

"Did I say several stupid things yesterday?" he asked me.

"Mostly it was incoherent babbling," I said.

"I rarely babble incoherently. I usually babble lyrically."

I sipped my coffee. Chick absently tapped the pack of Camels on the table, pondering something.

"That wasn't me yesterday," he said. "That was some guy with a gut full of bad medicine and a head full of damaged wiring. Caused the set screw on my mouth to shake loose."

"I never pay attention to you anyway," I said.

He nodded. "You shouldn't have to listen to that kind of crap from me."

"It's okay. I made a bunch of nine hundred calls from your cell phone."

"Well, I shouldn't have done that. Next time I want you to smack right in the mouth."

"Happy to," I said.

He grunted. Took a drag from his cigarette, then watched the exhaled cloud of smoke drift off into the growing dawn.

"I hadn't been shot in a while," Chick said. "I didn't like it."

"Nobody does."

"Used to not bother me."

"Maybe you got more reason to live now."

"Maybe I'm just getting older."

"It's about time."

He smiled.

"What's the deal with you and Darnell?" I asked.

"I'm irresistible. And charming. Handsome. And gentle. And—"

"Full of crap," I said, finishing it for him.

Chick blew another cloud of smoke into the air above us. He shrugged. "There's that."

I told him about my talk with Peter Braithwaite. Chick was uncharacteristically quiet after I finished. I watched as he chewed on the corner of his lower lip.

Finally he said, "That's a tough thing. For the kid and the dad both."

"Yeah."

He let out a breath and rocked back and forth. "Shit," he said, more to himself than to me. "Why does it happen?"

"I don't know," I said. "I don't have an answer. Thought about it a lot, though."

Chick nodded. We both understood about the depression that sometimes visited. A damnable shadow that left a cold ache like a frozen knife against an old bruise. A leftover from the Little War Nobody Loved. Peter Braithwaite's father didn't have anyone to share his with, and it took him down. Could've been Chick. Could've been me. Still could happen. Chick knew that. I knew that. It was hanging over us, and there was little either of us could do about it.

"You meet the new bodyguard?" I asked.

"Yeah," said Chick. "I talked to him. Filled him in on what has transpired so far."

"What do you think?"

"He'll do," said Chick. "He's big. Tough. Got his shit together."

I took another sip of coffee. "We still don't know who shot at you."

"Or where your buddy Rory is."

I nodded. "Turns out Michael was coerced to throw a game years ago. He didn't."

"What's that got to do with this?"

"I don't know," I said. "Maybe nothing. But it gives us another connection with the KC wise guys. Valeri Darnell's marksmanship is another factor."

"Maybe that eliminates her," Chick said. "A good shot with a rifle would have done a better job instead of spraying bullets all over the place."

"Unless she was nervous," I said. "She doesn't look like she shoots people on a regular basis."

"Besides," Chick said, "she didn't know about your rifle."

"Yeah," I said, agreeing.

"And she's a good kisser."

"That's certainly a consideration," I said.

"She wouldn't shoot me," said Chick.

"Not on purpose, anyway," I said. "But I don't think it's her."

"Good."

I looked across the horizon and watched a crow fly off the ridge. A starling followed the larger bird, harassing and pecking at it. Something tugged at my memory. I closed my eyes. I had it. I set my coffee mug down on the table and looked at Chick.

"You got something, don't you?" said Chick.

"Right in front of me all the time."

"What?"

"I think I know who shot you."

FORTY

had been so busy trying to figure out who I didn't want to think would kill Fogarty that I hadn't considered the whole scenario. Part of me hadn't wanted it to be Valeri Darnell or Rance Caraway. All of me didn't want it to be Michael LeBeau. Caraway had been a possibility, but he was on the set when Chick was shot. Maybe Chester, the male secretary with the big pecs, would like to see Fogarty out of the picture. A lot of suspects. A lot of hate.

But the wild card was my rifle. Besides Rory Marchibroda, only one other person had been close enough to my truck to have known about the rifle. Only one person had been inside the truck. And I had overlooked him.

Kerry Kane had been sitting in the backseat of the Jeep the night we accompanied the quartet out to the honky-tonk. He'd had an opportunity to notice the booted rifle under the seat. Maybe his foot had bumped it while he was sitting in the backseat. He definitely had reason. Fogarty treated Kane like a stray dog. He had been the butt of the star's abuse and the bottom rooster in a twisted pecking order. Kane was a disposable personality in Fogarty's world. But even Kane would have his point of stress, where he would either be broken for good or twisted into retaliation.

When I was in the service, we had a guy in our company, name of Simpkins, a skinny guy with a bad complexion, an Andy Gump chin, and a painful speech impediment that made him sound as if he were talking with a mouthful of marbles. A couple of failed abortions from the Bronx, guys with sand for brains and a vocabulary they'd learned squeezing out relatives in public toilets, picked on the kid relentlessly. I interceded a couple of times, but like my corporal told me, I couldn't be around all the time. They would trip up Simpkins from behind on patrol and urinate in his helmet liner when he would leave it unattended. When Simpkins would protest, they would imitate his speech impediment or slap him upside the head. They called him "Simp the Wimp."

One night the Bronx pair had loaded up on Jack Daniel's whiskey and Cambodian Red and passed out in their dugout. While they were unconscious, Simpkins bound his tormentor's hands and legs and taped their mouths shut with tape stolen from the medic. Once they were immobilized, Simpkins propped both men's legs up on sandbags. Then Simpkins climbed into the back of a Jeep and jumped off onto each man's exposed leg, snapping shins like dry plywood and shattering kneecaps as if they were robin's eggs.

One of them bit his tongue off and suffocated before we could get the tape off his mouth.

You never knew where a man's boiling point was.

I left Chick, who was not thrilled that I was going to confront the shooter alone. I pointed out that he was in no condition to back me this time. The hired bodyguard was waiting outside the trailer. He greeted me, and I asked if he'd seen Kerry Kane.

"No," he said. "He just left. About ten minutes ago. He and that bearded asshole took the rental. They didn't look the type used to being up this early. Said they was going to see the fat kid. The one stayed in town last night."

"How long have you been up?"

"Couple hours."

"Have you seen Fogarty this morning?" I asked.

"No. He's still in the rack. They were up late drinking and smoking dope. That movie star, Meagan Ames, was with him.

They were arguing about something but ended up in bed together. What's up?"

"You better check on him," I said.

"Why?"

"Chick was shot with my rifle," I said. "Which was under the seat in my truck. Kane may've known about the rifle."

The guy nodded. "Okay," he said. "I'll be right back."

He opened the door and disappeared into the trailer. After a few seconds, I heard him yell for me to come into the trailer.

I tore open the door and ran to the rear of the double-wide. The bodyguard was hunched over a figure on the bed. Fogarty. Meagan Ames was next to Fogarty, her nose pushed to one side of her face and a nasty cut like a huge fingernail slice across her right cheek. Like Fogarty, her mouth was taped, but unlike Fogarty, she had a breathing hole cut into the tape. There was something obscene stuffed up her nostrils.

Condoms.

Someone had shoved condoms up both nostrils. I moved around to the side of the bed, pulled the prophylactics from her nose, and checked her breathing. It was labored, but her vital signs were good. She moaned and rolled her head but remained unconscious.

"She's okay," I said. "So much for safe sex."

A spray of crimson marred the satin pillow next to Fogarty's head. The room was saturated with the stale smell of marijuana and cigarettes and the thick aroma of drying blood, which smelled like meat thawing on summer concrete.

"They cut his fucking ear off," said the bodyguard. There was blood all over his hands. "But I can't find it. Must've taped his mouth shut first so he couldn't yell out."

He ripped the tape from Fogarty's mouth, which made a sound like a wet towel tearing. "Aw shit," the guy said. "They stuck the ear in his fucking mouth. He's still breathing, but it's shallow. Get a doctor, and I'll give him CPR. Hurry!"

Using the cell phone, I hit 911. That done, I left the trailer and ran to find Geoffrey Salinger and the production company's doctor.

"Dammit, Storme," he said, opening the door. "You don't have to beat down my door."

He let me inside. He had been looking over some still shots, which were spread like fallen leaves on the table.

"Somebody tortured Fogarty and Meagan Ames," I said. "Fogarty's missing an ear, and Ames has a half-moon slash across her face."

"I'll get the medic over there and call a doctor," said Salinger.

Back at Fogarty's trailer, the bodyguard had managed to revive the wounded star. I asked him what kind of car Kane and Volts were in.

"It was one of those foreign jobs," he said. "An Infiniti or something like that. One of the fancy ones. Dark blue."

Chick came limping up on his crutches as I was getting into the Jeep to see if I could run them down.

"I'm going with you," he said.

"No, you're not," I said. "Doctor said for you to take it easy. Call the police."

I left them, started up the Jeep, and bumped down the rural road, a plume of dust trailing behind. I saw Chick in the rearview mirror, leaning on his crutches.

The morning dew glistened on the meadow grass and the thick weeds as I clicked down the country road. Plumes of fog seeped from the tree lines, and steam rose from the ditches.

I took a calculated gamble that Kane and Volts had lied to the bodyguard and weren't really going to visit Braithwaite in town. So when I hit the two-lane county blacktop, I turned left, instead of turning right, which would have taken me to town.

One mile down the road, the state maintenance ended, and the pavement collapsed into a rocky back road, which led deeper into the rural countryside. There was a black skid mark where the blacktop ended. I got out of the Jeep and checked to see if he had turned around. The road was narrow at this point, and I could detect no depression in the thick, wet grass where Kane would have performed a three-point turnaround. If he had turned around and headed back for the highway and town, the police were much better equipped to find him.

If they stayed on the gravel, Kane and Volts could continue about ten miles on a rough washboard road that would take them out of the county, where they could hit state 169, then jump across to Highway 71 leading either north to Kansas City or south to Joplin. If they reached KC, they could lose themselves in the bustle. If they went to Joplin, they could catch a bus or charter a private plane. Either way, the police might not think to cover 71, which was sixty-five miles west of Bailey's Crossing with no good way to get there.

I stayed on the gravel and prayed for a break.

I got one.

Three miles down the gravel road, there was a hairpin corner hidden by a sudden rise and the unmaintained weeds along the side of the road. The rise in the road and a tractor path in the middle of the curve gave the illusion that the road continued in a straight path. No problem for the locals who drove the road daily in their pickups and tractors, but a sudden adjustment for a city boy taxed by fatigue, drugs, and anxiety and sailing down the pitted road at highway speeds.

I saw the car. It lay on its back, the broken wheels at odd angles, like some prehistoric tortoise.

The car, a Lexus, sat overturned in a fallow pasture of weeds and fescue grass. The car had ripped through the barbed wire as if it were dental floss and then had taken a quarter revolution, digging a wake of dirt in the field before rolling.

I parked the Jeep and walked through the field to the vehicle, the damp weeds swishing against my legs and darkening my jeans to mid-thigh. I looked inside the damaged blue hulk. I saw

Volts in the passenger seat. His neck was elongated and hyperextended, the back of his head parallel and lying on the same plane as the line of his shoulders. His face was covered with blood, his mouth agape as if screaming at something in another dimension.

Kane was nowhere to be found. There was blood on the driver-side door and a depression in the grass where he had apparently pulled himself from the vehicle. Leading away from the car was a trail of bent fescue grass as if a gigantic slug had slithered through the damp vegetation.

Kane's trail led to a thicket of second-growth underbrush and centuries-old timber that covered the rolling hills and ridges for several square miles. In Missouri one could leave prairie and rolling plains and be suddenly plunged into an area as primitive and untouched as a primordial forest. As I stepped out of the sunlit pasture into the darkened forest, the air was damp and heavy with the smell of standing water and the syrupy aroma of decaying leaves. Pools of inky shadows stained the floor of the woodland, the refracted light seeping through a canopy of oak and locust trees as thick and dark as thunderclouds. I pushed through the brush, the wood limbs harsh against my hands and forearms.

Kane's trail was not difficult to follow. There were boot prints in the damp earth and fresh breaks in the skin of the brush, revealing the burnished white core and droplets of blood on leaves and smeared blood on limbs at waist level where he had pushed through.

Kane's footprints were halting and at varied lengths and directions due to his injuries or his indecision about which way to go. I found a spot where he had fallen, bruising a sapling at its base, and another spot where he had slid down a muddy bank, the trail of his body digging ruts in the bank.

I traced his sign for one hundred and fifty yards before I spotted him. He was lying on the ground in a washed-out depression.

I knelt behind a dead and broken locust tree and watched him. At first I thought he might be resting, but after watching for several moments, I ascertained he was injured and could not walk.

I had been in a hurry when I'd left and had not brought a weapon. I circled behind him, careful to keep a tree or other cover between us when possible. Finally, I was within spitting distance. He was unaware of my presence behind him. A crow squawked overhead. Kane was rocking back and forth and whimpering like a lost child. His hands and forehead were smeared with blood, his hair matted with mud and sweat, and his left foot lay at an odd angle. He had no weapon in his hands.

I stepped closer and said, "Didn't get very far, did you?"

He jerked around as if he had been yanked by a cable and yelped in surprise. He howled in agony when the involuntary movement scraped his injured leg along the ground.

"Oh shit!" he whined. He lay on his back, eyes squeezed shut and his chest heaving. "Oh shit." His chest spasmed, and his shoulders shuddered. "I think I broke my ankle," he said, sobbing. "Man, I'm fucking dying. It hurts. Ooohh, it hurts."

"I'll bet it does. I'm having a difficult time garnering any sympathy," I said. "You didn't extend much to Fogarty and Meagan Ames."

"I didn't do that. That...that was Volts. He did that."

"Why don't I believe you?"

"The...truth." He sucked in his breath between clenched teeth. "I need a doctor."

"I'd say you did too. But you don't shoot me straight, all you're going to get is gangrene and left here to contemplate the pain that is going to increase moment by moment"—I pointed at the ankle—"when the shock wears off."

"Okay, okay," he said. He sucked in his lower lip. "Here's what happened, you gotta believe me, man. Meagan came over and started coming on to Volts. She was trying to piss Fogarty off, but it wasn't working. He just laughed at her. Then she got Volts all worked up and hot before Fogarty took her away from him."

"How did Fogarty do that?"

"Like he does everything. He just nodded at her, and she jumped up and left Volts with the blue balls and breathing hard." He bit his lower lip and closed his eyes again. "Oh man, this hurts. You gotta get me some help."

"Not yet," I said. "Then what happened?"

"Volts got pissed and said it wasn't right for her to do him that way. Leaving him with a boner like a phone pole. Cam told him to go knock it down with a hammer, then things settled down, but you could see Volts was pissed. Cam kept digging at him, laughing at Volts and telling him to go yank on it or find one of the horses. We got to smoking dope and drinking tequila. Then Cam and her got into the ludes, and they went to his bedroom. They were staggering around barely awake when they went to the back. Anyway, Volts started eating PCP and greens and getting hisself all wired up. Then he started talking shit about the way Cam treated him and me and how it was time we did something about it."

"Which was cutting the two of them up?"

"Yeah. But Volts did all of it by himself."

I shook my head. "You'd better be a little more forthcoming, or I'm going to tie that leg to a tree and leave you here while I get the police."

"I didn't cut his ear off," he said.

"But maybe you slashed him some and stuck his ear in his mouth."

"You don't know how he is. He's a bastard."

"Yeah, I know. Recognized it right off," I said. "What irritates me most is that you shot Chick."

"I didn't do that."

"You're a liar."

"Honest, man, I didn't do it."

"You had to," I said. "You're the only one who could've known about the rifle."

He swallowed. I watched his face. He wasn't going to confess. He knew that was the end if he did.

"Well," I said, "you can explain it all to the sheriff. I'll fix the leg and get you out of here."

I looked at his leg. It was swollen and tender to the touch. I splinted the injury using a couple of branches off a fallen tree, then lashing the wood to his leg with my handkerchief and strips of cloth I tore from his shirt. He helped by moaning and whining the whole time.

With his arm over my shoulder, we limped out of the thicket, a three-legged beast inching and hopping along. When we reached the creek bed, I slung him over my shoulder in the fireman's carry and hauled him across. By the time we reached the point where I entered the woods, I was sweating freely.

I leaned Kane against a huge, gnarled oak tree, whitened with death, and paused to catch my breath and loosen the knot in my shoulders.

That's when I heard a noise. Behind me.

FORTY-ONE

Rory Marchibroda was driving out to the movie set when he spotted the Jeep barreling down the highway. Couldn't believe his luck.

"About time I got a break," he said out loud as he watched the football player's Jeep turn off onto the two-lane county road. Shit, the guy about took the corner on two wheels. What was his hurry?

But it didn't matter. What mattered was that he'd made the guy, and whatever was on Superstar's mind would make him less likely to see Rory tailing him. It would help that he'd ditched the Caddy and hot-wired a white Chevrolet pickup in a Walmart parking lot. Must be about a million of these crates here in yokel valley. Wouldn't even stand out. It had mud-splattered sides and best of all, a gun rack with a loaded Remington pump shotgun hanging on it. There was a baseball cap on the floorboard with a tractor logo on its crown. Rory had jammed it on his head when he'd left the Walmart parking lot. No way would Superstar recognize him in the old truck with the shitkicker hat on.

On the floorboard he had something special he had brought for the occasion—a cut-down baseball bat.

He continued up the road before turning around to follow the Jeep. The plan was to follow at a safe distance, which wasn't a problem, since the football player had his foot clear through the firewall of the Jeep.

It was starting to rain when Rory spotted the Jeep pulled over to the side of the road. Rory backed off the pedal. He couldn't tell if the guy was still in the Jeep, so he pulled the brim of his hat down further on his head and turned the windshield wipers off. As the truck rolled down the rutted road, Rory eased the stolen .357 closer to his leg, getting it ready in case the guy recognized him, which he didn't think would happen. Just some old farmer guy out to check his cows or hogs, or whatever the clodhoppers did. Ease by the Jeep, ask about the weather or some other hay-seed bullshit, nobody here but us country bumpkins, then raise the Magnum. Surprise, motherfucker.

But there was nobody in the truck. Off across the field, he saw a blue car upside down. Had rental plates on it.

Rory got out of the truck to take a look. Nobody around. Where'd they go? He stuck the Magnum in his waistband and walked around the wrecked car, where he could see the footprints and mashed weeds leading off into the woods. He also saw a dead guy he didn't recognize inside the car with his head pushed into his armpit. Rory walked back to the pickup and got the shortened bat out of the truck. He hefted it and smiled. Yeah, play a tune on asshole's head, see how he liked having it turned around on him.

It was starting to rain harder when he followed the smashed-down trail through the weeds to the woods. His fingers flexed on the bat handle as he walked along humming a Tony Bennett tune. He stepped into the woods and after about fifty yards, stopped and gave it some thought. Thought about the night at Superstar's cabin. The football player lived out in this shit like he was fuck-ing Kit Carson. If Rory followed him farther into the woods, he would be on the guy's terms, which might not be a good thing.

While he was thinking about it, Rory saw someone coming up through the woods. He ducked behind a thick tree that looked like it was about three hundred years old and watched the two men approach. One of them was being half dragged, half carried by the other guy. The other guy was Storme. They weren't mak-ing any effort to conceal their approach. Of course they weren't, Rory, you dope, they weren't expecting anyone.

Least of all, they weren't expecting Rory Marchibroda. Superstar had finally made a mistake. A big one. And this time Rory wasn't going to underestimate the guy. No talking this time. First take him down, then you can do what you want. That was the way to do it. Get a good lick in on him, then talk.

As they got closer, Rory could hear the guy's breathing. He was carrying the other guy now—son of a bitch was strong as a horse—and they were going to pass right by the tree Rory was hiding behind. Rory tightened his grip on the rain-slick bat.

Storme stopped and set the other guy next to a tree. When he did, Rory stepped out, raised the bat, and brought it down across Storme's back at the point where the shoulder and neck converged. A noise came out of Superstar like someone had punctured a trash bag full of air, and he fell to his knees, rolled over on the ground, and didn't move. Damn, maybe he'd hit him too hard. He didn't want the guy to die. He wanted to mess with him some.

Then he heard the big guy groan and stir on the ground. Good. Superstar was okay. For now.

The guy with the messed-up leg started to scream, but Rory stopped it by smashing an elbow into the guy's face.

"Shut the fuck up," Rory said as the injured man lay on the ground, mewling and moaning.

The guy looked familiar to Rory for some reason. Where the hell had he seen him before? He looked at him for a while, then he remembered.

"Yeah, I know you," Rory said. "You're the guy shot up Superstar's buddy. I appreciate that. This is going to be more fun than I thought."

FORTY-TWO

Just as I leaned Kane against the tree, I heard a rustling sound behind me that sent a wave of realization and fear down my spine. I felt a whisper of air by my ear right before a heavy, dull pain shot through my shoulders and neck like an electric current borne on steel cable.

And darkness flooded into my head like a shadow.

…Rain against my face. Moist, silty taste of mud, which was gritty on my lips and between my teeth. My left arm felt numb—as if it were a long way from me and not a part of me—almost as if it were in another dimension.

When I moved, a bolt of pain shot through my arm and back as if someone had jammed a long, steel needle through my shoulder. I sucked in my breath and squeezed my eyes shut, teeth clamped together. Then, blessedly, the numbness returned.

I heard a voice behind me, whimpering like a sick calf. Kane. Heavy thud against my rib cage, sending shivers of agony through my body.

"Wake up, asshole," said a voice. A voice towering high above me. "You don't get off that easy. Your Uncle Rory's here."

I rolled over, and looking up, I saw Rory Marchibroda, nine feet tall and framed by tree limbs, rain slapping off his shoulders. "That's right," he said, smiling, "it's me. Didn't think I'd forget, didja? And this time I got the bat. How do you like that? Some great shit, huh?"

Then the smile disappeared as his teeth gritted together, contorting his face into a mask of hate. He kicked me again. A low noise escaped between my teeth. I tried to roll away from him and get to my feet, but the shoulder betrayed me, and I lay there in the mud and the damp like a broken toy.

"Does that hurt?" he asked me. "Yeah, I think it does. Remember when you fucked me up in the nigger's coffee shop? Yeah, you do. How you like it?"

"What...do you want?" I said.

"What do I want? I want your ass, Superstar, that's what I want. I'm going to bust you up." He brought the bat down on my thigh before I could roll away. It felt like he'd slammed a garage door down on me. "A piece at a time. That's how it's going to happen. And there ain't shit you can do about it, dick head." He brought the bat down two more times. "Come on, say something smart." He kicked me in the stomach. A string of saliva hung from his mouth, and he was breathing hard. "Ain't you got something funny to say? I wanna hear it."

I tried to cover up. The feeling returned to my left shoulder. I bit down hard so I wouldn't scream.

Kane started to whimper. "Oh shit, oh no. Oh shit, oh God."

"Shut up, you little pussy," said Rory, turning his head to look at Kane. He raised the bat and took a step at Kane.

"Nooo!" wailed Kane. "Don't hit me, please."

While Rory was turned away, I rolled his direction and took a swipe at the back of his leg, just below the calf, in an attempt to knock him off his feet. But I couldn't get any leverage with the bad shoulder, which burned and howled with pain, and I was only able to stagger him. When he tottered, I tried to push myself off the ground and grab his jacket or belt but fell short on the attempt. I wrapped my arm around his knee and tried to pull him down.

He dropped to one knee and came around with the bat, smashing it against my ribs again. I felt something give way like a rubber thong popping loose. I was unable to keep from crying out in agony. I rolled into a fetal ball and hugged myself. There was a metallic taste in my mouth like I had a mouthful of pennies. Blood. I had bitten my tongue. I spat and felt warm liquid trickle down the side of my mouth.

He prodded me with the bat. Gently, as if testing meat to see if it was tender enough. "You better not try that shit again, Superstar," Rory said. "What's your hurry, anyway? We got all day."

I didn't say anything. Tried to keep my head together, not think about the pain, and think of a way out of this. I was miles from anywhere and two hundred yards from the road. It was too early for some farmer to go to town for supplies. I hadn't seen any cattle for a farmer to come and check on. Just a beat-up football player, a scared kid, and a social deviate alone in the silent forest. The rain beating down.

The rain didn't care.

"Just...get it over with," I said.

Kane began whining again. "I thought I told you to shut up," said Rory. He kicked the kid hard, and Kane wailed. Rory ripped up a handful of weeds and shoved them into Kane's mouth. Kane choked and coughed and spat.

"Now keep your fucking hole shut, or I'll jab a stick in your throat. Y'understand?"

"Leave him alone, Rory," I said with difficulty. "It's me you want."

"You're a noble bastard, aren't you?" said Rory. "But you're wasting it on this piece of shit. He's the one shot up your buddy, what's his name."

"How...how do you know that?" I asked. I searched the ground for a rock, a branch, anything I could use for a weapon. Keep him talking, buy some time. I spotted a rock about the size of a baseball four feet away. How to get close to it, though?

"I watched him do it," said Rory. "I was sitting up on a hill with a scoped rifle when all of a sudden, it's amateur night, and junior here starts popping caps. Course, he ain't good at it, so he don't get it done. But it put your buddy out of action, and that's all I needed."

"You're wrong about that," I said, ready to try anything, even a bluff. "Chick's here with me. He's not hurt all that bad. He circled around to see if he could cut off the kid. He'll be coming back this way anytime now. Sheriff will be along too."

"That right?" said Rory, big smile on his face. "You're a lying sack a shit, you know that? I saw you on the road. You come alone. Who you think you're talking to here? Some hick with cow shit on his shoes?"

"No," I said. "More like some gutless jerk-off with paste for brains who can't face me man-to-man."

For my comment I took another boot to the side, but it allowed me to propel myself closer to the rock I'd seen. An arm's length away now.

"If I were you, I'd show a little more wisdom before I opened my hole again, y'know? I mean, you only got so many more things to say before you don't say nothing ever again. That connect for you, Superstar? Now," he said, kneeling beside me, "like that jig said in that Tarantino flick, 'I'm gonna go medieval on your ass.'"

"Anything beats listening to you talk," I said, coughing. But I felt fear creeping into my head, slimy and cold.

He stood up, looked down at me, and said, "Well, smartass, it's time you learned to keep your mouth shut." He brought the bat down, and I rolled away from it and grabbed the rock. I sat up and threw it at him. It struck him in the chest, and he reeled backward, his eyes closed. With my good arm, I pushed myself to my feet and ran. I figured my only chance was to run. I was too beat-up to launch any kind of attack.

I crashed through the brush, branches slapping and raking my face. My insides felt like broken glass moving around in there. I was unable to gain any appreciable semblance of speed due to the cracked ribs and bad shoulder. I staggered and lurched ahead like a drunken man rather than a former professional athlete.

I heard Rory pounding behind me, cursing. Thunder boomed and rolled.

The forest jumped ahead of me, tilting and bouncing like a bad dream.

Though the injuries slowed me, I knew if I could stay ahead of him, I would eventually wear him out and escape. He had to know that also. There was light ahead of me where the woods opened up to the field.

If I reached the field, I might make it. If I didn't fall, if my knee didn't give out, I might live.

Unless he had a gun. Then he would just shoot me. At least it would be quick. Amazing what you'll settle for.

We scrambled and staggered through the woods, pain stabbing through my body with each step, the labored breathing of my executioner behind me. Branches cut my face, and the pain in my ribs and shoulder was unwavering. I was nearing the edge of the open field, where my longer strides and better conditioning would be an advantage to me.

I was going to make it.

Then I felt a sudden impact between the shoulder blades; a heavy, solid object struck me as if a large fist had punched me, the force of the blow causing me to pitch forward and lose my balance. I banged off the side of a tree and tripped over a sapling. I landed on my back, arms and legs splayed out, my head thumping the ground.

When my head cleared, I saw Rory picking up the bat he'd thrown at me. He walked my direction, then stood over me, purple-faced, his hands on his knees, sucking in big gulps of air, the sweat dripping out of his raven-black hair and rolling down his dark jowls in rivers. If I had been able to extend the chase just a few more yards, he would have been too exhausted to continue.

I looked across the open field. So close. Almost there. But now it was fourth and long, and I wasn't going to make it.

Nothing was said for several moments while he regained his wind, and I lay there in the clearing soaked with rainwater and perspiration, unable to move. I felt the first pangs of despair at the inevitability of the situation. My body was damaged and drained of the ability to respond. I couldn't think of anything heroic to say, felt only anger at having to die at the hands of a cretin like Rory Marchibroda. It wasn't the way it was supposed to end. But then, how was it supposed to end? Whether it was the silent bullet in a jungle on the opposite rim of the world, the truck barreling down the on-ramp with a white-knuckled driver, wired to the teeth on some pharmaceutical, or pushing the button for the nursing home orderly while arteriosclerosis squeezed and clicked with metallic talons, the end result—whatever torment or circumstance or sick irony precedes it—remains the same. You're just dead.

"Well, asshole," said Marchibroda, his breath still coming in bursts, but more controlled, "you've been way more trouble than this is worth." He put a hand to his chest and winced. "That's gonna raise a welt like a grapefruit where you hit me with that rock. Gonna hurt tomorrow, but that won't matter, 'cause I'll have the memory of beating the shit outta you to make me feel better. Before this is over, you're gonna be begging me to kill you. And when you reach that point, I'm gonna make it last a little longer."

I didn't speak. I concentrated on steeling myself against what was to come. The only thing I could do now was deprive him of the satisfaction of hearing me scream or beg or cry, though the inevitability of the moment when I broke was a more chilling thought than death itself. Pain makes cowards of us all. I'd seen it too many times to believe it couldn't happen to me.

The blue-gray clouds overhead framed Rory like a mythological warrior as he raised the bat to the sky. Lightning crackled and flashed overhead. I curled into a ball and felt my teeth grind together in anticipation of the unthinkable.

And waited for the gruesome finish.

Then I heard the sweep of footsteps, as if a large animal were running swiftly across the grass, and the sound of a man grunting with physical effort. I'd heard the same sound a thousand times waiting to haul in a pass while a cornerback measured me for a hit.

I peeked through folded arms just in time to see Michael LeBeau take out Rory Marchibroda with a full body block. Marchibroda had heard him and managed to turn an instant before impact. Rory got the bat between them before they crashed to the ground. The air whooshed out of Rory when he hit the ground, but LeBeau lay on the ground as if he had fallen from a tree.

LeBeau looked at me, and I saw the purple knot across his forehead where he had made contact with the bat. Through the middle of the purple knot ran a jagged ebony crease, which was bleeding. His eyes were dilated and glazed.

"Fucking nigger," said Rory, getting to his feet. Reaching into his jacket, he produced a nickel-plated revolver. LeBeau tried to sit up, but Rory shot him in the leg. LeBeau yelled and grabbed his leg.

"I had enough of this shit," Rory said, wiping sweat and rain and mud from his face. "First, Rastus gets his, then you, Storme."

LeBeau rolled his head my direction. "I didn't throw that game, Wyatt," he said, between clenched teeth. "I...didn't."

I tried to speak but couldn't make the words form. My head hurt, like someone shoved an icicle behind my eyes.

Rory clicked back the hammer of the gun, and I made a gut-tearing lunge at him, which became a sickening feeling when I fell short. He kicked me in the head, and the world began to spin away from me. Nausea tickled my throat. I felt a rain of stones against my back and shoulders, pushing me against the earth and grinding the air out of my lungs.

Through the pain I heard an angry wasp sizzling overhead, then a noise like a ball bearing striking a carpeted floor, followed by a popping sound off in the distance, as if someone were shooting off firecrackers. I looked at Rory Marchibroda, who was swaying like a scarecrow in a high wind, his hand over his heart. He had a puzzled expression on his face, as if pondering something strange and mystical. When his hand came away from his chest, it was syrupy and crimson with blood. He looked at the hand with the same puzzled look.

He held the hand up for me to see. There was a faraway look in his eyes. He gave an odd half laugh and said, "Where...Can you believe it?" He took a couple of faltering steps before his eyes rolled back in his head and he slumped to the ground.

I looked at LeBeau through blurred vision and tried to speak again, but instead my mouth worked like a beached fish's. I looked at Michael LeBeau, and the countryside behind him seemed to swim and shimmer and spin.

"Chick," said LeBeau. "He came with—"

But that was the last thing I heard before the spinning landscape whirled and spat and shrank away from me.

FORTY-THREE

I was alone. Alone and a long way from home. It was a land of distant lights and strange voices in the sky and colors without names. I was changed and confused, yet not always afraid. There was a white beach. And a sea like silver discs. I sat on the beach and watched exotic birds float across the rainbowed sky and disappear like so many subconscious thoughts. I was thirsty and tried to drink the seawater, which had the consistency of mercury, and when I raised it to my lips, it had no taste. I picked up a handful of sand, and it sparkled and slipped through my fingers like fine gold dust.

Then the sun burst into a long, white flash, hurting my eyes.

I awoke in a pastel room of neutral aromas, with the smooth, low hum of climate-control machinery and the gray hiss of a television. My left arm felt heavy and swollen, and there was a tightness in various places on my body as if I were bound with something.

I croaked something unintelligible and saw the silhouette of a man stand and move toward me.

"Well, I'll be damned," a familiar voice said. "There is a God."

"Thirsty," I said.

I heard the clink of ice and the tiny rush of water poured from a pitcher. A plastic glass with a straw in it was placed near my mouth. I pulled on the straw and felt the moisture cooling and lubricating my mouth. I had never been so thirsty.

"Hey!" Chick Easton said to a young woman in a nurse's uniform. "Need a doctor in here. He's awake. Hurry up."

My eyes cleared, and I saw Chick standing over me. He was wearing a shoulder holster with a cocked automatic pistol sheathed in it, the hammer thong unbuttoned. "You would wake up in the middle of *Days of our Lives*," he said.

I blinked my eyes, then widened them. Couldn't lift my arms. One arm was bound in tape and plaster, the other had a tube protruding from it, leading to a clear bag hanging upside down from a metal tree. Wires led from me to a machine with a monitor that blipped like sonar on the screen.

"Where am I?" I asked.

"MU Med Center," said Chick. "They life-flighted you here. You've been out like a light since yesterday morning. Sandy's on her way."

"Michael?"

"He's all right. Had a concussion, and they put three stitches in his forehead. The bullet passed through his leg, didn't hit a bone. He's stove-up for a while, though. He's one tough son of a bitch. Even with the bullet wound, he helped me drag you back to the truck. He was bleeding all over the place. He's in the next room."

"How…," I began. "What happened? Where's Marchibroda?"

"Glory Rory? I had to sort of dispatch him a little. I rested the Contender on one of my crutches and busted him right through the heart and one lung. Two hundred fifty yards. Didn't even have to walk the bullet up. Hell of a shot. And you didn't want to take me with you."

"Thanks," I said.

"You haven't seen my bill yet. Heroic deeds cost."

"Why're you carrying a weapon, and why is it cocked?"

"Oh, that? Aw, the police got some crazy ideas about me answering questions about what happened. We had a disagreement about where we were going to do that. They wanted me to go downtown, and I said they could ask the questions here. Then they got all indignant like cops do and asked for my gun, and we had another disagreement about that, and we've been more or less arguing for the past several hours. Them telling me I'm going to jail, me saying not yet. Them threatening to take me by force, me telling them what a good shot I was and lying about how many extra clips I have on me."

"You shouldn't have done that."

"We still aren't sure Rory wasn't hired by Bobby Frank Ventura, so I thought I'd stick around a while. Your buddy, Sheriff Statler, smoothed things over with the locals. They finally took my statement here in this room. The head nurse didn't care for it, but it got done. The cops're still grumpy, but they'll get over it."

A fiftyish man with wavy brown-and-silver hair, wearing a white doctor's coat, bustled into the room, followed by a plump nurse with a severe expression on her face that became more so when she saw Chick.

"Are you still here?" she said.

"That's her," said Chick. "The one I told you about. Hot damn, I'm crazy for her."

"You need to leave now," said the nurse.

"Not yet," said Chick.

The doctor thumbed my eyelid wider, looked into my eyes, shined a penlight into them, and asked Chick how long I'd been awake. "Five minutes," answered Chick.

"I'm surprised you didn't shoot us when we came in," said the severe nurse, her hands on her hips and glaring at Chick.

"Thought about it some," said Chick. "But I figured with us getting engaged and all..."

The nurse made some kind of dismissive gesture that included an unspoken obscenity, then she and the doctor checked my blood pressure and other vital signs while Chick kept talking.

"Fogarty's going to be all right. They flew him out to the coast so a plastic surgeon in LA could save the ear. Sheriff Statler found drugs in the trailer. Statler has issued a warrant for Fogarty's arrest and is filing extradition papers. You know Statler won't let go either. Marchibroda was responsible for the convenience store killing. Also for killing two teenage boys over in Gilmore." He explained how Marchibroda had killed two drug dealers, stole their car, and then hired the two teens to drive it back to Kansas City. I remembered what Statler had said about my lack of cooperation leading to the deaths of two teenage boys. I wasn't very proud of that.

"Something else," said Chick. "Apparently, the Paradise police were already on to Rory. He roughed up some teenage kid. Guy's a one-man crime wave."

"I should have let you take care of Marchibroda," I said. "Then maybe those two kids would still be alive."

"Can't think like that," said Chick. "Rory's off the bus for good."

"What about Kane?"

"He's in critical condition in the Paradise County hospital and has been placed under arrest for attempted murder, felonious assault, and reckless driving." Chick looked at the head nurse. "Reckless driving," he said to the austere woman. "That's a joke."

"Well, I wouldn't know," she said, ignoring him. Chick smiled, enjoying himself.

The doctor stood up. "Your vital signs are good, but I want to run more tests." He looked at Chick. "And I'd like to take a look at your wounds," he said. "You need to get some rest." To me, the doctor said, "Your friend's been awake since you got here. And he ripped open his puncture wounds when he dragged you and the other man back to the truck. I don't know what you two have been doing, but I'd recommend you avoid it in the future."

"I thought you said Michael helped you drag me," I said to Chick, who was pretending to watch television.

The doctor looked at Chick, then back at me. He shook his head. "It seems your friend is clinging to this story for whatever reason. Truth is, LeBeau had a concussion and was in shock from the leg wound. There was no possible way LeBeau could have helped. I don't know how he did it, but you wouldn't be alive now if your friend here hadn't dragged you out."

I looked at Chick, who shrugged. "So I drove the Jeep down to you. It was easy."

"And in the process opened up those wounds again. I redressed the wounds," said the doctor, "though he was difficult, even surly about it. He refused vaccination."

"I'm afraid of needles," said Chick, digging a pack of cigarettes out of his shirt pocket.

"He accused me of trying to sedate him at the request of the police."

Chick placed a cigarette in his mouth.

"Put those cigarettes away right now," said the nurse, her hands on her hips. "There is no smoking allowed in this hospital."

"I would never smoke in your gulag," said Chick. "I just like to hold it in my mouth."

"You have been smoking, because I smelled it," said the nurse. "He has been smoking late at night, Dr. Cummings, and ordering in takeout food and liquor. That's why I had the phone disconnected."

"She's too clever for me," said Chick, taking a sip from a pint bottle of Jack Daniel's and pulling his cell phone from his jacket pocket. "You want a pizza, Wyatt?"

After an hour of further tests and looking at X-rays, a nurse wheeled me back into my room. Chick stayed with me during the entire session. When we returned to the room, he sat back in the visitor's vinyl chair and folded his arms on his chest.

"Besides the cracked ribs and the damage to the shoulder, there are multiple contusions and lacerations," said the doctor. "There isn't any internal bleeding, which surprises me. You're a tough individual. You sustained a concussion that has me concerned. The CT scan showed no blockage, and the X-rays don't reveal anything that cannot be healed with rest and time. But these types of injuries are tricky. And dangerous. In my twenty-five years in medicine, I have rarely seen anyone so badly beaten without sustaining permanent injury. You are very fortunate the blows to the head did not cause long-term damage."

"He wanted me conscious during the beating," I said.

"Well," said the doctor, "we're going to keep you around here for a few more days. But I think by the end of the week, you'll be able to go home, and after about six weeks of total rest, I think you'll be on your way to a full recovery. Are you hungry?"

"Yeah," I said.

"I'll have them send something up."

"He's going to be all right then?" asked Chick.

The doctor nodded. "He will be if you don't sign him up for the rodeo or rec league football for a few weeks."

The doctor left the room. Within moments the food arrived, and I didn't even notice that it tasted like cardboard. In fact, I became preoccupied with the task of cutting, forking, chewing, and swallowing.

When I'd finished eating, Chick and I talked for a while.

"How'd you and Michael get there?" I asked.

"I appropriated Salinger's Jeep," said Chick. "He was hesitant at first but became more enthusiastic while I was pinching his lower lip. LeBeau drove me."

"How'd you know which way to go?" I asked.

"Really didn't until we saw a white pickup truck barreling down the road. We took a chance and followed it. Paid off. It was Rory. He'd stolen the truck. We got there and saw your truck and the pickup and the wrecked car. LeBeau jumped out and followed the tracks. I told him to wait, but he wouldn't listen. So, I thought I'd circle up ahead and try to cut Rory off, which turned out to be a mistake. I was about two hundred yards away when I saw LeBeau tackle Rory. Gave me time to get a bead."

"That was a quite a shot," I said. "Had you missed, that was it."

He nodded. "Yeah." He said it in a soft voice. "I thought about that. Tried not to. Did a lot of that kind of thing back…But it was the first time there was really anything at stake if I missed." His lips formed a thin line, and through the aperture I saw his teeth grit together briefly.

"I just couldn't miss," he said.

"Well, thanks."

Chick had that funny look again, like the day I'd told him about Braithwaite's father's suicide.

"You okay?" I asked.

"Huh?" he said. "Yeah. Sure." His front and bottom teeth were set in an even white line, as if in pain. "I thought this movie thing would be like one big party for you and me. It would've been weird if I'd have been killed by accident and you'd have been killed by some guy out of your past. All that time in during the wars, sneaking around, getting shot at…I expected it then. After I got shot, I started getting gloomy and dismal about being crippled up. It made me feel impotent. Didn't like the feeling."

I nodded.

He looked away, pretending to watch television again.

I dozed off, and when I awakened, Chick was slumped in the visitor's chair. He was doing something I hadn't seen him do before.

He was asleep.

Later, he even snored.

FORTY-FOUR

Chick was in a festive mood.

"Please fasten your seat belts," said the soothing intercom voice. "We will be arriving at Los Angeles International Airport as scheduled, which is four oh five Pacific time. The weather in Los Angeles is warm and sunny. The temperature is eighty-seven degrees. We hope you enjoyed your flight, and thank you for flying Southwest Airlines."

Chick and I picked up our luggage, picked up keys at the Hertz desk, then shuttled out to the rental lot to pick up the red Chevrolet the travel agent had arranged for us. We stepped off the shuttle, and I felt the heat shimmering off the concrete baked by the Southern California sun. The temperature in Missouri had been in the forties when we left KCI. It had been a month since the incidents in Missouri. Chick's limp was gone, and the soreness in my ribs had subsided, but I was still moving slowly and experienced some trouble with migraine headaches, though they were subsiding in intensity and frequency with each passing day.

Chick swung the Monte Carlo into the stream of traffic on the expressway. Los Lobos was playing hot Mex-rock on the radio. A sooty haze hung over the traffic, and the bumpers from a million cars gleamed in the sunlight.

"You think he'll be glad to see us?" said Chick. He was sipping beer from a green Heineken can he had pirated from the plane and singing along with the radio.

"I don't see why not," I said.

"I'm going to be glad to see him," said Chick.

"I can see that."

Chick drove directly to the county sheriff's office to check in. He was wearing his bounty hunter persona today. The LA County sheriff's office wasn't anything like Carney Statler's office back in Truman County. LA County looked more like a city police station than what I was used to—guys in suits and ties, shoulder holsters worn over trendy shirts rather than brown uniforms and cowboy boots. Chick was looking for a deputy he knew named Ramirez. We found him in the break room, getting a cup of coffee.

When Chick told Ramirez why we were in California, he said, "You're going to do what?"

"I'm going to pick up Cameron Fogarty," Chick said. "He skipped back in Missouri. He and his lawyer have been sidestepping extradition, but the bondsman is out big bucks. So, I'm taking him back." Chick lit a cigarette. "I'm hoping he resists."

"Yeah," said the deputy, a handsome Hispanic man with dark hair that curled in front like Superman's. "I'd like to see that. We've had some trouble with that gringo in the past. He called the undersheriff 'a cheap hired geek' because we processed him for a disturbance complaint. It'd be nice to bust his door down."

"You might as well come along," said Chick.

"Man, that'd be all right," he said. "But the sheriff would fry my butt if I was to go rousting movie stars accompanied by out-of-state bounty hunters."

"Gonna miss the fun," said Chick.

Ramirez looked around the station. Smiled. "You know," he said, "I've got a supper break coming up. I might accidentally eat close to where you could find your skip. Let me make a couple calls. I'll be right back."

Five minutes later Ramirez returned. He had a big smile on his face. "I've got the perfect place. Great restaurant over in Bel-Air. It's out of our jurisdiction, but the place could use a little seasoning. I'd say a Chicano cop and a couple of Midwest hicks would be just about right.

"You're going to love this. Fogarty and Salinger play racquet-ball together twice a week," said Ramirez. "Five thirty, Mondays and Thursdays. They'll be out there. I can get you inside the place, got a friend who works there, but after that you're on your own. And I mean on your own. You don't even know me if anybody asks."

"Can you get me a piece?" said Chick. "You know, for old time's sake."

"A gun?" said Ramirez. "You and a gun at the Bel-Air Racquet Club? Hell, no."

After eating we followed Ramirez's plain Jane Ford to the Bel-Air Racquet Club, an exclusive tennis and racquetball center complete with swimming pools, live plants, weight room, and all the glitter that money could rent.

As claimed, Ramirez was able to get us past security and inside the complex, which was a combination of the Astrodome and the Taj Mahal. Sleek Californians in designer tennis out-fits and sleek, liquid-colored tights gave us curious looks as we passed by.

"Have you noticed we're the only ones here wearing pants?" I said.

"You need to work on your tan," said Chick.

"Are you kidding?" I said. "I feel right at home here. I'm thinking about joining."

"Yeah, you blend. It's what the place needs. Some gimpy guy looks like a Busch beer commercial."

We found Fogarty in an interior cafe bordered by glass-walled racquetball courts. He was wearing a white tennis outfit with a matching headband. The reattached ear was sticking out at a strange angle and looked to be a half inch lower than the other side. The headband made it worse.

Meagan Ames, also in full leisure regalia, was with Fogarty, and another young beauty was seated. Chester, the beach boy secretary, was also with them—he was not dressed for sport, as he was the hired help. There was a bottle of wine in a clear ice bucket. The three Hollywood types had goblets of the golden vintage in front of them on the table. Fogarty and Salinger and Ames looked like they belonged on the cover of a Southern California tourist guide—sun-bronzed flesh, capped teeth, their practiced personalities polished to a high sheen. It took your breath away.

As we approached the table, Fogarty looked up. Recognizing us, he closed his eyes, shook his head, and said, "Shit."

"Told you he'd be glad to see us," said Chick.

"Why are you here?" asked Salinger.

"Thought we'd catch up on old times," I said, "Maybe get in a game or two."

"This is an exclusive club," said Fogarty.

"Aw, c'mon, Cam," said Chick. "How exclusive can it be if you're a member?"

"Look," said Fogarty. "What the hell do you guys want? There's no reason I ever have to see you again. You understand that? Shit, what idiots."

"You skipped bail back in Missouri," said Chick. "Sheriff's kinda mad at you. The prosecutor's kinda mad at you. The state of Missouri's upset also. Worse, the bail bondsman is extremely perturbed. You left him holding the bag."

"Yeah," said Fogarty. "So, who gives a shit, huh? Why don't you two lame assholes hop a Missouri donkey and head back to hillbilly valley."

"Mule," I said. "We have mules in Missouri. We had a jackass once, and we followed it back here."

"Great job on the ear, Cam," said Chick. Big smile.

Fogarty's hand raised instinctively toward the damaged ear. He caught himself and put his hand on the table.

"We can do this nice and easy," Chick said to Fogarty. "If you'll just be compliant and serene, it could go that way."

"Get lost," said Fogarty.

Chick smiled. "I knew you wouldn't let me down." Chick reached under his shirt. There was a flash of silver, and before Fogarty could react, Chick had snapped the Smith & Wesson handcuffs on the actor's wrist.

Meagan Ames jumped up out of her chair. "You can't do that. This isn't done."

"Take it easy, sweetheart," said Chick. "This is way over your head."

"Get security," said Fogarty as Chick pulled a struggling Fogarty up out of his seat. Fogarty tried to swing at Chick with his left hand, but Chick blocked the punch, then clamped the handcuffs shut on the free wrist.

"You can't do this," said Meagan. A broken record without a script.

"Sure I can," said Chick. "Already have."

Meagan Ames looked like a heart attack in the making, her eyes wide, mouth falling open. Fogarty began to struggle, but Chick jerked the cuff chain, causing Fogarty to wince. Using his thumb and forefinger, Chick pinched Fogarty's lower lip, then twisted it. Fogarty's back arched, and he came up on his toes.

"Be nice now," said Chick. "You need to know I'm really enjoying myself here, so the more you struggle, the more I get to subdue you. Even a moron like you can understand that, can't you? Blink your eyes if you understand."

Fogarty blinked.

Chick nodded. "Good. Well, boys and girls, we've gotta go now."

Meagan started to say something, but Chick held up a hand. "No," said Chick. "Don't ask us to stay."

"Stop them, Chester," said Meagan.

Chester sat quietly. He looked amused.

"Did you hear what I said? Get your ass up and make them let Cameron go."

"No," said Chester. "I don't think I will."

"You are sooo fired."

Chester stood up. "You guys need any help taking him out of here?" he asked us.

"No," said Chick. "But thanks for offering."

"Chester, you shit," said Meagan. "You get out of here right now."

"Sure, Meagan," said Chester. "I'll leave. Before I go, though, I just wanted to let you know that I agree with Storme. You do make love like a washing machine. It's mechanical. You're nearly as good as masturbating, though."

Chester turned and walked away, head erect, massive shoulders square. Meagan looked like she'd been slapped.

"You assholes are in big trouble here," said Fogarty as we led him out of the club. The club members stared at us as we left.

"How you figure that?" said Chick. "I'm a legitimate officer of the court. Everything is legal."

"I'll pay you whatever you want to let me go," said Fogarty.

Chick shook his head, saying, "I don't think I could put a price on this." He waved at some patrons who were staring at the three of us. "I really don't."

The End

ABOUT THE AUTHOR

W.L. Ripley is the author of two critically acclaimed mystery series, one featuring Wyatt Storme, an ex-NFL star and atavistic cowboy, and the other featuring Cole Springer, an enigmatic ex-secret service agent. Both series are published by Brash Books.

Ripley is a native Missourian who has been a sportswriter, a successful high school and college basketball coach, and a well-respected educator. He enjoys watching football and playing golf, spending time with friends and family, and enjoying a good cigar when his wife, Penny, allows it. He's a father, grandfather, and unapologetic Schnauzer lover.

Ripley writes daily from his western Missouri home.

CPSIA information can be obtained at www.ICGtesting.com
Printed in the USA
LVOW10s1655170415

435059LV00002B/125/P

9 781941 298664